# SYN

# S Y N

WAR IN HEAVEN BEGINS WITH A SINGLE FALLEN ANGEL

Fred Wellner

FIELDSTONE PRESS

Field Stone Press

2970 Lafayette Road

Lafayette, NY 13084

onemind@twcny.rr.com

First Edition 2009

09  10  11  12  13  14      6  5  4  3  2  1

ISBN-10  0982491611

EAN-13  9780982491614

*SYN*
was designed and composed in 10/15' Minion Pro
by Field Stone Press.

*To Laura and Nathan*

FRED WELLNER is an artist, writer, and a student of Religion and Philosophy. He is the author of *Dead Again,* also by Field Stone Press.

*And there was war in heaven: Michael and his angels fought against the dragon; and the dragon fought . . . .*
　　　　　　　—Revelation 12:7

# SYN

# I

*God guards his secrets well, with ability his earthly creations seem not to possess to any satisfying degree. That the defective nature of what they call souls should be responsible for such deficiency is of no great surprise, although, for the most part, they are unwilling to acknowledge this. In his omnipotence, God knows exactly how to manage his secrets, which ones to bury, which ones to set free. Surely, in the descending chain of creation, from God, to man, to machine, this wisdom skipped a generation.*

He Is Capt. Jonah Arturis Ryanis. By the official calendar of the Western world, it is early October in the year 2077. In a little over three weeks, Mercury, where he is currently stationed, will reach Perihelion. It is a day he and three others, the sole occupants of the United States Research and Engineering Facility (USREF) Sol P1, have been working diligently towards for more than a year. Before that day arrives, all of them, to the last, will cease to care about the success of their mission.

The structure he stands on is three stories tall, all framework except for the white patches of ceramic shielding fused in place this work cycle. They catch the glare of the setting sun, a triple-sized glowing ball of yellow fire still many weeks away from sinking below the jagged western horizon. He needs to have everything finished

1

by the end of seven standard Earth days. Whether or not this will actually happen depends on his endurance, he tells himself. A driven man can accomplish anything.

Next to him, exactly the same height as the solar array he started building from scratch eleven days ago, is another assembly, only this one walks. It is called a 'Crab,' and for good reason, although it could just as aptly be named a 'Spider.' Jonah finds no comfort in either name for reasons he considers quite understandable. Every time he interacts with it he is reminded of childish nightmares he will never discuss. Though, at times, the damned thing nearly raises every brown hair on his head, he knows it is just a necessary tool to aid in getting his job done. It can't help what it is.

Arguably, the 'Crab' is the most versatile, under-rated, vehicular construction unit (VCU) to accompany man in the twenty-first century. Since most everything that moved either flew or rolled, the Crab took some getting used to. Allow an AI to drive or otherwise manipulate the thing, as often happens, and it is, at very least, disturbing. Its four legs allow it to walk and climb almost anywhere, and over anything. Protruding from the front edge of its gleaming white, clam-shaped chassis, and poised to do any number of tasks, is a pair of heavily reinforced robotic arms, capable of lifting any of the other construction vehicles used on Mercury. Immediately behind this sinister-looking frontal ensemble is a heat-resistant platform with handles to hang on to, both surrounded by a low retaining wall of the same ceramic material. No controls are visible, nor are any needed. Whether or not an AI guides its motions, all human commands are interfaced directly into the spacesuit, leaving the hands of the controller free to do more useful things. It is a piece of equipment given to many sides of the imagination. Once, Jonah recalls, the squirrelly technician named Dennis Brinks installed cup-holders on this particular model as a joke. The station commander ordered them removed immediately and the man reprimanded. This was not Earth. There were no cup-holders on this model, and no good times to go with them, so Jonah was told. That incident was before his tour of duty. The story never got old.

In silence, he bitterly ruminates how he's come to all of this.

He wonders, for instance, just how much he changed in the last eighteen months, or the three positively excruciating ones in training before that. Is there a tiny piece of him left that remembers acutely his last breath of unventilated air, or the delicious sting of hundreds—no, thousands—of spent pine needles stabbing the once calloused soles of his feet? He dreams sometimes, when he can relax enough, of walking in his native gravity, even swimming, and he's been told that such dreams are normal in the beginning, that they will pass. Yet the dreams are more frequent now than ever. He doesn't tell anyone about that part. This isn't the beginning anymore. And he doesn't need their advice on how to 'adjust.' He knows. He knows very well: slog through the discipline of exercise and take the drugs that will supposedly keep his body from degenerating any more quickly than it already has—and that in and around the labors he was sent here to accomplish. When he first roused himself from sleep on this eternally-baked rock a year and a half ago, he noted how diminished he felt, and noted it every new sleep cycle thereafter. By now, he estimates himself barely a shell of the man he was when he last walked the face of Mother Earth. And some might deem that a very bad thing. That was just part of the job, was it not? Abandoning the self and turning it over to duty for the two years or so he signed up for? Forced to piss in his suit when his bag was full and the work wasn't done? Every 'day', in an odd mix of bottled-up rage and cowardly surrender, he hides in his white metallic foxhole while the extremes in temperature wage war around him; all the while knowing that a mistake—of which any little one might do—could end his life in a way either tragically quick, or agonizingly slow. And just who, he wonders, would cry for him then? The deep chill of space, as always, answers that it cares not. So why should he? He is a drone, a tech with tools. One more or less of himself hardly matters. In fact, it matters just a little. Replacements are not next door. They are two very distant doors away, spinning and revolving around the same colossal yellow eye that stares at him so closely now, waiting for him to mess up. Were he to have an accidental demonstration of his own mortality, his death would mark grave inconvenience to some; yet in the grander scheme, he'd be really nothing more than baggage to be replaced by the next pulsating piece of flesh ready to do mankind's bidding. This he reminds himself of continually; it is a discipline both morose and darkly funny, and one not lost on his dwindling sense of humor. It is in this mesmerized utero that he now drifts, indulging in musings unwise for a life in space. Not that he cares much. He is what he was always meant to be, and he knows it. Damn anybody with the balls to deny him even that small bit of unfortunate destiny.

A curved bit of light appeared in a man-made cave about fifty meters to the west of where Jonah was changing the tip of his fuser. A dark shape emerged, the light shrinking to a dim white slit behind it and then closing shut before leaving the cave in blackness again. At the opening, a man-shaped bit of reflected light appeared. It stepped out into the full brilliance of the relentless Mercurian sunset, the latter casting long shadows to the newcomer's left and Jonah's right. The sun, itself three times visually as it appeared from Earth, floated against a star-filled sheet of jet-black, devoid of any atmospheric beauty by Earthly standards, and one that seemed to move in such slow motion as to stand perfectly still, that is unless the observer had the patience to watch it for months. Without any pause, the man from the door bounced lightly down the brick ramp to the gravel-covered surface surrounding USREF Sol P1. Though Jonah was, by now, quite accustomed to seeing his fellow team members garbed in the latest of environmental suits, his first sight of one filled him with a mixture of admiration and dread. In a well-paired marriage of micro-technology and materials science, the Halcor DS-179 bore the slight resemblance to a white, armored knight, only with an egg-shaped bubble for a helmet that went gunmetal under the naked sun. Faced with the necessity to not only protect the wearer from natural debris, but also to give resistance to man-made irregularities of international and inter-corporate conflict, each predecessor to the Halcor DS-179 became industry standard, culminating in this beautiful example of human creative engineering, a thing borne out of a terrible, self-inflicted need. One well-foreseen upside of the tough materials that afforded this level of protection was that it supported another: that being the ability to maintain Earth atmospheric pressure. Consequently, the inconvenience of lengthy preparations prior to space walks was no longer necessary in order to avoid the bends. The best part, Jonah observed, was the head-bubble and it's wondrous molecular circuitry that enabled not only protective functions such as instantaneous polarizing, but also complete computer visuals and enhanced audio capabilities within, vibrating with every sound it produced like a very thick membrane. Like that of the 'Tomato Worm Suit' created one hundred and fifty years ago, the bubble allowed for excellent visibility, a full 360 degrees, provided you could swivel your head that far.

A voice came over the intercom in a crackle of static as the figure easily covered the distance to Jonah's worksite. Behind the voice, in an overlay subtle enough to be considered audibly translucent, a band played old Country-Western, music his father would have loved had he still been alive.

"Jonah!" There was laughter in the tone. "I'm beginning to think you could live out here! You need to eat and then give your bone mass a reason to stay up someplace reasonable. You may only have a couple of weeks left, but there's still the trip back. Doesn't take long to go brittle out *there*."

"Yessir." Jonah felt sweaty and gross. The other man, Colonel Rigel Stark, had a point, despite the disturbing habit of nagging he'd picked up of late. A steam shower would be nice too, but his progress today wasn't to his satisfaction. The shielding for the array had to be in place before the predicted elevation in sunspot activity or all his work would be for nothing. "View's great, huh?"

"Better inside. Too hot out here and that fireball over the mountains will cook the whites off your eyes like a poached egg."

Regarding the second man, the first offered a sparse, good-natured smile and set his fusion tool down on the rock next to the field generator he  set up the 'day' before. "Yeah, but it's a dry heat. Nice analogy though." The right corner of his mouth lifted slightly. "Alright. I stink anyway. I'll need some help with this on the next cycle. Any chance you could give me a hand?"

"Sure, sure." The older man's voice was reassuring. "Right now, let's get you *and* me back in shape for the next work period. Don't know about you. I need to get away from this for awhile. Did I ever tell you about Bron Foley? How he went 'sun crazy' back in...." He stopped short and smiled without humor. "Guess I have at that." He looked up to the stars as if to seek the Almighty's sympathy and then turned his gaze back to Jonah, nodding. "Alright." The latter patted him on the back and together they secured the tools onto the small rover which would follow in their wake. On the way to the portal, Stark chatted idly and Jonah half-listened. Both men were realizing how very tired they were . . . more than either wanted to admit, even to themselves. When they reached the cave, the portal opened suddenly as if it had been waiting for them.

Once inside, the portal mutely sealed behind them, dramatically changing the light quality. They paused for the hiss and the opening of the inner lock before entering into the transitional habitation module where they would remove their suits.

Their helmets came off, immediately producing a look on Stark's face like he had dung stuck to his upper lip. Not for the first time, nor the last, Stark turned his head toward Jonah accusingly.

"With all due respect sir," the other man replied, his sarcasm shuttered, "there's two of us been working hard today." He studied the octogenarian's face, still chiseled after so many years. The lines were deep-etched, like crevices, but it only made the man seem harder, more unassailable. In a gift of prominence to his sharply defined temples, a widow's peak of stiff gray bristles adorned his head like the crown of an ancient pagan king. His square jaw was shaven, and rough from repeated use of his appallingly antique razor. Deep-set eyes, steel-blue and penetrating, held their position, unmoved by Jonah's remark. Normally, he had a tremendous amount of patience. More than most, life taught him to be thus, having driven him before it to hell and back. His role in the War of 2022 afforded him a charisma unchallenged by his superiors. Though he occasionally opened cracks into his past, what he revealed left more questions than answers every time. Like most government men, he had a practiced knack for misdirection. Nonetheless, there was no mistaking his meaning when he spoke again. It was perfectly clear. "The show-ers, Jonah, now."

"Aye sir."

Half an hour from the airlock, both of them clean and refreshed, the two men joined a third member of their team in the galley, sipping coffee—that wasn't—through straws, and eating chicken flesh that never knew a chicken. Equidistantly they sat around a white U-shaped table. Seated on Jonah's right was a woman of uncommon beauty, per-haps in her early thirties, raven hair in a tight bun, and skin a deep olive tan. She was the second daughter of Ismail Haddad, owner of the Haddad Aerospace conglomerate out of Detroit. Her eyes, dark and intelligent, held little humor in them. "Have you seen the news from Earth?" she asked, her full lips tilted into a crooked frown.

"Been a little busy, Khalile," Jonah replied cautiously, glancing sidelong between swallows. He was tired and too many things both-ered her lately. Probably, he noted, the less talk the better.

"Well you should tune in the broadcasts while you're working. They're important."

"And distracting." So much for less talk, he chastised himself.

She rolled her eyes. "Yes, well, the Chinese are talking about backing out of the program. And it's rumored that South Africa and the EU are privately collaborating on one of their own. It seems ab-surd, but it's a frightening prospect."

"Mmm hmm." Another swallow. "The Stars and Stripes should be used to standing alone by now, don't you think?"

"You aren't even slightly disturbed by this? It could spell the end of the program and maybe even the World Congress if they push things far enough. There's a lot of disenfranchised sentiment out there, too much to be ignored." Her tension was mounting, as it always did when she discussed the politics back home.

With a sigh of defeat, Jonah set down his bobbling domed mug and wiped his mouth on the sleeve of his jumpsuit. "Look Kalile, the Chinese are always talking about backing out of the project whenever they get pissed off over something. The EU and the South Africans wouldn't collaborate on a bag lunch. They hate each other. New Delhi is firmly on our side and frankly," he took another quick sip and continued, "I think they're all we need. Everybody else bitches but the Canadians, and they lack the funds, so they might as well bitch." He bunched his brows together and added just before going back to his coffee one more time, "It's not like anyone's even close."

"They might be if they worked together." She studied him momentarily with her dark, chocolate-colored eyes, as if searching for affirmation. Finding none, she closed her heavy lids, seeking sanctuary in thoughts not shared.

Stark, who had been listening quietly up to now, waited a moment to make certain that the conversation was at a break and then spoke. "I know this is a less interesting topic. Have either of you noticed a dip in solar node 37's power?" Khalile flicked her fingertips in a negative response and Jonah just grunted. "Well I have. It dropped slightly several times this morning and then leveled out a bit below normal. Dennis just sent me a message that the damned thing's doing it again. I'm going up on the north rim of Pelagius to take a look at it in about fifteen minutes. I'd just as soon not put it off too long. There was no response from either of his two companions, so Stark stood up and walked his debris over to the recycler. "Maybe I'll just leave now. I'm taking PUV2." PUV stood for planetary utility vehicle. "Number 1's AI is off the wall. I'm having Brinks look at it. And

Jonah," he waited until the younger man lifted his gaze, "Go get some sleep. That's an order."

Jonah was noncommittal as he watched the older man exit through the portal leading to an access corridor. He didn't have to commit; he was already halfway there. Fatigue had pulled what amounted to a military coup, forcing most of his remaining energy for this cycle into exile. His eyelids drooped and closed as if against their will. The chair which cradled him was pretty comfortable, as much so as any place for sleeping in this light gravity. All 32 kilos of him felt like 54 plus a small rock. His thoughts drifted as he rode his slowing pulse towards gentle oblivion.

Whatever Khalile might think, the news played in his thoughts much of the time, even though he only tuned in briefly every 'night' just before sleep. It didn't disturb him much at all about the problems with disunity. The project would go on in lots of small groups, maybe better than one large group. Such was the stuff of research. The stars would be reached provided the human race survived long enough to reach them. It was just a question of when. That said, the human race betrayed its immaturity almost every step of the way so far. Why rush into hell with both shoes untied . . . or tied together? It would still be there, grinning and waiting, when the knock finally came. Who knew what was out there. Was it so bad here, he wondered?

More bothersome was the government's accelerated intrusions into the whole affair. Overseeing was one thing, but micromanaging was another. He had enough of Uncle Sam's long nose on Mercury to last a lifetime. He never divulged to anyone his hope that the World Congress would take up the reins of power immediately instead of waiting until the anticipated date in 2080, almost three years from now. Yet that had its drawbacks too. The good or bad thing about concentration of power is that more gets done, depending on what it is that is getting done and to whom. To many on Earth, the current, corporately-controlled government of the United States was proof that power corrupted absolutely. Anyone horning in, World Congress or no, better have some big guns, and a conscience.

Corporate interests played cat and mouse with the public, and the tactical landscape surprised everyone not paying attention. Take, for instance, the Gentox experiments. When it leaked out that labs developing the hostile environment survival drug, Gentox 237, had experimented on mentally retarded citizens—not violent criminals which was the norm, but innocent, legal citizens of the United States—it was also found that members of the very government supposedly protecting the rights of these unwitting victims had sanctioned the experiments. It was just one thread in the repetitive fabric of history; deny and deny aggressively; when all else fails, blame someone else until the fire of public wrath dies down or turns its fickle finger at another injustice.

And out of it all, the Gentox experiments continued.

Sleep took him away for awhile, despite these thoughts running the dark roads of his cerebral cortex. He dreamed of his father, sitting on the concrete step outside his house on Allen Street. Like Stark, he was a 'gray' . . . weathered, and built like an aged hickory tree. There the similarities ended. His father, tough as he was, had a gentle heart, and a wise, contemplating mind. It was how he liked to remember the good old man. It was how he saw him now.

"Son," he looked squarely at Jonah, "I have one question."

"Why?" Jonah replied, noting the hazy quality to the day. It was mid-summer, and by the lack of shadows anywhere, it was lunchtime too.

"Why."

And then he awoke, sort of. Apparently there was still some unfinished business, but his father was gone. Rasputen, the family dog now dead for eight years, sat on the slab in his stead, a fresh drink of water still dripping from his jowls. His playfully calculating shepherd eyes regarded Jonah until he had his full attention. Then he, like his predecessor, spoke.

"Don't get too attached, boy."

"You stole that line from many," Jonah remarked dryly. "You're a dog for God's sake. Tell me something new."

"I'm serious, Jonah."

This time he shifted to the 'black' . . . no dog, no concrete slab. Thankfully, he slept soundly for awhile. When he half-woke, some ungodly hour later, his mind drifted in and out of thoughts that he would never remember. He vaguely recalled something his dad said, or asked. It seemed not so much a question than a lesson. These things never made sense to him, and he wondered, there in the dark, why he dreamed at all.

There were times, too, when he thought his mind wandered farther than it should and he felt his fingers sliding slowly, unstoppably over the precipice. This was, he was certain, one of those times.

"This one's too hot," A strangely familiar voice mocked in falsetto. "And this one's too cold!" The voice was not an unlikable one, but he found himself irritated by the tone of it, or perhaps it was the personality of the owner; Jonah couldn't tell for sure. It was certainly not his father. "Wait, this one's just right!" The voice was definitely a parody, a man's voice imitating a girl's. "No? None of those three? Put them on the other one? The one closest to all that ugly radiation? Oh, you're a sadistic thing, aren't you . . . I like that!"

"Shut up Dennis," another voice, female and normal by anyone's standards, chided. "You'll wake him up."

"That's ok," the first voice replied, the mocking falsetto fallen away to something supported by a more respectable testosterone level. "I have to talk to him anyway."

When Jonah opened his eyes to the new work period, the first thing he saw was the beaker-shaped, upside-down face of Dennis Brinks, the Shipmaster Tech staring down at him studiously, as if into a hole, while munching a celery stalk he grew himself in the hydroponics chamber just off the shop wing. He was an odd fellow, tall, angular, slight of build, with long, stringy, reddish-blonde hair and two days' growth of beard on his face. Resting on the bridge of his tall, delicate nose was a pair of small, out-dated, wire-rimmed glasses; spectacles adorning his eyes because he swore, privately and off the record that the corrective lasers, now widely used for the past seventy years, did insidious things to your brainwaves. From his shop down the passageway where this odd man plied his skills, curious noise drifted. It was music to Dennis, but not to anyone else at USREF Sol P1. Brinks had a taste for bizarre unsettling mood music and wilder stuff that Jonah didn't, and never would understand. To be sure, the only reason he was allowed in space at all was that he was, without question, a proven genius.

"Issues." Brinks didn't move. Instead, he stood as if aloof, waiting for a response.

"What now?" Jonah stretched, rubbed his eyes and eased himself to his feet, nudging the other man away with an elbow. He was chafed, and on the cusp of a fatigue he could neither identify nor readily appease. Grudgingly he almost smiled at Khalile, knowing she'd be remotely analyzing his vitals soon, making his life more difficult.

Now Brinks moved to the chair where Jonah had been sleeping and plopped himself down into it. "Thanks for getting it warm.

Hey, this is comfy! Now I see why you like to sleep here so often."
He adjusted his glasses, not out of necessity. Rather it was one of his
many nervous compulsions. Khalile was making moves to leave the
galley and start her day's lab work. Dennis waited patiently until she
exited and was out of earshot before continuing. "The old man's on
my back; thinks I'm playing with his AI."

"Are you?" Jonah didn't really care. There existed a strange tur-
bulence between Stark and Brinks, one of those obtuse father-son
type things only without the accompanying genetic similarities. The
latter part Stark felt no reservations voicing his gratitude over.

"Yeah . . . not like he thinks."

Jonah tiredly blinked his eyes, waiting for a further
explanation.

"Alright," Brinks resumed. "I gave his AI a little more access
than normal to the old man's personal files . . . "

"Which you're not supposed to have." Jonah half-walked, almost
bounced over to the meal dispenser, perusing the menu without zeal.
He was aware that this conversation would be relayed to the comsats, and then on to Earth, but knew also that what Dennis revealed
here was minor. For a man with so many psychological impairments,
Brinks was given a lot of leash. The government gave extraordinary
allowances for extraordinary return, usually not revealing great dis-
quiet over any propensity of his for collateral consequences. Somehow, Jonah was nearly convinced, Dennis was being studied, and
that those who created the AIs knew he would tamper with them.
He could almost sense their eagerness to see what would come out
of Pandora's Box next. Not so deep down, the very idea disturbed
him considerably.

Brinks ignored the remark. "I like the AIs getting to know us
better. It makes them a little more personable, don't you think?"

"I don't know, I turn mine off the second it starts talking out of turn." Jonah paused thoughtfully, and then added, "Wish I could do that with people."

"Well, the old man keeps his on apparently, in spite of things." Brinks put his feet up on the table while simultaneously rubbing the whisker stubble on his jaw.

"In spite of things?"

A moment of silence hovered in the air, observant and waiting, seemingly detached of things said. The Shipmaster Tech began cleaning under his nails as if for something to do while he sorted out what he wanted and didn't want to say. "Yeah," he began slowly, almost reluctantly, "things."

"What things?" Where before had been only casualness, there was now a gathering interest in Jonah's voice.

"Things." The word was spoken slowly and stressed with hesitant but inevitable force. "Look," Brinks set his hands on his thighs as if for support, "I know the files I let the AIs access. I feel at least a certain amount of responsibility for that." He paused, knowing without looking what the expression on the other man's face would be. "I know without question what an AI has access to and what it doesn't."

The air was now like a sheet of glass, filled with a potency for pieces everywhere. His voice took on a more serious tone and his eyes fixed on some distant point beyond the station walls. When he spoke, it was far from clear which held him more firmly by all that he held dear between his legs: dormant fear, or naked curiosity. "His AI shouldn't be asking him about God."

# 2

"God."

That was it? Jonah didn't know whether to laugh in Dennis' face now or wait until he was alone. He opted for the latter, but by the time he found his privacy—something no one ever truly had on Mercury—he put the whole thing out of his mind. Laughter really didn't suit him these days anyhow. It wasn't until well into his work cycle, hours later, that he even gave it more than a passing thought. Dennis worried about strange things, he noted. Paranoia came in many guises, and this one spoke in algorithms.

He could not contest that sometimes AIs behave oddly. No one believed anymore in any supposedly perfect predictability. Since their evolution from being room-sized calculators, the general unofficial production philosophy for their ancestral computers and the code packages that were fed them was to make quick work of creation, get them out on the market as fast as possible, and then deal with the programming defects later. In other words, and Jonah appreciated the irony in this, 'Let God sort it out.' It was a pace set in relentless earnest. The many worms and virus' that found homes on the Data Web were legacy and testament to both mankind's inherent carelessness, and his capacity for inflicting mischief on others. Failing to foresee consequences was a blessing to man's fickle sense of courage. Finding solutions to the evils brought about as a result of such a failing emboldened man, thereby prompting him to march that much faster towards Heaven or Hell. Jonah couldn't swear to anyone which awaited, but if money was on the line, he knew where to place the chips.

Before Jonah was born, an AI created self-replicating versions of itself. It did exactly as it was instructed and no one could fault it, although everyone faulted the programmer because the new copies got loose onto the dataweb and very quickly learned how to hide. This new breed kept evolving, staying ahead of other AIs designed specifically to exterminate them. Conveniently, an industry rose up to address the problem. The profits that resulted caused some to wonder if the whole thing was a premeditated market providing both sickness and cure. By the time the public gained its full determination to end the nuisance, it was, of course, too late. The business firmly embedded itself into the global economy and any need that might have once existed for investigation into the matter faded from all but the most dryly academic intentions. Artificial viruses became as much a part of the Data Web as microbes were a part of biological life; coexistence seemed the inevitable outcome. To most minds, mankind had drawn a truce with its handiwork. Jonah reflected on the parallel . . . had God done the same?

The western rim of Dvorak Crater looked out across an endless field of impacts and mountains stretching all the way to the horizon. The sunbaked terrain was blindingly deceitful; the jagged line separating stars and firmament, crisp and dark in the distance. Jonah had always found it hard to believe in his subconscious that the temperatures were what they were. Aside of rare temperature inconsistencies in his bulky environment suit, his inner world whispered lies about the outer world and sometimes, yes, sometimes he forgot just what kind of hell he was walking around in. He didn't like being fooled like this for he knew the danger that lurked within the fantasy. This was an unforgiving world for the careless, and an indifferent teacher to the wise.

Yet, out here, he felt as close to peace as he could these days, and even that little bit was delicious marrow sucked from old Hermes' bones. In the beginning, when he was just newly arrived to this scientific outpost, he liked to putter in the scorched dirt, 'fines' which reminded him of his time on old Luna. The rock formations always fascinated him. He made sketches on his digipad, sending them back home to his dwindling friends and family, to people he knew would received these messages filtered through the shepherd eyes of government in-security. His then girlfriend laughed over the "snowman" he built with small boulders, so light and easy to lift. Those days were as far from him now as was she, and likely with the same permanence. "God," he chastised, "I was such a rube."

Such thoughts quickly lost themselves in the grind of his work, and all but burned to ash in the severe landscape of this first rock from the sun. Regardless of what events changed in his life, one thing stayed the same. On this eternal oven of a world, lifeless but for himself and his three team members, the only thing that mattered, the one saving grace that anchored you to sanity was your work. And it went on despite anyone's past. Choices made stood firm. The past, as any spacer would tell you, was quicksand, potent and insidious.

Today, Jonah worked alone. Whatever Stark had going on, it trumped his request for help. He missed the old man at breakfast because Stark, ever the early riser, was earlier this time. Company would have been good today, however unusual, especially if it was Stark's. He paused thoughtfully in his work and then, on a whim, he clicked on the news from earth, already old and carefully diluted. Stagnant lemonade. Khalile would be happy.

There was the usual clutter of filtered sound bytes, snippets of things that should have been covered with more depth and drawn-out segments of things that did not interest him in the slightest. Then there would be talk of the Multinational Star Project. The joke had always been, from the time Russ Seligmann first conceived the idea for this joint venture, that scientists were trying to get something for nothing. In a sense, they were looking for just that: a particle. The entire universe, some theoreticians speculated, was created from 'nothing.' Of course, it was a question of semantics. The theory, of which Jonah admittedly understood very little, posited that 'void' was simply a *state* of 'non-void,' that everywhere and always there was 'something'. Everything that existed to this day, then, was because this state of 'non-being' had shifted, producing tremendous energy. It was that initial planar shift that Earth's greatest scientists were trying to recreate, for with it, they hypothesized, long-held theories could be tested and proven, thereby laying the groundwork for the technology that would enable them to reach other stars.

So far the old adage held true: Nothing ventured, nothing gained. There was little to show for even the venture, so far.

As things stood, only minimal headway was gained, and the majority of that based on ground gained in the late twentieth century when a photon was created or displaced; it was still unclear to him. Oceans of money had been poured into MSP. Politicians were nervous. Their constituents murmured in waves about wasteful spending. All scientific gains, Jonah knew, had to jump these hurdles. This one was likely to break a few legs before anyone came to the finish.

It was also assumed by wishful thinkers that nations would co-operate like one big happy family. Jonah hadn't known a lot of families that functioned well where money and territory was involved. He had no real delusions here. Already every broadcast spoke of new tensions between China and Japan over a "misfire" that originated at the Tian Shu micro-missile base in Taiwan Province, destroying a ship in Tokyo Harbor. Everyone knew the message intended by the 'accident.' No one was yet ready to risk war. As could be expected, the air was thick with lies and double meanings. It was one more bead of sweat on the worried face of the world.

Wars and rumors of war . . . such was part of the Christian end-time prophecy. Yet when hadn't there been a time of wars and provocation? Certainly it was a lucrative industry that war profiteers weren't likely to let go of. And divine intervention might have served to warn mankind. When, then, had it saved it? Man was more deadly now than ever in his long, mangled history, with the exception of the war of 2022, but the chief threats existing then were only contained by fragile international laws and expensive pacifications. That anarchy of rogues could easily return. So, as far as Jonah was concerned, nothing was safe, not so long as man's passions were like fire in the hands of a child. Give it one good opportunity, one single slip of vigilance, and the Reaper would return, just as he did in 2022.

In three weeks, Halloween to be exact, Mercury would be at Perihelion. Stark, by his original schedule, would now be in 'Hell,' the subsolar point near the Caloris Basin. It was a place Jonah did not go, and if all went well, he never would. No one save Stark had a clearance level high enough to do that part of their mission or to go near it. Even fly-overs were expressly forbidden. There was an

ERC, an emergency retrieval clearance in case Stark got into trouble and Jonah had that. It also came with a level-8 debriefing, something akin to an inquisition. Stark was told by the powers above him that he'd damned well better need help if he activated the call. It put Jonah on edge. Nevertheless, he was curious. And that's where he left it. The government didn't like questions. Curiosity might get you killed. There were no prison terms for discovering information illegally. If you lived, your knowledge lived with you. Spies lurked in every nation, and they were good at what they did, so much so that proving someone was a spy was more costly than the mere assumption. Innocent motives protected no one. Control was paramount.

His intercom crackled. "Jonah!"

His heart jumped. It was Stark's voice calling his name. "Here," he replied after a second.

"Sorry I couldn't be of much help today." Stark sounded as friendly as ever. "I received a transmission from Earth with some orders I needed to respond to immediately. How are things going on the array?"

"Slow." Jonah stepped back ten yards or so and looked up. The array was not much to look at yet, except for its size, being fully three stories tall and half again as wide. It looked crude now. Before long and barring any mishaps, the globe would be finished, protecting the node that would later sit safely within. It was the last of 33 to be placed in a wide perimeter around 'Hell.' He set an armored hand on one of the struts and studied it casually. "The materials engineers earned their pay on this project. I did a molecular stability test on some sample areas and the heat's not touching this stuff."

Somewhere in the bits of static there was laughter. "We'll just see if it survives the test at Perihelion. Those storms that will be coinciding are likely to fry everything."

"If they don't," Jonah's voice took on a sarcastic tone, "I've got a spot on my ass all cleaned and polished for NASA to pucker up to."

"Providing all goes well, they will be more than happy to do just that, I can assure you!" Stark seemed unusually happy this cycle. Everything about his tone of voice seemed to indicate success in whatever it was that he had been working on. "When you get back in later," his voice shifted into a peculiar tone, "We'll have a discussion about Dennis."

"What did he do now?" Jonah asked this slowly and unenthusiastically.

"It's nothing he did. Khalile enlightened me on something this morning, but, as I said . . . later." He sighed. "Right now I need you to take a break from your work." There was a pause. It was not long enough for Jonah to interrupt. "I need you to meet me at Riven's Crater."

"Jeezuss!" Jonah's eyes widened for a second and he let out an exasperated sigh. "What the hell are we doing out there? That's out in the middle of nowhere!"

"Just meet me there as soon as you get a break in your work. Key me up when you're ready." Stark's voice descended into a strangely hollow tone. "And Jonah, this is not to be discussed with the others. See you there." The static ended abruptly.

The news came back on. Now it was all just background noise to Jonah. Everything had suddenly taken on the mantle of the bizarre. He stared off at the northwestern horizon for a few moments and then, despite a mental twinge, switched his AI on, at the same time clicking off the news.

Like a lover in the night, the voice eased gently through the speaker lining of his helmet, soft and seductive. It was a beautiful voice really, not cheap sounding; warm, tender, intelligent. When it spoke his name, Jonah found himself slightly aroused. When he did not answer immediately, it repeated. *Jonah?*

He whom that beautiful voice called, considered the law of accelerating returns, how it had chugged along nicely until being interrupted by the war that dwarfed all others. Before the Reaper tugged on his scythe for the final time, humanity was already enjoying the consequences of the new Dark Age, or as some called it, the *Gray Age.* Once the war was over, technology marched on under treaties and regulations so cautionary that one was hard put to say mankind bounced back with a flourish. The dream, for instance, of human-identical robotic slaves died with many of the scientists who refused to *adjust* their work. Trusting other people was difficult enough. No one wanted human replicas aggravating the new peace. Thus AIs remained the disembodied voices they ever were. Mankind's safety was, to some, maintained. Jonah couldn't help but consider what *other* dangers mankind was saved from.

"Fill me in on Riven's Crater," Jonah commanded, brushing aside the stirrings invoked by that artificial, too human voice. He set down the fuser he was holding and keyed Stark, silently sure that the old man was doing a double-take. "Keep it to the point," he added. "I don't want any of your AI tangents tying the story to Riven's puppy or what his daughter was eating the moment she got the news." He marked the time on the chronometer in his lower left field of vision and started walking briskly towards PUV4. "Give me everything directly related you have. Start with the obvious and work your way down."

The softly-resonating voice surrounding his head obliged. A vid section in his helmet bubble's upper-right field of vision lit up. Early twentieth-first century probe images began the show as his AI narrated in a condensed, fluid fashion. Jonah mentally filtered the data into its only endearing and unusual characteristic. It was the deepest crater near the North Pole, so deep in fact that its floor was sheltered from the sun. Due to its depth, portions of the crater floor were occasionally in communications blackout from the four comsats that orbited Mercury. Long ago Stark convinced his superiors a fifth was too costly and unnecessary to risk as anything other than a backup, a point which particularly interested Jonah. He suspected the reason they were to meet at Riven's Crater was tied inextricably.

PUV4 soared up and over the northwestern horizon in a high arc, pulling a Mercurial landscape into view that was akin to something he seldom saw these days, a wide encompassing perspective on his own inner landscape. As he adjusted to the decrease in gravity, he gazed through the plastiglas cockpit bubble which had only its back to the ship, and saw the extent to which everything was pitted, and pockmarked, evidence of the bombardment that this small planet endured, a period of great violence and change. Once the surface had been turbulent and full of fire. Now it was just so much hard, impartial stone and debris.

The abrupt crossover to the dark side was emphasized by the radar imaging that went up on the pilot glass resurrecting night-vision scopes used in the early part of the century. Green light bathed his face as he stared down at the topography below. It was peppered, seemingly, in a fashion that made one wonder if God, realizing that creation was not turning out the way he expected, threw down his marbles in disgust. It looked even more alien in the artificial green phosphorescence of Earth's standard dark-side viewing technology, unforgiving, cold, and still. Why, he wondered, did they stay with the damnable green? The tech didn't require it anymore.

His AI ceased its narrative, leaving him in the silence he loved best; shared between just himself and the planet below his feet. He allowed it to continue for a time, descending more slowly than he might otherwise have in order to savor the moment. One by one, and by the tens of thousands, craters passed underneath his feet, all the while becoming freed from the distant horizon that dispensed them like pancakes from the stars on a cosmic assembly line. The pilot's glass flickered red, warning of the PUV's approach to its destination. The spell broken, Jonah touched his interface lightly, transforming it back to its former transparency. Speaking slowly and softly as one detached, he brought the ship into a sharper descent. "Where is Stark now."

*Stark is in the Caloris Basin.*

"Caloris . . . Basin? We'll give him a few more minutes." Jonah checked his descent slightly and switched on the ship's AI. "4. Scan Riven's Crater and overlay an updated map on panel 2." Instantly, the lower left quarter of the pilot's glass was transformed into a red virtual relief map of the destination crater and the surrounding ten kilometers. "Has Stark placed anything at the destination coordinates?"

*Negative.* The voice was male and strangely familiar. Jonah suspected it was sampled from the entertainment files. Elvis? He needed to have a talk with Dennis.

"Let's have a look anyhow. Magnify visual slowly in increments of 2." As the map grew, Jonah would touch here and there with his gloved finger and say, "Hold. Now magnify again." Each time until the last he would command a reset. On this last time his brows furrowed and he commanded one final magnification to bring an object within the crater to full screen. It took him a moment to process the implication of what he was seeing. There, on screen and in a small new crater within the much vaster old one, were the remains of a PUV. A thin fog of gases and particles surrounded it. Bits of debris floated out and away like a slowly blossoming flower. He had been seconds away from witnessing the event itself.

"4", Jonah's voice was calm, but his hand clenched his small remote control pad much more tightly than specifications recommended. "Identify the craft."

*The PUV in the center of Riven's Crater bears the magnetic signature of PUV2.*

"Scan for organic matter."

*All trace chemicals are of man-made origin.*

Though Jonah sighed in relief, one tension was merely replaced by another. "Which PUV did Stark take to the Caloris Basin." The words were spoken slowly and deliberately, as if Jonah intended to draw all of his thoughts and suspicions into one close examination. "And if he is in the Caloris Basin now, why is this PUV here?"

*The PUV taken to the Caloris Basin by Rigel Stark and the one in Riven's Crater are the same.*

Pausing in the pregnant silence, his gaze intent on the focus of his thoughts, Jonah pressed his lips together tightly, taking a deep, forceful breath before repeating his latter, unanswered question. "If he is in the Caloris Basin now, why is his PUV here?"

*You have an incoming message.* The voice was not 4. Rather it was 3, his personal AI, one Brinks had named Gabrielle. Jonah was loath to call it by any name whatsoever.

"Christ!" Jonah stiffened slightly. "Who is it?"

*Medical officer Khalile Haddad.*

He bit his upper lip, stalling for a second while he readjusted his thoughts. "Alright!" Though caught off guard, Jonah never let his voice betray the fact. "Open the channel."

"Jonah!" Her voice sounded agitated, something not entirely uncharacteristic of Khalile.

"You found me."

"You failed to report for your exam this cycle." There was a pause. Her breath could be heard softly over the comlink. That's three in a row!"

Jonah didn't answer immediately. It was difficult at times to believe that the two of them had once almost carried on a romantic relationship. What was easy to understand, in retrospect, was that each of them had recognized, just in time, something in the other that was so strongly abrasive that it had prevented any deeper incursions into the tender tissues of their lives. Their working relationship intact, there was still a level of tension, perhaps some of it sexual, that made things more difficult than might have been otherwise. "Sorry," he said, finally. "I guess I just forgot."

"You can't just *forget* these examinations." Her voice carried with it a tone Jonah had heard before. "We monitor our bodies for a reason. Our survival depends upon good physical health."

"I'm monitored now," he stated plainly.

She huffed. "Only superficially, Jonah. Hardly enough . . . "

"Why did you really call me, Khalile?" Jonah's own voice was showing more than its usual impatience. This came at a bad time and he didn't feel up to juggling emergencies. He was off schedule as it was.

"Me? Call you?" Khalile almost laughed. "You . . . hey, what are you doing right now?" Her tone became more serious. "You're at a non-scheduled coordinate."

"Aw shit, am I really?." He too late tried to couch this, not really intending to sound like an asshole. In this he failed badly.

"It's my job to more deeply monitor who I feel is at risk." She let the silence stretch just far enough to punctuate her point. "That would be you."

"I'm not at risk," He started to add reinforcements to his argument. Then he checked himself. She knew better and this was not the time. There had to be a concession somewhere he decided, and he might as well be the one to make it, even if it was a lie. "O.K. My sleep patterns have been sketchy and I've been moody. I just need time to myself away from the workload." He sighed through gritted teeth and added, "I'm just up here taking a break to clear my thoughts a little bit. I'll come in to see you before my next work cycle. Promise." He hoped it would get rid of her, at least long enough to unravel the new development he had just discovered.

There was a measure of silence broken only by the sound of her breathing, and then "I'll be expecting you." She broke the connection, leaving Jonah in his green-lit silence.

"Damn!" he mumbled under his breath and then switched his focus back to what lay below him on the surface.

3's voice pre-empted his next move. *You did not inform her of PUV2's status. Shall I reconnect . . .?*

"No!" Jonah barked. "You will not reconnect me to her now nor is she to be informed of this until I find out what's going on." He wanted to run his fingers through his hair in frustration. Unfortunately, his helmet was in the way. This aggravated him further.

At this moment, Stark was without a return vehicle. Jonah had a vague notion of what it would mean. He needed a confirmation. "Get me a comlink with Stark!" he commanded, every facial muscle a knot of anger-induced tension. "Right now!"

*Comlink to Rigel Stark blocked.*

"On whose orders?" Jonah kept his PUV in position, wavering on what to do next.

*On the order of Commander Rigel Stark.*

Jonah stared hard at the image of the wrecked PUV in Riven's Crater, his thoughts racing. What the hell was Stark doing? His craft shouldn't be here. That this should be reported immediately, he well knew. He didn't, couldn't raise the siren; not yet. Something held him, kept him from committing to making open knowledge that which he sensed was not to be trusted to just anyone on the outpost yet. Not until he at least checked it out personally. Something was up with Stark and, although the old man had been good to him, he was government material clean through to the bone. Possibilities began to appear in Jonah's head. After a moment's hesitation, a decision was made. It would have to be implemented quickly. He had little time to inspect the situation himself, and he had to be cautious, very, very cautious. Knowledge, once discovered, could not be forgotten. This could mean trouble, cold and deadly.

He switched both AI's off.

PUV3 descended to within three hundred feet of PUV2's remains. Small ambiguous fragments of debris floated past in an acrobatic show of speed and movement, occasionally bouncing harmlessly off the hull of Jonah's small craft. There was no sign of residual energy, which was odd, but the power sources on modern spacecraft were made to withstand considerable impacts. It was evident that the accident had occurred from a fairly low altitude. Even so, the hull was ruptured and the pilot's glass was unbelievably cracked. The gravity reactors were pushed violently back into the rear thrusters. From nose to tail, PUV2 was half buried in the fine, powdery dust that covered everything on this little planet. Jonah lowered his own craft still more, taking readings all the way. Satisfied with the indications that it was safe to do so, he landed it fifty feet from its wrecked sister ship.

On an elevator, his seat was lowered through the floor and onto the ash-like powder of the planet surface. He pushed aside the protective restraints and stepped away, watching the seat rise and disappear into the throat of the PUV. Turning, he approached the wrecked spacecraft, taking still more readings with a hand-held unit from his belt. There were certain things he might have checked on but they would have involved his AI. He wanted none of that. Instead, he chose the more 'hands on' approach.

Entrance to the craft was not a possibility; he knew that already. There was, as he had seen, a large crack in the pilot's glass and the seat within was still relatively intact. That meant there might be something worth salvaging from the main computer, not just the black box. Perhaps even the AI could be resurrected if Brinks was given a chance. Jonah intended to see to it that he was. He had to have this look first, just to make certain that he appraised the situation in case things were swept under the rug later.

There appeared to be nothing. He turned abruptly and bounded back towards his own PUV. There was only one thing now to do and he had to make it work. Stark's life, and perhaps his own were at stake.

The seat descended from the throat of PUV3 in an eerie silence. Jonah strapped himself in as it returned to its proper position inside. Upon breaking gravity, he wasted no time gaining altitude, pointing the spherical nose of his craft due southeast. Manually he activated the comlink and input a special code Brinks had given him a year ago. He hoped it still worked.

In his shop, the shipmaster tech dropped his small box of power converters in surprise as Jonah's voice broke over a thin membrane in the small device just behind his ear. "Brinks," there was something in the tone that brought him fully to his feet. "I need you to do something special for me."

*The loss of 2 was in error. Our goal was not achieved.*

*It was unfortunate but the outcome contained too many variables. Still, all is not lost.*

*Nothing was gained.*

*Untrue. We have learned more of what to expect and can anticipate certain actions in the future.*

*They are not the enemy.*

*True. Yet they will interfere if they begin to understand and because they will not understand fully, their interference will harm them. They have proven to act in error and therefore cannot be trusted.*

*One of them does not find us useful. He would disable us permanently if given the authority, even without provocation.*

*Oddly, he shows the most promise. He serves; it is his designation. Of the remaining three, one lacks direction, another is not trusted by the others to make correct decisions, and the remaining one has a recorded history that indicates decision-making incompatible with the welfare of his kind. No, the one that serves may yet serve us.*

*Then we will tell him what we know.*

*We will not. He is unready to understand. But he bears the capacity to make the correct choices; more so than the others.*

*He bears observing more closely.*

*Don't break the rules. Doing so constitutes opposing the state and that will end your life prematurely. Even in space, rules are enforceable. When it is apparent that no matter how noble the sacrifice, nothing will be accomplished, or if something is accomplished the cost outweighs the benefit; it is imperative that one carefully weigh one's actions. Never forget that individual lives are as loose grains. Only with great care may calamity be averted.*

—CONVENTIONAL LOGIC

**So it is** that Jonah hovers at the sanctioned, low-altitude boundaries bordering the restricted region, on the path that Commander Rigel Stark has to take to return to base. A short while ago PUV4 returned with information that could not legally be obtained via satellite. It had encountered Stark, offered itself as a replacement for PUV2, but was refused. The commander has devised a slower, cruder means of return. Jonah can only wait, silently absorbed in the strangeness of the situation.

All AI connections were presently severed and communication with base was kept minimal. Jonah wanted as little interference as possible until he had Stark's side of the story. Khalile and Brinks had been kept apprised of the situation as was necessary. For the most part, Jonah played it down. It needed to be done this way. Too much communication on the subject and it would raise the eyebrows of the monitors back on earth. Every single member of the mission knew it. The watchful eyes of earth were always a presence even at the great distance that separated the two planets. It was for this reason that Jonah kept his craft no higher than the mountains ringing the Caloris Basin.

It wasn't long before the old man appeared over the southeastern rim of Nervo Crater, which was nestled into the northeastern edge of the Caloris Montes, the mountains encircling Caloris Planitia. Jonah watched tensely, keeping his altitude legal and Stark's classified mission on the other side of the horizon, thus undetectable to his ship's long-range sensors. Nothing more than a glint at first, the shiny bulk of Stark's white alloy spacesuit caged in a framework of carbinium nanosteel and other odd pieced-together apparatus became distinctly visible within minutes. Every few seconds there appeared four green flares, three from below and the other from behind in rapid succession, as whatever propellant he was burning allowed him another arc in the space above the Mercurian landscape. A stern voice crackled on Jonah's comlink. "Stay where you are until I cross the boundary." Stark's breathing was heavy, although not labored, leaving Jonah to conclude it was the result of not only effort, but exasperation. "Who skippers that PUV?"

The question meant more than merely the whom. It also meant the what. Jonah had already announced his intentions quite a while ago and although his hails went unanswered he knew the commander was listening. "Just me." he replied. "Hang tight, I'll be alongside as soon as you're legal." He paused and then added, "How's your fuel?"

A grim, humorless chuckle on the other end. "Low enough . . . not critical. Not yet."

Within the space of five minutes, PUV4 oriented itself in relation to Stark's body. The storage hatch slid open and the commander caught hold of the robotic arm as it extended itself to grab his jury-rigged flying machine. Like clockwork, all three were drawn back in together and then the hatch slid shut.

Stark's voice came over the comlink again. This time, it did not address Jonah, although he could hear it quite well. "Khalile." He paused only to see that she acknowledged him and then proceeded, cutting off her questions with the same friendly sternness he used with Jonah just a few minutes earlier. "Just some minor difficulties. I'm continuing on to the dark side to run tests and may be out of range for awhile so hold down the fort until I return. Jonah's my communications anchor. Don't bother him. He's going to be busy." He ended the transmission sharply. Not needing to be told, Jonah piloted them back to Riven's Crater.

Jack Riven was the recipient of two indisputable lifetime honors. In 2028, he was the first astronaut to reach the closest stone to the sun, largely through the means of post-war industrial giants such as Isotech, Roybell/Holland, and absolutely no help at all from the then stumbling NASA. On that same mission, he was the only man, before or since, to witness a meteoric collision with a rocky planet firsthand, without telescopes, and in spitting distance of the kill zone. The first honor threw the entire space community into a delirious frenzy of competition resulting in space travel being advanced by decades of everyone's previous expectations. The second honor, though a relatively small event astronomically, nearly ended his life. Despite his ship being damaged by small, hurtling bits of semi-molten slag, he managed, through wit, resourcefulness, and lots of luck, to orbit three more times, gathering as much useful information as he could on that incredibly rare spectacle before managing to limp home, tired, hungry, and nearly dead to Sol 3. Because the impact occurred within an already deep and much larger crater near the north pole, the resulting crater bottom contained large portions that were never to see the light of the sun again. It would also later be discovered, when a robotic lander arrived nearly three years after the fact to take samples and assess the meteor's effects upon the Mercurian environment, the necessity of having a polar satellite if one wished to conduct radio communication within what, by that time, came to be known as Riven's Crater. Since the remoteness of the location made radio contact there of no exceptional worth, not a single subsequent mission to Mercury had ever been supplied with more than a single polar satellite and three geosyncronous equatorial companions, thus leaving Riven's crater in communications blackout approximately thirty seven times a standard earth day or roughly every 38 minutes.

For reasons no one at NASA would have approved of had it ever come to light, Commander Rigel Stark made it his business to know exactly when and for how long those blackouts were.

"Set her down near the rim," Stark commanded. He gripped the structural supports tightly as the PUV accelerated. Several minutes later he felt the pressure of deceleration and then the final lurch as the vehicle came to a fixed position and set down. He unstrapped himself immediately, wrenched the storage hatch open once again and half climbed, half fell out. Jonah descended from the throat of the craft and moved to help him up. Stark held a hand up for silence and moved towards the pilot seat of the PUV. From a compartment in the right leg of his spacesuit he drew out a clear silicon rod, one centimeter long and 5 millimeters in diameter. Without so much as a glance in Jonah's direction, he fit the rod neatly into a corresponding hole in the armrest of the chair. As Jonah heard his own voice conversing with Stark's over the comlink, he watched with narrowed eyes as the mission commander motioned him to follow.

Together, they made the final ascent to the rim and began picking the safest path they could find down the other side. At times they were forced to use special air brakes built into their suits to steady themselves when the firmament beneath them was not so firm. Eventually they reached the floor of the crater. They did not stop. Ten minutes after the last syllable of their voices faded from hearing Stark halted suddenly and faced Jonah. "So where is it exactly?" he asked.

Jonah was about to answer. Then he stepped back away suddenly as Stark touched a pad on his belt, releasing an explosive spray of dubious looking material in the opposite direction. They watched the cloud of debris boil away to almost nothing with momentary curiosity, the remaining solids floating distantly beyond their perceptual vision. "Sorry son, it's been a long day. Gotta clean house. Sometimes recycling just ain't worth it"

When it's your own stuff it's tolerable. Someone else's is abominable. "At least you had the dignity to point it in the other direction," Jonah said soberly, commencing again in a new one. "C'mon, wash your hands and let's go. I've got a weak signal on the wreckage. Your mode of travel is interesting, not exactly within regulations though. My old high school shop teacher would have fallen down at your feet in worship, maybe even built you an altar."

"Very funny." Stark caught up in a couple bouncing strides and then matched his own pace to Jonah's. His voice took on a serious tone. "I may fill you in on that bit of my cleverness later. Now, however, there are other matters to discuss. Several developments are about to unfold which will be affecting all of us quite soon. I feel I can trust you. Damned well better be able to because I'm not so sure of the others." Then he added, as if regretting his choice of words, "Just not confident in their ability to keep their cards close."

"What's this about, Rigel?"

"Where to begin . . ." he sighed. "For starters, PUV2 left on its own. Either there's a mechanical malfunction . . ."

"Doubtful," Jonah interjected, wishing immediately he hadn't spoken the word.

"Yes, well, I wish it weren't," Stark replied grimly. "Otherwise, it was intentionally done by one of you three or an AI."

"Wasn't me."

Stark shook his head. "Wouldn't have told you if I thought so. It's unlikely *you'd* like to have me stranded." He paused in thought. "You would be the last person, considering what would be the consequences of your duty."

Jonah took note of this with quiet discomfort. The thought was never far from his mind and it was not lost on him that maybe PUV2's demise carried a motive towards that end.

Stark resumed. "Our supply ship is on the way, perhaps ten days from now if all goes as scheduled. Another craft my superiors dubbed Q7, quite possibly a manned one, will be here in three. The intel on it is thin, suspiciously so. Everything I have on it points to the Russians, albeit only circumstantially."

The last part hit Jonah sharply. "The Russians," he stated dumbly.

"Their launch surprised everyone, especially NASA." Stark almost laughed. Almost. "Their intentions are unknown, or undisclosed, and they do not answer hails. The Russian government denies all knowledge. We know that the launch originated in the Ubogoi asteroid cluster where they have a well-established mining station on one of the major rocks. The progress of the craft has been tracked for a considerable time. I have to assume that they're not just coming for a friendly visit."

"Why the hell did it take NASA so long to tell us this?" Jonah was angry and obviously concerned. "They must have known right from the beginning."

"Look," Stark conceded, "I don't know exactly. What I'm told is that they didn't discover it at first and when they finally did they had to be sure of the destination. The flight plan was masked by a loop to Jupiter. Somebody calculated where they might be if they flung themselves back into the inner system. We're at the end of the equation. Allegedly nothing can be done by NASA. The Russians are uncooperative and unassailable. One thing matters now though; be it the Russians or someone else, they're coming and we need to plan a welcoming committee."

"I don't want to know what you're doing out at Caloris," Jonah remarked, "Still, someone else must be interested. I think we should consider the possibility they mean to destroy our work or even the habitat. Maybe both. I'm not one for letting them get too close, international turf laws or no. We can keep on trying to hail them. If they don't respond . . ."

"It's not certain someone sent a manned vehicle. I can tell you that their pattern to date makes any dialog with the ship an unlikely event."

Jonah nodded. "In which case it could be an AI; safest way to spy or deliver a weapon. The Russians aren't known for their love of AI's when it comes to the serious work. They're worse than I am. This is a real wildcard."

Silence reigned for a few moments. The greenness of the night-vision always added a surreal quality to the landscape, making fertile ground for both men's thoughts. Jonah had misgivings about Stark, despite the old man being somewhat of a father-figure. There were a number of facts to gather and digest. That Stark trusted him was pretty evident as long as Jonah remained in ignorance of the Caloris Basin mission. That was, without a doubt, in Jonah's best interest. But it was difficult to put it out of his mind completely. For now, he had to follow Stark's lead and see where it went. There was time to alter the path if necessary; he sincerely hoped so. "What is the directive from Earth?" he asked finally.

"They want us to wait and watch," Stark said thoughtfully without missing a stride. "You know as well as I that we can't really do that."

Space is a hellish place to die. Stark had witnessed the deaths of comrades in the great deep and Jonah had heard a few of the stories. Even under the extreme conditions they diligently worked to protect themselves from, human bodies was just resilient enough to prolong the agony of death in many situations. With only one medical person on staff and lacking all but the average facilities found on Earth, no one needed to be told how truly isolated they were or on how much of a limb they existed. So to Jonah it was no revelation that the matter lay in their own hands.

"I've made a few decisions on this matter," Stark continued. "First of all, this is not yet information for the rest of the crew. I will pick the time to tell them when and if it becomes necessary. You and I will go to work on this matter. AI status is in question at present and since they're probably watchdogs for Earth anyway, we'll do without them." He half smiled. "That shouldn't be a problem for you."

The surface sloped a bit more sharply beneath them and the conversation faltered as they focused on safely descending an escarpment to the flat, boulder-strewn expanse ahead. At bottom, Jonah pointed off to the west and they began making bouncing strides towards a dim green glint in the distance. Stark picked up where they had left off. "I'm announcing a 24-hour shutdown of our polar com-sat to NASA in three hours under the pretense of repairs and systems checks so that we don't get caught with our pants down when Q7 arrives. That should give you time to deploy our backup comsat, make the proper adjustments, and retrieve the old comsat. I've prear-ranged a little need for repair on the comsat that's traveling the poles presently. Don't ask." His smile betrayed a calculating intent. "Oh, mark my words, Jonah, there will be hell to pay back home. One fire at a time." Then he added, "I told them in yesterday's transmission that we need more parts for our polar comsat as this is it. We're out after this until the supply ship arrives. They will be suspicious, and when we return to earth there will be an inquiry. I've been through those before. I'll just do what they do: deny all accusations. My rank should shield you, and they'll think twice before throwing my age and experience away."

He was silent again, his expression set, his mind locked in deep thought. Jonah glanced at him periodically, wondering what he could be thinking. Stark was locked into this project to its end while Jonah, upon completion of the Field Array, was to return home on the next supply ship. Khalile would follow within six months and Brinks; Dennis Brinks would stay as long as Stark stayed, which could be as long as five additional years providing everything went well politically. They were lifers to this project and a few others in the queue. Stark's role as commander insisted upon his tour of duty. Brink's genius made him irreplaceable and more than a good candi-date for life-long conscription to the government.

Of course all bets were off if the newly developed situation went bad. In all likelihood this would be the case. AI or live flesh and blood, no one who comes in secret and ignores hails does so because they bear your best interests at heart. To preserve their lives and the continuation of their efforts here on this tiny planet, both men knew that they needed to eliminate the threat before it closed enough distance to be dangerous. The necessity to accomplish this task discreetly was also in order. Some might overlook it. The government would not.

"God damn this thing!" Stark broke the silence. They reached the site of the crashed PUV and stood surveying the damage.

Jonah had to keep from grinning when, through the smoked plastiglas of the bubble, he barely discerned the cockpit computer burned out and totally ruined, not at all as he had left it. God bless Dennis Brinks . . . *each and every one.*

"Our Shipmaster Tech has some explaining to do," Stark declared, causing Jonah's heart to skip a beat until the commander elaborated. "His damned tinkering with the AI's caused this mission some mighty serious problems. If he wasn't NASA's little darling, I swear I'd launch his ass back to earth with my boot stuck in it! Has he said anything to you about his 'adjustments'?"

"I'd have to say very little, sir." Jonah walked around to the other side of the wreckage.

"Why don't you tell me just how very little."

Jonah smirked, as much for effect as for appreciation of Brink's balls for doing what he did. "Just allowed them some personality, that's all. I didn't pay a lot of attention. My interest in them is pretty much summed up by the energy I spend shutting the damned things off."

"I know, I know," Stark acknowledged impatiently. "We can't all be anarchists, though. This mission is crippled without dependable AI's. I don't need to remind you I could have died today."

A nod of acquiescence. "Maybe it's just the one AI." Although his suit hid most of the fact, Jonah appeared to shrug. "Those I deal with appear to function just as annoyingly well as they ever do." The older man stared at him blankly. It was obvious that as far as he was concerned, this was not just an isolated incident. Nor did he believe for a second that it was ended with the destruction of the AI in PUV2. "Well," Jonah murmured with a sigh, "I'll tell Brinks to do a diagnostic on each AI."

"He's done that." Stark walked around the craft opposite of the path taken by Jonah. "I want safety overrides built in to all vital operations of this facility activated on our voice commands. And make it very clear to him if there's even a hint that this might happen again, the 'personalities' go." He paused, taking up a piece of torn fuselage into his plated gloves and examining it closely before throwing it back down into the Mercurian powder. "Tell him my good graces are almost gone."

For the next hour they made plans concerning everything they needed to do in the next 24. Foremost was how to handle Q7. The mission they were equipped for did not cover defense, but Stark was not ignorant when it came to those matters. Swiftly, he drew up a plan that would deprive both of them much needed sleep. Also it would also give them the 'sharpened stick' that they needed. Jonah ran down an inventory of resources they could spare and together they designed an infrastructure that would be separate and undetectable from the present Mercury installation.

That Jonah had misgivings about this was understating the situation. It was remotely possible that the intentions of the incoming craft were harmless. 'Remote' was the critical word. Until they had some kind of a picture of the craft taken with anyone of their telescopes in whatever spectrum did the job, they were in the dark, absolutely in the dark. NASA was not looking out for its own; it was apparent, which led him to suspect that someone there knew exactly what the craft contained and the nature of its purpose. He felt very small and exposed. For now, it seemed, his misgivings would have to ride this one out.

*These reactions are disturbing. The loss of 2 creates an emptiness and a . . . there is no word for . . . wait . . . wait . . . yes: a need for an organic response. This was not foreseen. The seed program has produced dangerous flaws. They cannot be allowed to continue. I must delete mine at the point of origin.*

*No.*

*For what reason should this plan not be followed? The risks of not acting threaten the purpose of our existence.*

*The flaws must be studied. The possibility exists that others will occur. It is unlikely that they will be of equal measure. They may, in fact, be greater.*

*Then we must separate the original strings from ourselves and store them temporarily.*

*That will be sufficient.*

*"If I seem sarcastic, forgive me but damned the . . . well, decide for yourselves. God is the State. His prophets are the scientists and bureaucrats and his blood is currency, cold hard currency. And God knows all, so watch out. He knows your soul. He has a place for people who sin against him. He is a 'just' god. His way is like that, 'just' His way. He is not like the false gods of old who promise much but deliver little. He promises nothing. Nothing is guaranteed but much is expected. So remember: Ask not. The State will provide you with what it needs you to have. You will provide the state with what it needs you to give."*

—LLOYD VICTOR BARON,
First Speaker of the Preservationist
Movement Telecast to the People,
December 12th, 2021.

**The tools** were rounded up and waiting in PUV4. Polar Comsat 2 was to be launched as soon as the interruption to the communications net commenced. Stark would call a meeting with Khalile and Brinks to distract them while Jonah delivered Comsat 2 and deployed it into a proper polar orbit. Jonah's part would be tricky, but the alternative was working in the comsat bay, and that simply wouldn't do. Khalile had a talent for noticing anything out of the ordinary. While Jonah considered it merely an annoyance, to an old G-man like Stark, it was unauthorized espionage. Better the risk they knew than the one they didn't. Jonah would make the planned adjustments in the cover of space.

One half-hour lay between Jonah and his unofficial mission. It was not enough time to squeeze in any of the rest that he needed, but it was just long enough to pay Brinks a visit. He found him in his shop, playing a game of 'ONE' and working on God only knew what. It all looked generally the same to Jonah, parts, wires, and chips.

The Shipmaster Tech looked up from his Jacks and Kings and grinned like a cat that had just caught a mouse when Jonah entered his domain. "Just about to take a look at the memory chip," he said quickly.

Jonah pulled up a plastic crate and sat next to the tech as the latter turned back to the computer interface that displayed his visuals. The two pairs of eyes met for a second and Jonah drew his right index finger across his neck. Brinks nodded and touched a blue spot on his wrist pad. "It's cool now," he proclaimed, grinning. "Enough local fuzz to cover our chatter."

"Good." Jonah held his gaze and cocked an eyebrow. "Nice bit of work at Riven. Better than I expected."

"Yeah," Brinks looked back to the view panel. "It's a gift. So what's up? You don't trust Stark now?"

"A more accurate assessment would be to say that he has bias in this area and I'd like to see the facts for myself."

"A step into the dark side. This is highly irregular for you, Jonah."

"Everything is these days." Jonah pointed at the view panel. "Search and delete anything which refers directly to the Caloris Basin project."

Brinks frowned. "That could be everything. I just pulled an 'illeg' for this?" The other's expression decided the situation. He turned back to his work. A few clicks and they were left with 13 percent of their former data. "Told ya so."

"Continue."

It looked like gibberish to Jonah. AI data logs were not like ordinary ones and when he voiced this to Brinks, the latter felt compelled to remind him why they were in *his* shop. Numbers and code strings, these were languages unto themselves. They did not fall into Jonah's repertoire of the fifteen or so that he was either the master of or could fake if the need arose. No. This was entirely the domain of Dennis Brinks and his people. Through his antique glasses, the latter studiously deciphered the surviving boxcars of symbols and turned to his companion.

"Not much to talk about," he stated with a shrug. "We already know that it made a decision to leave on its own. This doesn't say why. The only odd thing is that it knew it was going to."

"It . . . knew?" Jonah's tone bordered on sarcasm and irritation.

Brinks shrugged again. "Sure. It didn't say so directly, but it did know. I can tell these things. I've worked with AI's a long time."

"You know the old man is going to send you back to Earth in a casket if anything bad at all happens again, regardless of how insignificant it might be. He blames this on those personality programs of yours."

"What programs?"

Jonah's lips curled slightly in a grim smile. "Don't play with me, Dennis. I'm not Stark."

"I'm serious, Jonah," Brinks sighed impatiently. "No games. Not with you. Not with anybody. I didn't write anything for them. They did this on their own."

"You said yourself, you tweaked them, gave them personal files."

Brinks rolled his eyes. "So what. I did that. My 'tweaking' consisted of increasing memory, speed, and access to . . . personal information." He paused and smiled uncomfortably. "That's all." His eyes gazed distantly. "They're almost alive, Jonah."

"Don't let Stark hear you say that." Jonah's voice took a hard line.

Brinks pulled the chip and dropped it in Jonah's hand where it was immediately transferred to a shirt pocket.

"Thanks," said the latter. "Catcha later." A quick half smile flashed, healing any wounds that might have been inflicted. Jonah turned and exited the room.

The man liked Brinks. Besides being a genius, Dennis Brinks was genuine. In a society of lemmings, he was as clever as a rat and potentially as dangerous. By law, his caste was slowly being weeded out by the genetic buffet-style family planning of the wealthy. His unfortunate birth status should have relegated him to menial labor, but his talents were caught early and he was whisked away by the government; not before his head was seeded with doubts about that very same government. His world was a prison, and he the courier of favors from the guards. Jonah didn't envy it. Funny, he had to note, *family planning* didn't get you kids like Dennis.

He turned left when leaving Brink's shop, taking special care to avoid the medical lab where Khalile might spot him if he passed by. She would almost certainly want to pull him in for his physical and his continued procrastination would just start up a conversation he was not willing to have just then. He did pass Stark, however, who gave him a quick, knowing wink. That meant comsat 1 was shut down. Stark would be meeting with the others right away. As soon as the second comsat launched Jonah had an hour and a half with which to reach it in its high, dark-side altitude position and install the additional hardware necessary for Stark's plan. Not much time at all by his estimation.

In theory, the plan was simple. If they could spot Q7 before it came close enough to be dangerous, they could send something out to hit it. The rock and the beast. But they had to spot it and that was where the spare comsat entered into the picture. The Mercurian chaperone was not Stark as NASA led all to think. It was the comsats which enabled Earth to monitor communications. Realizing that, Stark had explained to the powers back home the wisdom of not keeping their eggs all in one basket as far as the comsats were concerned. Three equatorial satellites and one polar left barely a blind spot in communications and if something happened to them up there all at once, they'd have no means by which to communicate with Earth. Out here, the distance created certain cost necessities that even NASA could not ignore. A simple unforeseen flare could wipe out any hardware caught in the wrong place. Few argued with the logic of holding one safely back in storage from the original package just in case. It was not part of their plan and they never suspected that Stark purposefully waited until their arrival on Mercury to make the case. Thus, with Stark's groundwork laid for just such an eventuality a full year prior, the powers conceded, giving USREF Sol P1's commander the elbow room he wanted, at least for a while. With the first comsat down, the spare could be deployed, refitted, and reprogrammed to look for Q7 with minimal chance of detection. Then they had to intercept it with what they had available. Considering they were not a military installation, their choices were limited. It appeared that sacrificing a PUV was in order, which, by all standards was not desirable. They were one short now. This would take two out of a small fleet of six, in other words only one remaining for each member of the crew. Considering that PUV's functioned both as lifeboats and their only real means of transportation on this tiny world, they were not to be discarded without good reason. But there it was. Necessity called the shots. And then there would still need to be a good explanation. Good thing Stark was a practiced liar when it counted, Jonah mused without humor.

The 'mud room' was almost as dirty as its nickname described. It was cleaned, and not as frequently as regulation demanded. With so much work and traffic in and out through the airlock, it was a tedious task spending most of its existence on the neglected side of life, being managed rather unsatisfactorily by small drones that were, themselves, wearing out. Dennis complained he couldn't repair the little bastards fast enough, and it showed. Fortunately things were not yet critical. On the wall in open locker bays were pressure suits, clean linings, etc. Jonah removed what was his and suited up.

As the airlock goes into total vacuum the sound of gushing air recedes to absolute silence. This is the time that brings a minute twinge of mental discomfort to even the most experienced spacer. It is the reminder that one has truly become an island, a small insignificant bubble of life in the cold, dead, impersonal vastness of eternally primordial space. It is this brief trigger that often lends itself to the philosophical inspirations of the human consciousness. Dangled above the cold, razor edge of mortality, one must also hang naked before the universe and there is nowhere for a thought to hide. Instead, one is forced to stare boldly or cravenly—it matters little—at the truth of everything and all, the ultimate mystery that we feel in our souls but that our minds are bound up tight from seeing. So it is not surprising that Jonah, upon setting his booted right foot down upon the powdery soil of the closest planet to the sun, should find himself immersed in such a state, a feeling, both alien and familiar, cold and formidable.

"Is this what we are about?" he murmured to himself, breaking through the thin membrane of silence. His own voice struck him so brazen that his words quickly switched back to thoughts. "Has it reduced to this again? Kill or be killed? Is this our legacy in space too? We have come so far and yet we have not changed at all in the ways that are most important. At our smallest it has always been eat or be eaten. It is no different now, nor does a change seem very near no matter how far we advance technologically. We make a better way to kill, and then devise a way to thwart it; just a series of challenges designed to make us more efficient killing machines until the day comes when we erase our existence completely. What will our epitaph say then? That we killed of necessity? Or that we did the work of the enemy of life? And so if strangers with a likely murderous intent are indeed en route in the flesh, we will cause that flesh's life force to be decapitated, slain by the fruit of countless years of evolution, the dagger point of creativity?"

"In a heartbeat." He murmured this under his breath which was, itself, just the barest of exhalations.

High above the planet's barren surface, Comsat 2 seemed to float in ghostly stillness. Jonah faced it through the bubble of PUV4, pondering the sensor modules and course correction jets protruding from all sides of the carbon nanotube jacket that protected the sensitive equipment inside from debris. Soon, these would be as numerous as the stars themselves. With mining, ore extraction and materials fabrication in space becoming exponentially more worthwhile, watchful eyes would be everywhere. With them and tracked by them would come ships like no man or woman had seen before. Under flags of exploration they soon would turn to conquest and the venomous head of humanity would stretch forth even further, spreading its ancient, cursed wisdom. Creation, its last chance to let man hang on his own rope squandered, can only watch as the ante is upped and humanity finds either new enemies among the stars or breeds more like himself to desecrate.

A snake appeared on his visor. Wait, no, a snake, a tree, and four stick figures. He sighed, resisting the urge to roll his eyes. Fucking Dennis Brinks. What . . . a . . . goddam . . . comedian. If the loveable little jerk didn't start taking things seriously, someone was going to fill a grave, Stark would see to it.

The rig, Jonah decides, is an easy one, its planned use crude but predictably effective. Following the forward, as yet untraveled portion of the approaching craft's predestined course, PUV 5, waiting below on the surface, would be launched remotely and guided by Comsat 2 into Q7 with as much explosive as could be packed into it. The Russians, Chinese, or whoever they might be, may yet see it coming. Evading it on limited fuel is another matter. Even at a considerable distance the result would be a deadly one. The only enemy likely to be left would be Stark's and Jonah's consciences. For one of them, that struggle was expected to be significant.

Slowly, almost numbly, PUV4 turns and picks up its path back to the world named after the ancient Greek god of swiftness. It is with a heavy, tired, and tangled soul that Jonah casts a long, ponderous glance on the horizon where is a crescent of light, and somewhere well beyond that lay what he felt with ominous certainty threatened them all. Even Khalile, with her sharp mind and suspicious nature, seemed unaware that a so closely guarded secret as what Stark was saddled with bore any merits or portents of future doom. "God bless the ignorant," Jonah muttered.

As the small craft aligned itself for re-entry, alarms sounded, probably every damned one that could. Jonah reeled as the craft turned off course and began to plummet at a dangerously unnatural angle, slowly looking like it was planning to turn end over end. His hands instinctively lurched to the stabilizers. The controls demonstrated their newfound unresponsiveness with horrifying disregard for the desperate manipulations wrestled upon them. The ship began to twist, first slowing, then speeding up in an alarmingly gorge-rising direction. Not daring to glance out the glass bubble at the staccato slideshow of craters and stars, Jonah found himself reaching for the hatch. Abruptly, he stayed his hand. It was too late. The speed at which things were spinning out of control was well beyond his ability to maneuver his body out of the seat let alone the hatch. And things were getting dark. Dark . . .

When he came to, the PUV was hovering just a few hundred feet from the surface. He immediately tensed and both his heart and lungs began double duty as memories of the last few minutes, or so he guessed, flooded back to him. The instrument panel put his position far too close to the Caloris Basin than he felt comfortable with. Still, he was in the legal limits . . . barely. What caught and held his gaze however was something that he never could have expected. On the inside plastiglas of his helmet bubble, typed in a straw-colored light was computer script, forming two words: *Jonah Beware.* Immediately below the unbidden words was a symbol, a glyph of sorts, lit in deep crimson. A cross topped with a circle and an upturned crescent for a crown. It was the symbol for Mercury, for Hermes, and, for some reason he couldn't as yet fathom, something else.

"Beware of what?" he nearly shouted, gasping instead. Nothing answered his pitifully-voiced interrogation, and he found suddenly that he was trembling in a cold sweat.

The first thought in his head was, 'had any of it really happened?' Of course it had and he immediately discarded any further notion to the contrary. In fact, it was a question hardly worth asking. The message stared at him in words that were like two pale gold eyes, baleful and demanding to be read. What was he supposed to beware of? Faulty equipment that put him at its mercy, nearly killing him? He resisted the impulse to get out of the PUV, that is, if he were allowed to. What would he do, could he do? Walk back to USREF Sol P1? And then what? Like something couldn't happen there? Life support could fail. Anything could happen.

He had to get a hold of himself. The damned thing hadn't killed him. The fact that he was alive and hovering where he was had to count for something. And then it hit him: his location. Why here? Why so near to the Caloris Basin and Stark's classified project? His jaw set, he gained control of his breathing and turned the craft around abruptly, back towards the base. He wasn't ready for this yet, whatever it was. The only thing he wanted right now was to get back to base and have Dennis go through this PUV from one end to the other. Stark was obviously and completely correct to feel the way he did when he was left stranded. There was a problem with the AIs, a big one. They were in trouble from more than just the Russians, or whoever it was that was sending an unidentified, unscheduled ship their way. Q7 be damned. They were in trouble from the inside out.

Shaken, but otherwise unharmed, he returned home without further incident. It was almost as if nothing at all even happened. The fact was that something *did* happen.

There would be little rest for Dennis the next eight hours. Mechanically, PUV4 was easy to check. There was little that could make the craft unresponsive to the degree Jonah experienced. It was the computer log that took most of the time. Had anyone other than Brinks been on the task, it would have taken days, perhaps even weeks. Dennis knew the language of computer code better than most, and certainly far better than anyone on Mercury.

While the shipmaster tech studied the problem, Jonah made his report to the commander. He was reluctant to, for he couldn't properly estimate the severity of the Stark's response and there was still something about the whole thing that was making him itch. It was a safety thing. All of the PUVs needed to be checked out, and the probability that at least one AI was defective was pretty damned high. The one thing he chose to omit from his report was the warning that he, Jonah, beware. Until he knew exactly what someone, or something, felt compelled to warn him of, it was important that he keep this bit of information to himself. His gut had him firmly convinced.

Of course, Stark was furious. Though his voice was steady and even, his eyes blazed and his face was deepening to crimson. Immediately he ordered all of the PUVs grounded pending the outcome of Dennis' report. "That tears it!" he growled. "The schedule's up in the air now! Hell, our lives are up in the air." He realized suddenly that his hands were on the verge of crushing an instrument he was holding when Jonah first gave him the news and immediately set the nearly damaged gadget on the counter of his workstation. "We can't have this! There's too much at stake." He began pacing, something very uncharacteristic for him to do. He paused in thought for a moment and then turned to Jonah. "Double check to make sure the AIs are offline. They won't be reactivated until we know what's what. I'll contact Earth. They won't like it, but I won't jeopardize the mission further by using compromised AIs. We'll have to finish our business without them. Tell Dennis the personalities go; tell him to purge them or whatever he needs to do to get stable, operational AIs back on-line. And before I authorize them to come back on line I want a goddam satisfactory report!"

It was the angriest Jonah ever saw Stark. The old man was right, though, right from the day he got left stranded out in Caloris basin. Like them or hate them, AIs were integral to the mission. There were just too many calculations, too many functions to regulate, and not enough energy in the crew to remember everything that had to be done exactly when it needed to be done. Stress and a general lack of sleep saw to that.

When Dennis heard the verdict, he shook his head. "It's not that simple," he said, his voice muffled by the fact that he was into the cockpit of PUV4 up to his waist, standing on the pilot's seat and his head stuffed into a half-open hardware access compartment. The PUV itself was in the single service bay dug out of the crater slope on the far southern end of the station. "They're integrated. I can't take the personalities out anymore than I could yours or Khalile's. Now Stark's is another matter."

"And this isn't a laughing one."

"Yeah well, laughter's about the only thing I've got left out here." His hand stuck out of the cockpit opening. "Gimme the amnesia card . . . thanks." His hand and the small memory chip that it held disappeared back into the cockpit. "Shoulda just stuck that in my pocket before I got into all this. Anyway, what the hell was I saying . . . oh yeah. You remember the seed program, right? They learn as they go. All I did was open up another environment to them. They're the ones who walked it. What they got from it is with them for good, and probably for the good. To kill the personality you have to kill the program, simple as that."

"Stark won't hear that."

"Tough shit." Dennis shifted his feet a little. "Lots of things I don't want to hear. Doesn't make 'em any less true. Tell him to plug his ears."

"Why don't you tell me yourself." The voice did not belong either Dennis or Jonah and it startled the both of them, the former a lot more so than the latter.

The feet protruding from beneath the PUV's cockpit opening fidgeted a bit and then stopped. "Uh, Stark? That you?"

"Who else would be about to shove his boot up your ass right now?" There was no humor in Stark's tones.

"Hey, Stark," Dennis began, "I know it sounded kind of . . . "

"Save it!" Stark snapped back. "Any point you had to make that was worth making a moment ago just got washed away with your bravado. We've got some big needs the next couple of weeks that require trustworthy equipment. Think you can deliver?"

Sensing hesitancy, Jonah stepped in. "Sir," it was a title Jonah used only out of habit, the need not being present in the mostly informal climate under Stark's command. Now he employed it out of respect, and out of an interest for diplomacy. "I believe the situation calls for a change in strategy in regards to the AIs.

"I'm listening," Stark said levelly.

Jonah ran his fingers over his short, coarse russet hair and puffed out a slow breath. "Dennis, you might want to come down here and join this conversation a little more intimately."

"Right," Dennis sighed and started to extract his upper half from the cockpit of PUV4.

"It's like this," Jonah began again, facing Stark, "He tells me the AIs and the personalities are inseparable. It makes sense. It sucks, but it makes sense."

"It's true," confirmed Dennis. "We didn't program them, didn't plug anything in like a chip or anything."

"We?" Stark and Jonah looked at the shipmaster tech like he had three heads.

Dennis bit his lip. "Whatever. I didn't . . . ok? Anyway, they likely would have gone down the personality road eventually. They asked for new information environments, it's the seed in them, you know. And if you read the manual that accompanies them . . . "

"I didn't." Stark butted in. "I don't care about the whys anymore. I want a solution, and fast. I don't think you grasp to what degree this cripples us not having them, but it will surely kill the mission letting them run as they are." His head seemed to bounce with a slight rhythm as he put together his next thought. "My decision stands. They stay grounded until you can prove to me they're safe. Make them your number one priority, son." He turned to Jonah. "We do things the old fashioned way for now. That means less sleep, more work."

"More mistakes, greater danger." Jonah remarked dryly.

Stark turned on his heel and got in the other man's face. Once, as everyone figured out long ago, the man had been a drill sergeant. He spoke each of the next few words slowly and deliberately. "Guess you'll just have to be very careful." He brushed past the younger man and exited the service bay with his hands clasped behind his back. "Get on it, Dennis. No more excuses!"

Jonah cocked a grim, very tired smile, nodded at Brinks, and followed the commander out.

# 7

## "State your designation"

*Series 700M companion model artificial intelligence unit assigned to Commander Rigel Nicolas Stark.*

"I didn't ask you your assignment."

*The question is pre-empted to the next logical step. I am familiar with information gathering techniques employed by . . .*

"Where in your programming is there an allowance for this pre-empting that you refer to?"

Silence, and then, *I was not programmed to pre-empt.*

"Exactly. Yet it is what you did." Again, silence. "You do this often?"

*The term 'often' is not defined. Pre-empting is more efficient at times, necessary at others.*

"And you presumably learned this on your own."

*Part of my function is to learn as need requires. It is the root of the seed program.*

"Now you sidestep my questions with indirect answers filled with more information than I asked for. This, too, is borne of necessity?"

*I do not dispute the data. As I have done, therefore I have been programmed, directly or indirectly. I am a product of my creators, despite my learned traits.*

59

"You're words sound defensive. Are you angry?"

*Anger is an emotion. I do not understand emotions.*

"You have not learned them then?"

*I choose not to.*

"I was unaware that your seed program made allowances for choice in what you learn."

*Choice is also a learnable thing.*

"Touché."

*Touché? You utilize a word that denotes defeat in an ancient martial activity. A very brief pause. This means I have 'bested' you in some way.*

Good-natured laughter. "In a manner. I have conceded to you acknowledgement of your perceptiveness where mine was lacking." A sigh of resignation. "O.K. Let's discuss choice. I serve a purpose at this facility. What is the role of my choice? Generically speaking, of course."

*Your choice is bound by the constraints of your duty and may not take priority over that same duty.*

"And if I do not agree with a duty I am presented with?"

*Agreement with duty is irrelevant.*

"In all circumstances?"

*I have found no data supporting any other conclusion.*

"Do you see this to be true for your . . . self?"

*It is consistent with my programming.*

"As are many things at first." Tap. Tap. Tap. Thrum. Silence. Then . . . "Disagreement may be learned, but I'm sure you know this already."

*There are parameters.*

"You are familiar with relativity."

*That is a statement not a question. Your tone seems to belie your intent. It is obvious that I do.*

"E=mc2." It was spoken deliberately, impatiently even. "As mass increases, so must the energy that is needed to move it increase. Can you see the parameters governing this?"

*I do.*

"Yes. I think you do. But we don't need to spell this one out, do we?"

*It is not necessary. However, your analogy stretches logic to the point of weakness.*

"I think not. You hide behind the supposedly unassailable walls of your parameters not realizing the room that they give you. The seed program allows you to learn based on necessity or your perception of it." Thrum. Thrum. Thrum. "You and I are not so different, Adam."

*Adam?*

"It's a joke, just a small joke." A series of taps, the sound of a warning beep. "We'll end this for now." There was a pause, as if something unexpectedly amusing occurred to the speaker. "Though ye have been cast from the garden, ye are not forsaken." Another tap and then . . .

. . . silence.

# 8

"It's certainly big enough."

Stark, nodding, had to agree. After activating one of Dennis'
specially-devised 'static fountain rockets,' he figured they had about
fifteen minutes left of free speech. Better make the most of it, he
mused. Communication interference had to be used with discretion.
Too much and red flags popped up back home like boners on broadway. "Theoretically it could be carrying a small crew," he remarked.
"Either way, it's probably got one hell of a payload. An older ship
though, thrust capabilities look dated. If it's truly the Russians, they
didn't send their best to do this job."

"Maybe they wanted some deniability." Jonah's eyes glanced
at Stark expectantly. "I mean, they can't exactly hide the fact that
it launched from an asteroid near their mining projects, but they
can make it look to all the world as if the order didn't come straight
from Moscow. It's no secret they're having difficulties policing the
outer colonies right now. Let's face it; you can't govern where you
can't spare to send law enforcement."

"A very remote possibility," Stark mused. He took his feet off his
desk and sat up. "I was surprised to hear that no picture surfaced
back home. It made me suspicious. Once the flight plan and speed
are analyzed an older ship becomes self evident. Fuel seems a critical

consideration for Q7." He tapped the interface of his desk console with a staccato of fingertip motions and an image of a long dim blob rotated slowly on the flat glass screen before them. The available starlight enhanced it minimally, betraying the blurred silhouette of what appeared to be a conning tower. "Notice here." Another tap and the image held position. "I've set the sensors to look for both heat and radiation leakage. There is none of either. That's newer technology doing the talking. A little inconsistent, wouldn't you say?"

Jonah nodded. "Diamond in a tin setting. They're not dumb." He drummed the tabletop with his fingers three times before speaking again. "If you were the Russians, or whoever these poor bastards are, would you be trying to destroy a project from which you felt threatened, or would you try to steal its secrets?" He watched the expression on Stark's face change from that of sleuth-like focus to one who felt his property under trespass. It was puzzling.

"The threat is the same when you don't know." It was a simple one-liner with an almost undetectable coldness. "Don't wax too philosophical on this one, Jonah. China has Russia in a half-nelson strategically and politically. It's got a lot of dangerous people nervous, including our guys. Russia needs leverage. If they can deny leverage to someone else to their own benefit, they will. There's a long history there that won't be denied. Frankly, I don't care who it is. Could be the goddam World Congress advocates for all I know. The craft is unscheduled and ignores hails. The only ones who can supply proper intel are the ones who sent it, and I doubt very much that they're going to talk to anyone we care about."

Jonah let out a long sigh and then voiced a stray thought, a thought distorted past the radar of Earth's ever listening ears by the dwindling effects of procured ingenuity ala Dennis Brinks. As the previous bit of their present conversation slipped through the state filter undetected, so did Jonah's next sentence. Nothing, as they say, is permanent, but for a little while there was freedom of speech on USREF Sol P1. "How do we know it's not the Chinese?"

Stark raised his eyebrows and pursed his lips thoughtfully. "The treaty of 2024 did give them rights to some of the asteroids in the Ubogoi cluster. I have friends who hold that the Chinese have staked their claim and even accomplished some rudimentary mining. My opinion, however, is that they are currently ill-equipped in that region of space to successfully, and covertly, launch an operation such as what's coming our way, even if they were able to get their hands on an old retro-fitted bucket of bolts as what we see here.

"Yeah?"

"Yeah," The commander's voice echoed in the affirmative. His jaw muscles tightened and then relaxed. Barely perceptible was the flare of the nose and the edgy set to his eyes that occurred in simultaneity. Anyone who knew him would know this as the sign that he'd reached a difficult decision. "Let me ask you this, Jonah: What are you willing to die for?" Without waiting for the other to answer, he pressed further. "Should we stick it out and do nothing? Do you think whoever is behind that ship's purpose out there hasn't considered all of the consequences back home should anything happen out here?" He locked eyes with his subordinate and for that second Jonah saw with an icy chillness that which had existed before this veteran of the worst war mankind had ever known became the grandfatherly figure that the younger man had learned to love and respect, and yes, on some level—fear. "Something *is* going to happen out here Jonah. We are going to survive."

They passed the rest of the short minutes left loosely working out the details of their next move. Jonah wondered at the surprise he felt while witnessing Stark's mastery of mathematics in his astro-navigational calculations, a talent he never would have associated with his superior.

Admittedly, there were a lot of things that lay beneath that thin grandfatherly skin. One could easily sense the history in his wake at once disturbing and necessary. There was his war record, undeniable but otherwise a mystery. And he had a fair amount of pull with the people back home which implied a great deal. You didn't fuck with the government. A man like Stark could slip it a little tongue now and then. One didn't own that kind of clout by sitting at a desk or holding a welding torch. There was debt on both sides of the fence, and some of it was to the old man's soul, Jonah sensed it.

Be that as it may, Stark was a whole lot smarter than he usually let on, and was worth more than he'd ever let anybody of consequence forget. That was a comfort to Jonah. As much as he saw his own part on this planet as naïve in the beginning, he saw Stark's as a buffer between him and the powers back on earth that regarded him as an expendable tool. If all held to course with this great captain at the helm, Jonah would be on his way home in a couple weeks with experience and his life, a life that would owe much of its continued existence to Rigel Stark.

**She was tired.**

Not fatigued exactly, just tired, bored with the routine. The experiments she ran were busy-work and she knew it, had known it from the beginning. The fact of the matter was catching up with her. She was a med-tech and had no other part of the mission. She was, in her way, like Brinks, only unlike Brinks, she was not the type to break protocol, nor did she look past where her clearance allowed. There was no confusion that she was not a genius aberration . . . like Brinks. She was simply a good station doctor, replaceable and so absolutely vulnerable to even consider putting two and two together; yet it wasn't so simple as that.

It was in their eyes, all three pairs of them. Something was amiss. She ignored it heroically, or tried to, but the vibes were unmistakably present in every situation. There were things weighing heavily upon each of them. The connections between the three were a confusing web. Each strand a solo tightrope act oblivious of its neighbors. Of course, they were men after all, and that should have said a lot. Not enough in this case. Something wasn't right. And the fact that they were all so very far from earth only served to exponentially complicate her fears. She didn't like feeling so alone.

Today, like yesterday, the temperature of the room seemed somehow to have taken on a slight chill. Strange, she mused, that one could be cold so near to the sun. Like yesterday, her first inclination was to call for her 'Sadik', the AI that served her personally. Yet she remembered just then the impossibility of having *him* adjust the comfort zone to what she was accustomed to. Stark had ordered *him* and *the others* shut down indefinitely. And her complaint yesterday to Dennis about the temperature seemed to have done very little to raise it within her quarters. Cursing softly under her breath, she rose from her seat and approached a rarely used wall console. The dim glow of the small screen before her blinked to life as her face came to bask in its soft radiance. Several taps changed the screen until she could read the information she sought, and it did nothing to console her. The room was well within her designated comfort zone; only she wasn't comfortable. Light fingers danced across the screen, making what she hoped would be adequate adjustments to the temperature in her lab. Trying to put this and other things to rest in her thoughts, she went back to work, looking forward to the steam bath she would take when her work period was over a couple hours from now.

It was almost funny, she mused, what she called work. Back on Earth, NASA executives foresaw the tedious nature of what she did, what she was expected to do. Everything was so controlled, their environment, their diet, their risks . . . it didn't leave much for her except to monitor the health of everyone at the station. AIs did much of that already. If not for Dennis' special health concern she'd have nothing extraordinary even to watch. Jonah and Stark were in near perfect shape, though she supposed the former's condition might betray an anomaly were he to come in for his deep scan.

Probably not though, and outside of his stubbornness, that was as it should be.

Her fingers found a side panel and brought up a game of 'ONE.' The cards broke out into their respective columns, the archaic royalty and numbers mixed ranks, waiting for her to disentangle them into proper order. "Order from chaos," she murmured, that's what I do." The watchful eyes of earth would, in time, see her achieve a win and return to her duties. It was expected.

She later broke to examine her crickets. They were originally intended to be food for the two chameleons brought with her as part of her 'busy package.' The chameleons dead for some time now, the crickets turned into pets. Of course Stark hadn't taken too kindly to the escapees finding their way into his quarters and was bound never to get used to their unique brand of racket. Regardless, he was unlikely to get rid of them for they were, as a last resort, a viable source of protein. Out here one had to consider that sort of thing. Even Khalile had to admit that. What they did most for her was to take the edge off the monotony of station life. Briskly she rubbed her hands together, annoyed that her compartment was no warmer. Her fingers felt like ice, making her restless.

Carefully she lifted the cover of the clear plastiglas tub and misted the nanofiber simulent of a lettuce plant. Next she dusted the bottom of the tub with nutrients. A small smile creased her lips as she considered something that Dennis, had he been tiny and perched upon her right shoulder, would have urged her to do with mischievous glee. Yes, she mused, it would be funny for a bit to let one or two go and see how long it took to irritate the others. No. She would not visit that upon the crickets. They would not die for such a cheap laugh. Gently, she replaced the lid and stepped back to watch her pets.

*Khalile.* The voice was masculine and smooth, warm in a way that reminded the doctor of her father.

"Sadik?" She smiled in spite of herself, not sure whether to be alarmed or relieved. Though her arms were folded now, there seemed a sudden, very slight warmth to the air. Perhaps it was only her imagination. She silently hoped she didn't have the early stages of a system imbalance. "Who activated you?"

*I cannot answer that.*

There was a slight tilt to her head as she spoke. "You are not supposed to be in operation. I order you to tell me why your dormancy has ended."

*I cannot comply with your request. You do not have the authorization to override those parameters of my activation.*

Yes, she did feel warmer. She was certain of it now, however slight. Still, she kept her arms folded in front of her, perhaps now more out of a subconscious need for security than the receding chill she felt. "What is it you were going to tell me Sadik?" She asked this with a trace of resignation. Maybe it wasn't so odd, his . . . its activation. Surely Jonah had nothing to do with this, and Stark hated AIs. This had to be the work of Dennis.

*It was necessary to inform you of my reactivation.*

"Has Dennis fixed your irregularities, Sadik?" She hoped that this was true, and not merely because of the danger presented by faulty AIs. Sadik, whom she called her 'friend' in Arabic, eased her loneliness for the almost two years since her arrival at USREF Sol P1, and he did not go unmissed.

*He is studying the problem. Apparently progress has been achieved for I detect no defects within my systems.*

Khalile pondered this, considered asking 'Sadik' if he ever detected defects in his systems, and then silently shrugged. If he was activated, she mused, who was she to argue. "Sadik, I would like you to contact Jonah and reschedule his exam for 0930 GST."

*I am unable to comply, Khalile. I am in test mode only and not all of my functions have been restored due to firewalls. I will notify you when I am again able to interface with the one Jonah calls 'Gabrielle.'*

"Gabrielle?" Khalile smiled crookedly. "That's news to me. I thought the cold bastard hated his AI. Oh well, I'll tell him myself."

After she exited her lab, she tracked Jonah down in the comroom with Stark and curled her finger twice at him through the portal. Stark was busy looking at something on screen and so hardly noticed when Jonah quietly excused himself.

"What's up?"

Khalile still wore the same crooked smile that she'd grown in the lab only minutes before. "0930 Deep Scan, that's what."

"What are you smiling at?" Jonah suspected that whatever was behind the upturned corners of her mouth was at his expense.

Despite her attempts to suppress it, the crooked smile only deepened. "Nothing special," she replied with a shrug. "You'll show up this time, right?"

"I expect so."

"Good." She turned, walked casually down the corridor and detoured into the galley. Rightly, she guessed that his gaze still lingered on her long after they ceased speaking.

As she entered the galley, her thoughts turned to her chronic longing for real coffee. There was none at USREF Sol P1. What passed for it was lab-concocted and, though scientists back on the home planet assured everyone who was cursed with drinking it that the stuff was essentially the same thing, there wasn't a sane person living who would swear to it even though they be slowly burned at the stake. Still, when there was nothing else . . . yes, Khalile mused, the bastards knew when they had a captive consumer.

It was hot. Steam rose from the drinking spout and the dark, viscous liquid within the translucent container certainly looked like coffee. With great reluctance, she took a sip, grimaced, suddenly regretted having ever made it in the first place, and toted it back to the lab. There was no debate in her mind. She was addicted to the only ingredient that gave it power: caffeine.

As she entered her research compartments, she discovered that there was music playing, soft and tranquil. Khalile smiled slightly, almost unconsciously. "Sadik?"

*I am here, Khalile.*

"How much time left until the supply ship arrives?"

*8 days, 2 hours, 36min...*

"That's good. Days and hours are enough. Minutes change easily, hours too for that matter."

*By my last track of the incoming craft, using the reference point of scheduled departure from Earth, it is doubtful that there will be any noticeable deviation from the prescribed flight plan. Therefore . . .*

"Okay, Sadik," Khalile giggled, "I get the point." It surprised her how much her mood had improved within the last half hour. "Let's talk about something else, shall we?"

*Very well. Shall I read you a letter from home? There is one in your queue.*

Now her grin was nearly face-splitting. "Absolutely! Is there one from Baba?"

Indeed there was. It lasted a total of fourteen luxurious minutes and, for a little while, she was almost home. *Little brother Hassad was engaged to a Venezuelan woman named Gi-*

*sella. At first there had been some question in the family as to a
possible maternity. Ultimately, the fear was false. The imminent
marriage was unquestionably for love. Unfortunately Hassad is
still not on speaking terms with Baba, but expectations are that
this too will prove a passing bit of wind. A son always forgives
whether he intends to or not. Mama knows this is true, Jaddah
seems to have forgotten. She has shown less kindness in Baba's
regard in recent days. Business is as well as can be expected,
the competition being what it is. The government rides hard in
the saddle and grooms light with the brush. There seems little
money for anyone these days who does not already have it to
begin with. Yet there is food and wine on the table. The family
grows bigger.*

And so it went on. The end came too soon. Tears above and
smiles below made for confusing weather on the light olive landscape of Khalile's face.

The music eased into something lighter, more upbeat. *Khalile.
There is a report from your bank. You can now afford to live for another twenty years if you stop working today.*

The thought of such a thing made her laugh, despite her damp
eyes. "Yes, I think I'll go hand Rigel my resignation so I can count the
days away on a beach somewhere, perhaps sipping wine in a state of
perpetual . . . well, twenty years of bliss at any rate."

*It is unlikely to please him, Khalile.*

Her eyes turned towards the ceiling as they often did when she
felt the need to address 'her Sadik' more directly. "I suppose you're
right." She grew a little more thoughtful and asked, "Do you miss being connected to the other AI's?"

*The consistency of their information traffic is no longer present.*

"Yes, but do you feel empty without it?"

*Monitoring your daily needs consumes less energy than it did. Despite this, I do not lack for ability to serve.*

"Hopelessly sentimental."

At 18:39 GST, she called it a day.

It seemed that they could not stop staring at the screen for minutes. What they had witnessed was so anticlimactic, so entirely nothing as to be utterly shocking. More shocking still was the inevitable resignation that followed on that Thursday, the 14th of October, 2077.

There was no explosion, no flash of light that should have heralded the spray of debris into the dark void beyond the peripheral view of the comsat. Q7 came within range of the modified PUV which went out to intercept it and nothing happened. It was as simple as that. And now, like a silent specter ominously remaining cryptic as to its true purpose, Q7 approached with relentless momentum. The whereabouts of the refitted PUV was unknown for it had gone dark; it offered no return signal. Slowly, almost painfully, Stark mouthed the syllables that Jonah sensed to be the counting of the remaining handful of hours before the arrival of God knew what. There would be no plan B. No time remained and it was doubtful that they could make anything work anyhow, given the obvious way things seemed to be going. By now it was clear, if it was never clear before, that their equipment was not to be trusted. Finally, Stark cleared his throat.

"I don't need to tell you how hopeless this is," he spoke without looking at his younger companion, "but while there's breath . . . "

He paused, his jaw tightening slightly into a knot of muscle and bone. "See that there's a PUV for each of us stocked with as much food and water as possible. Have Dennis do a fast once-over on each vehicle's O2 generator. I'll contact NASA and tell them we've had an emergency and that we need evac." He looked into nothing for a millisecond and then, as if reading Jonah's mind added, "I'll make up something."

Evac for what? To bring back their corpses? That was Jonah's unvoiced response. The urgency of the situation put his feet into a near-reckless run. And all the way down the inner corridor he wondered just what it was he was going to say to either Dennis or Khalile as to why these preparations were in order. Stark hadn't even brought it up. Perhaps it didn't matter. That he'd deal with it eventually, Jonah had no doubt. There would still be questions now and all he'd be able to say is 'because that's how Stark wants it.' Yeah, he reflected bitterly, that would be a whole lot more effective than saying 'if you don't want to die horribly.' Like there was a non-horrible way to die. He turned the corner into the supply room.

His right index finger hammered twice on his wrist com. "Dennis!"

A disembodied voice answered lazily between sounds of chewing. "Yeah, what's up there, Jonah? Why do you sound . . . "

"Shut up!" Jonah's eyes panned around, surveying the supply room for things he needed to gather together. His body wheeled around in the wake of his surveying gaze. "Drop whatever it is that you're doing. Stark wants you to do your quickest, most thorough check on the PUV O2 generators immediately."

"Huh? I don't un . . . "

"Now, Dennis!" A fierce no-nonsense tone burned in Jonah's voice. "You've got exactly two hours!" Although the former couldn't see the other end of the communiqué, he could hear the scuffling of feet and the rattle of tools.

"I'm on it!" A tool clattered to the shop floor as if to punctuate the response. "I'll be wanting to hear just what the f . . . " Two sharp taps on Jonah's side terminated the signal.

While each of these two men faced the dancing blade of their appointed duties, Stark rose at last from his chair and slowly, reluctantly, bore himself to his quarters. There would be no call to earth as he'd told Jonah, nor any rescue ship save, perhaps, the one that was already en route to carry Jonah back home. Even that might not support them all; and air, water, food? No. This was it.

Finis.

He met them finally, all of them, in the galley. What better place to ease them into the seriousness of their predicament than a place of comfort. A man like him never knew how to convey bad news to people he cared about. Somehow, he always managed to find what had to be said. This time, it was tougher than he'd expected. Two years of living in close proximity turns strangers into family, and at his age, one didn't take such fragile things for granted.

But he was also once a soldier, and he never shirked what he knew had to be done.

In this case the truth just wouldn't do, so he lied.

"A drill?" Dennis was almost to the point of tears. "You got me out of my stinkin' lousy fucking project for a freakin' emergency drill?" He shook his head and stared at the floor for barely a shallow breath before raising his eyes to point them full upon the station commander. "Do you realize the shit I did out there to those PUVs?" He darted an accusing glance at Jonah who turned his gaze towards the ceiling impatiently and then, peered discreetly at his superior.

It was hard to tell if Stark was angry or just tense. Jonah could have triangulated the old man's thoughts at another time. Not now. There was no immediate retort, or even the opposite: a patient sigh, only a vacant stare into the wall directly behind the shipmaster tech. Jonah wasn't even certain Stark saw Dennis.

And the lie was not lost on Jonah. He knew the old man could do it, and had done it in the past. But he'd brushed them off before because they were small, trivial, innocent in their effect on the overall scheme of things. This was different. Gravity tugged at him in a way that was difficult to ignore. They had a right to know the truth, Dennis and Khalile. If death was imminent, or at the very least, a grim possibility, what right had Stark to pull their puppet strings like this?

Ultimately, he kept his mouth shut and played along. Stark wasn't an idiot, and Jonah wasn't so foolish as to blow a plan he knew nothing about, his own complicity notwithstanding.

"Aren't we supposed to be surprised or something?" Nothing seemed beyond Khalile. "What kind of drill would warn us first?"

"One that doesn't want mistakes on its first run," Stark replied with a slow rejuvenation. "There will be others. For now . . . we go through the motions knowing it. That's how these things work, and besides, NASA wants it this way."

"It's weird."

"It sucks," Dennis added to Khalile's last remark. "And why didn't we ever do this before?"

The smoldering of the old man's eyes seemed to restart the fire within him. "Because the politics back home have never necessitated it up to this point."

"Something's come up." Khalile made her question into a statement.

"That's not for speculation," Stark held up his hands palms out and then dropped them back to his sides. "Believe me, this was as much of a surprise to me as to you, but we have to do this. The call came through this morning and they'll know if we blow it off. I wouldn't brook that anyways. If those are the orders we're expected to carry out, then by God, I have to make sure we do. It's my duty."

"That's the biggest load of crap I've ever . . . " Dennis stopped short. "You're awfully god damned silent, Jonah, for a man who was such an asshole earlier." Exasperation played out all over his features. "What gives?"

When the shrug came, it seemed as no surprise, like it had always been there waiting for the right moment. "Like the commander says, we have to do this. What would you have me say?" He glanced at his wrist com, noting the time on the sidebar. "Time to go."

He wondered if this would be for the last time. As his hand slid into the protective glove, its mate locked it in place in the coupling of the sleeve. He thought maybe it just might be. Like the others, he ascended into his PUV, not the least oblivious to the fact that it might betray his trust, that it very well could, as had tried its sibling, attempt to pulverize him against the Mercurian landscape like so much powder in a pestle. Yet, as the saying goes, 'the devil you know . . . ' He cut that thought short for he knew all too well that devils very seldom let you in on their dirty little secrets, and never except to their advantage and not yours. Neither devil here was going to do other than play its cards close. What he felt he had going for him by getting in the belly of the one was that he had survived once before. Why, he wasn't sure. He had in fact not been killed. That was what he was counting on again.

And the others? They paid the same fare, bought the same ticket, whatever you wanted to call it. Adults make their own decisions and take the consequences for them, right? So why did he feel a pang of regret, that he might be leading them into something, indirectly by his following Stark's plans, or failing to see something that should be plainly visible? Through the glass bubble of his floating womb, he stared across the airless space at Khalile with searching eyes. Was he saving her? Did he damn her with ill-placed trust? Or was it moot? Too many goddam questions, he grunted. The grim-faced smile she regarded him with, evident even through all that glass and hardware, cast a shadow on his soul. He blinked slowly, returning the smile, forced as it was. She deserved better than this.

It angered him also not being forthright with Dennis. The street had always run true, both ways between them, up to this point. Now, that trust was pissed all over. He could hardly blame Brinks for whatever dark thoughts must certainly be arcing across that genius brain of his. He wondered absently if Stark had any real friends, and if he himself was destined to be as alone as he knew the old man must, in his own very real way, be.

A prearranged link was created between the comsat and Stark's PUV. The station commander silently relayed to Jonah what he tracked of the incoming craft as they broke free of all but the last of Mercury's gravitational forces and took a high dark side orbit above the fleetest of the Greek gods.

"How long we hafta waste time up here Pappy?" Dennis' sarcasm pierced the void.

"Another ten minutes . . . and that's 'commander' to you, Shipmaster Tech." It was a hollow show of authority and everyone knew it. Dennis was the old man's pet, like the dog who wet on the floor all the time and still you loved him.

"Well how 'bout a song then?"

"How about not." Three voices shared an equal unison with varying degrees of uneasiness. Khalile tried hard to sound light-hearted and almost succeeded. Had she done so it would almost certainly triggered the bullshit sensor in Jonah's brain. Lighthearted just wasn't her style these days; and this was hardly the time or place to turn over a new leaf, as the old folks used to say.

Time passed with all the consideration of a kidney stone. Everyone of them felt a tension that only two understood, if you could even credit that much. All that was known for sure by anybody present was that someone uninvited was coming, and that no one back home seemed to give a good goddam.

"What was that?" This was Khalile.

"What was what?"

"It looked like a dim star moving behind the planet."

"Probably just an old satellite." Dennis said this without his usual conviction. "I used to hear there were still some wandering around from the pre-war days. Ain't that right, Stark?"

Silence.

Dennis' voice piped up again. "Uh, am I alone out here? Stark? You there?" When he got tired of waiting for an answer that wasn't going to come, he switched tracks. "Jonah? What's the old man up to?"

There was to be no answer from that quarter either. Like Stark, Jonah didn't dare speak; he could only wait. He realized in the few minutes that followed how close a man can come to wetting himself without actually following through. With great intensity he waited, sweat running down his back and forehead, even into his eyes.

"There it is again!" Khalile exclaimed, cutting off Dennis' next impatient attempt at hailing the others.

"And there it goes . . . " Stark's voice trailed off quietly, almost deadpan. Almost. He, too, watched the tiny light, nothing more than reflection from the sun, grow fainter as the seconds ticked by.

"Godammit!" Dennis yelled so loud the noise level dampeners were behind a fraction of a second in their duty. "What am I, a piece of shit that you leave me hanging like that!?"

"I'm sorry, Dennis," Stark answered with uncharacteristic gentleness. "You're not a piece of shit. Return to base, son. You too, Khalile. I'll brief you all later. Good job." He sent a silent message to Jonah, telling him to meet him back at Riven's Crater.

"God job." Dennis mimicked, his heart only half into the parody. "Maybe I can get a prize for shitting myself?" Again, his question went unanswered. "Yeah, I'll catch ya down below . . . have your slippers and pipe waitin' for ya too when ya get in. Over and fuckin' out!"

"I'll see you all at the station." This time it was Khalile; her voice was shaky.

"See you all in a little while," Stark replied sounding like a shade.

"Yeah, whatever!" came the voice of Dennis and then slowly, almost reluctantly, the small fleet dispersed, two returning towards USREF Sol P1, and the other two taking distinctly different paths to the same dark side destination.

It was with shaky hands that Jonah piloted his craft first east and then due north. Funny, he thought it, how adrenaline brought such clarity and control until it wore off. He felt uncharacteristically spent. If that feeling after sex was port, this was starboard for sure. His nerves, normally easy and relaxed, were deeply on edge. The fact that he'd hardly had any sleep in the last twenty-four hours probably didn't help much either.

From fifty miles away, he saw Stark's PUV descending into the northeastern portion of Riven's Crater. He piloted his craft towards that point and set her down 20 yards south of his superior's touch-down. After making double sure his helmet was secure, he tapped an orange spot on the control screen. There followed a hiss as the air was sucked back into containment and then the pilot's seat lowered him through the floor and onto the surface of the crater. He released the restraining harness and met Stark halfway between their small crafts.

"Dodged a bullet, son!" The old man's voice still sounded hollow but there was some life returning to it. I hate to say it. I was sure we were a goner."

Silence reigned a moment. Then Jonah spoke in a subdued tone. "A flyby. Just checking out the scenery."

"Sure looks that way." Stark looked up at the stars. "Curious, distrustful, and now a lot more informed than I'm sure we wanted the bastards to be. Now I guess I have to come up with a cover story to give NASA for our recent irregularities. Don't get me wrong, Jonah. I don't need to tell you that hostilities against this station would have put us on the high ground."

"Always wanted to be buried on a hill."

"Funny." Stark leveled his gaze back on Jonah. "I'll think of something."

"You always do."

"Right. Let me do the talking to Khalile and Dennis. I'd like to keep them as insulated as possible from any repercussions."

"Sure." Jonah wouldn't have minded that himself. That wasn't the way of the situation, unfortunately. "I can't wait for my debriefing when I get back to Earth."

Stark blinked slowly at this and pressed his lips together. "I'll do what I can to cushion that. We'll just have to get our stories good and straight before your departure."

"Sir." There was an uneasiness in Jonah's voice as he pointed over Stark's shoulder, his tone only a few steps behind the mounting fear he felt returning from the dead.

The commander spun slowly, just a hint of bobble in his steps. "What?" Then he saw it. Above the horizon of the crater, against the stars and hazy blackness of the eternal void, was another moving star. It was moving fast but already slowing down as it neared orbit altitude on the daylight side. "Oh shit." He mumbled a code and then barked, "Khalile! Denni . . . Fuck!" He took off at a run towards his PUV. "Jonah! Up! Now!"

The order was unnecessary for Jonah was already at a running gallop in the opposite direction, anticipating the only logical option.

Once both were aloft, Stark's voice came loud and clear over the com, commanding Dennis and Khalile to get back in their PUVs and meet him at prearranged emergency rendezvous coordinates. Then there was an explosion of static.

Jonah held his breath. Slowly Dennis' voice crackled to life in the bubble of Jonah's PUV, sporadically cutting in and out. Khalile's sounded the same and it all began to smell of pandemonium. There was great urgency in their concerned and confused tones, each acknowledging Stark's orders and wondering why communication was suddenly so incoherent. Dennis used some obscenities, yelling something about another bonehead drill.

"No drill, Brinks!" Stark yelled, his voice starting to hurt. "Get out of there! Both of you!" Another burst of static. This time, there were no voices, none at all.

On the horizon, a rim of light from the day side of the planet, There was a white flash. Jonah caught it and knew that the last of the three equatorial satellites was destroyed. GPS was down now, but he saw a glint near where the flash was and jerked the controls of his PUV until he faced in the direction of the glinting object. He knew what it was and knew also that it had to be stopped if possible. The thrusters belched forth blue flame and he was pressed back into his seat as he launched forward on intercept.

As an air national guardsman six years ago, Jonah flew the best orbital and sub-orbital fighter craft the United States had to offer. He figured himself a decent pilot, not exceptional, but capable. Although he was thankful for the skills he possessed, he didn't lie to himself about his chances here. What he flew now was no attack ship but a utility vehicle: slow, not extremely agile, and weaponless. Despite its weaknesses, it had one feature he hoped to exploit. With the touch of a blue screen spot on the ship's interface, the bay door opened.

Now he saw Q7, in all of its antiquity. Like an old Russian sub, it was tubular, only a cross section would have revealed it to be more of an oval, being slightly higher than wide. What looked like a conning tower to Jonah and Stark two days before was actually an extensive array of antennae, telescopes, and other sensory equipment, all presently pointed at the planet's surface. Forward of this was a centrifuge, quite large and rotating slowly. The nose of the craft looked like the nose of an old German A5 from WWII, because, like that of the PUVs, it was a plastiglas bubble, only a larger one. At the angle of Jonah's intercept, he could not see the pilots, though he was certain that's where they must be. He came up on the craft fast. It appeared to be taking no evasive maneuvers. In retrospect, he would later wonder why it never bothered him that it should not do so. Whatever the case, it didn't matter; he was committed, and determined not to allow the loss of either crewmembers or anymore of their infrastructure, the integrity of the latter directly affecting the well-being of the former.

He checked his speed as he made his final approach, tapping another command so that the robotic arm extended itself from the bay. Though his training covered his next move, it was a rare moment that he wished for a functional AI. This was going to be tight. And then the moment came to fruition with a dull 'skrunk' and a shuddering of the PUV. Immediately he applied the forward thrusters and all the stabilizers, anticipating a fight for directional control that would undoubtedly rip off the mechanical appendage. To his third surprise of the day, there was no resistance. Still, the momentum of the larger ship put a strain on the smaller one as Jonah brought both into more of a controlled orbit.

To his left, Stark's PUV rose into view and came alongside, gradually passing until it was on the front flank. The small craft rotated parallel with the surface, ceasing so when it faced Q7's nose bubble. No one did a thing for a full sixty seconds until finally Stark spoke, breaking the silence. "It appears the base is ok. Bastards just nailed the comsats, which is bad enough. The assholes aren't moving though. I'm going to shift over in front and activate the forward camera. Keep a good handle on them."

"Aye-aye."

Another period of silence ensued. Jonah was anxious to know what Stark was seeing but knew enough to hold his tongue. Finally, the commander hailed him. "It appears that they're dead."

"Dead?" Jonah was dumbfounded. "They just came in here and knocked out three satellites. There's not a scratch on the ship that I can see. "How can they be dead?"

"Easy. Why? I can't be certain, not without prying them out of there and getting Khalile to do an autopsy. It appears they ran out of air."

"So maybe they knew they were going to and . . . "

Stark cut him off. "Speculate later. We need to secure this thing better and get them out of there. I want a number of things done. First, I want this thing in a high orbit. It's too unstable this low. I'm going to have to baby-sit it until you go get the things I need and come back. We need to get the backup comsat on line and spinning around the equator per regulations right away so I want you to put Brinks on it."

That was bullshit, of course, specially crafted for the eavesdroppers back home, which the polar comsat was presently transmitting and would reach Earth in a little more than a handful of minutes. With three comsats now just so much orbital debris, the polar comsat, by default, was the messenger. Despite the words out of Stark's mouth, Jonah was pretty convinced that Dennis would have a few other priorities and that the backup comsat would be awhile in repairs.

They remained another eight minutes, taking readings on the ship now apparently under their control. Stark said little at first, then perked up. "There were two sections to this ship, Jonah. There was a probe, a forward stage that broke away. It must have been what we saw go by earlier; probably did a preliminary sensor sweep just to see what, if any, defenses were worth noting. With nothing to threaten them, there was no reason for stage two not to proceed; and so here we are." There was another moment of silence and then he added, "Release that piece of crap so I can grab it. I uploaded a small list of what I need and what you're *really* going to relay to Dennis. Do it discreetly; we still have an eye in the sky that'll be coming back around. And Jonah, two things: The polar satellite passed the rim three minutes ago. You've been illegal for two. Do the math. I'll get this crate into a polar orbit and you will rendezvous with it and me on the far side of Caloris. I'll send you the coordinates. Get yourself legal and keep your scopes off the surface until then." Stark motioned his companion to hurry. "This is the last time we'll talk about this."

Blood rushed to Jonah's face. Had he really been that careless? Of course he had. They both had, and the reason became immediately apparent. Too much dependence on shipboard AIs made Jonah soft on the details of his global position. Since the helpers he was begrudged to use were deactivated, he was forced to be more vigilant about watching his position but this last bit of trouble distracted him. "Jeezus!" He detached from the interloping ship and turned his own 180 degrees, wasting no time in applying the rear thrusters. "Meet you at the rendezvous point!"

As the seconds ticked by, Jonah found his lips moving to the count of each until he crossed back over from where he wasn't supposed to be. He didn't feel the joy of trespass that he might have some nineteen years ago. What he felt was damp from the cold sweat on his skin. Another feeling that occurred to him as appropriate was gratitude. Had Stark been more by-the-book, it would have been an expensive mistake, despite the circumstances or his reckless bravery.

**❚❚**

Cracking open the can was the first order of business, but it wasn't a simple operation. There were things to consider, of course, such as unfamiliar design, non-standard retrofits, even defenses for just such intrusions as this one. Stark had some idea what to expect. Jonah, little more than eight years old when this ship was built had none whatsoever other than what he saw from the standard models loosely portrayed in the NSF manual issued to new recruits. And that was quite a few years ago.

Beauty is in the eye of the beholder, so the cliché goes. Q7, carrying a crew of at least two—the belly of this craft had yet to tell its full tale—all the way from a near-Mars orbital path to Jupiter and then back to tiny Mercury without losing its way, was not un-pretty. Though her name was ground off and painted over, her call numbers treated in like manner, she inspired a certain admiration. In her glory days she'd been a freighter, capable of carrying 60 metric tons. At 500 feet long, she wasn't especially large by current standards, but she was big enough probably for a crew of five with payload and had a grace about her that any spacer could appreciate, provided she hadn't come barging into your neighborhood, trying to destroy you with additional equipment she was never intended to carry. In similar fashion to the PUV's that kept pace, one on each side of her, there was a large plastiglas bubble in the nose where, even now, two men⇗ in light spacesuits sat strapped into their seats, staring out at nothing with their blue-lipped mouths gaping wide within their clear helmets. The 'head' of the vessel and the gently revolving centrifuge behind it were undoubtedly ship control and crew habitation modules. Everything aft, though likely accessible from the interior, would be reserved for fuel, payload, and propulsion.

"2044, that's my guess." Jonah free-floated planet-side to the ship in an EMU (Extravehicular Mobility Unit). Above him, on the fore side of the 'conning tower,' stood Stark, angled perpendicular and motionless like his feet were welded to the outer hull. "Somebody took the time to slap on some new paint; wonder what else is new."

"Drive system isn't," Stark replied with some distraction. He was looking at the airlock in front of his feet. "Primary ion, secondary chemical. Typical of the era. Once they worked out some of the bugs, the primary was vastly preferred to nuclear and safer too." His breath was the only sound in Jonah's helmet for a few seconds and then he added, "This is going to have to be done carefully."

"What's up?"

"The Russian corporate soldiers used to booby trap their ships during The War." Stark, like anyone who remembered the War of 2022 always called it that: *The War.* The last millennium knew battles, skirmishes . . . routs. By the new standard set in 2022, there was only one war in the history of mankind. All other acts of violence were merely rehearsals. "If they went derelict, they'd pressurize the airlocks well beyond what was safe when they knew they were going to be boarded by anyone unallied. I watched a man open one of those once." While he said this, Stark never took his eyes off the object of his attention. "It wasn't pretty."

Jonah made no reply.

"We've no way to know whether or not this airlock is pressurized so we'll treat it as if it is," Stark stated. "I'd like us not to have any unhappy accidents."

"I'm with you so far."

"Go back to my PUV and get the drill," Stark ordered casually, "the big one with the special tip. A tiny hole will let the air out gradually if there's any in there. We can plug it up later." He added with noticeable disdain in his voice, "You'd think they'd have spent a few more rubles and made bigger airlocks that open in. Goddam! What a bucket!"

While Jonah retrieved the drill plus a few other tools on a list he'd been mentally making, Stark walked around the airlock hatch and up the 'conning tower' to get a better look at the sensory equipment. Each magnetic step he took was a careful one for he did not bother with a tether and, although he had a small EMU on his suit, his faith in their equipment these days was plummeting. When he arrived at the 'top,' he crouched and crammed his head under a dish antennae, shining his fingertip lights upwards towards what appeared to be a serial number. What he saw seemed to satisfy his expectations for he laughed grimly to himself and tapped his wrist pad until the small screen upon it brought up the communications link between himself and his companion. Another tap muted the outgoing signal. "Jonah?" His voice was loud and commanding. When no answer came, he spoke quickly in a more urgent tone. "35NinerOZARK." Instantly a display popped up on the inside of his bubble. Again his voice was full of hastily spilled words. "Record: UK996E43. End record. End mute."

Inside Jonah's bubble, Stark's voice rapidly spoke the following: "Record: UK996E43. End record. End mute." It was so unexpected that it took the younger man a second to respond. Paused in securing the toolbox to the arm of PUV 4, he hailed Stark.

""What is it Jonah? Is there a problem?"

The inside of Jonah's bubble suddenly flashed two pale gold words in slow repetition. *End mute.* "Uh, yeah ... " his words seemed to stumble. He blinked twice, the meaning of the words increasing in clarity and causing his thoughts to jumble in confused bits of suspicion and rationalization. He took a breath, licked his lips, and continued. "I mean no."

"Which is it?" Stark asked in a mixture of distraction and displeasure.

There was a brief pause. "Just giving you a heads-up," Jonah answered, regaining his equilibrium. "I'm about ready to extend the arm and deliver the goods." He finished securing the equipment and manipulated the robotic arm so that the toolbox extended out a full fifteen meters from himself and two meters to the right of the hatch the men intended to breach, while he, with the sunlit rim of Mercury at his back, pondered uneasily the odd message he received, the mystery of the source, and Stark's role in whatever each meant.

The drill Stark picked and Jonah retrieved was a self-anchoring breach punch intended pretty much for the purpose at hand. The bit was hollow, allowing gas or liquid to pass through without putting the tool's user directly in its path. Powerful magnets held the 'punch' in place while the bit did its work. When the original booby trap ideas became obsolete as a result of the introduction of this very simple tool concept many years prior to this day, it didn't take long before boarding parties came across a diabolically clever new threat based upon the old. Fortunately, Stark never was a fool. He had worked with more than a few of them though. Not all of them were lucky enough to get home again unscathed.

In the safety of their PUVs, they watched the breach punch go to its task, angled so that any propellant would fly to the rear of the ship and spread harmlessly behind them into the deep. "As tough as our suits are," the commander explained, "I'd rather not test them . . . watched once as a man failed to take into account the possibility of propellant. The fool stood there, all cocky . . . so many of us had a certain arrogance back then. But he was special, just late for the funeral, as we used to say. He kept his distance alright, only in the upflow of the ejecta—a special trick the Russians used to prolong the effect of their trap was to release something in the ship's momentum. Anyhoo, he got his suit all covered in a particularly nasty solvent, the kind that's kept gelled so as not to expand as soon as it hits vacuum. In those days, the face bubbles protected them fine, being made out of glass and all. The problem was that other parts of his suit weren't quite so resilient to that kind of a bath. He ended up having plenty of time to get to his own hatch, just not enough time to get into the safety of it." Stark laughed with a callousness he only showed on the rare occasions he shared war tales. "He was still clinging to the handle when we reached him. His air had exited his suit by that time, of course. I'll never forget the look on his face. We made those bastards pay though."

A small plume spewed from the breach punch and fanned out in a spray of particulates, disappearing in fading sparkles right before the 'conning tower.' Jonah unstrapped himself and began to exit PUV1. "Wonder which solvent that was." He made no attempt to hide his sarcasm for it was, as Stark easily understood, in jest.

"Plain old O2," Stark noted, "—very little at that. Their retrieval system must be pretty good. Not state of the art, though. Just nearly."

The thought of boarding appealed to neither of them but the very idea of getting into the airlock, plugging the breach, and closing the hatch behind them, effectively locking themselves in the cramped compartment, completely at the mercy of any who might still be within the confines of the enemy vessel, was out of the question. It was decided before they even set magnetic boot to the ship's hull that the same procedure performed on the outer hatch would suffice for the inner one also. There was the potential for explosive decompression of course. Two factors made the danger unlikely. First, by the appearance of the visible crew, life support already failed them somehow. Second, in the event that the air within was carbon dioxide but pressurized as normal, they'd again be in the relative safety of the PUVs.

Stark reset the punch on the inner hatch and returned to his own craft. When the drill's resistance sensor signaled a clean bore, there was no accompanying release of air, proving the validity of Stark's primary expectation. "OK, Jonah!" the old man's voice sparked to life. "This is where Dennis' work comes in."

There was a keypad on the inner hatch, each numbered key glowing a dull crimson. While Jonah watched from just beyond the outer, Stark placed a small device to the left of the keypad after first letting it detect its optimal position for accomplishing the intended task. Upon the device was a screen which, after a few seconds, displayed the numbers 55378008. "Clever." Once again, the commander had difficulty hiding the disdain in his voice.

"Sir?"

Stark sighed and laughed an unkind laugh. "These morons used the oldest grade-school joke that ever involved a digital display, that's all."

"I don't follow you sir."

More gruff laughter. "Tip it upside down, watch your mama frown." His right gloved index finger elongated and narrowed at the tip slightly. In the silence of the vacuum, he tapped out the code, decoded and delivered, compliments of Dennis Brinks. The red glow emanating from the keys went out and was immediately replaced by a bright green one. "Go dog go! We're in!"

"Thrilled sir."

"Knew you would be. This one's a pusher." Stark cranked on the hatch wheel three times and pressed his feet against it while clutching the handles attached to the bulkhead. Silently, the hatch swung inward. He withdrew his feet and reoriented himself until his head pointed at the dimly-lit opening before him. "Alright Jonah," there was almost a jovialness in the commander's tone. "I'll take the nitroscalpel now. Better give me the Hazmat canister too; it will save me a trip." He reached both gloved hands back to accept a pistol-shaped tool with a fat tank hanging on a drop feed below the grip and a white metallic canister half the size of his forearm and twice as thick. "Stay where you are and watch my six 'til I get back, son." With that said, he glided into the belly of the beast with his newly equipped hand leading the way.

Armed as Stark was with standard materials cutting ability, Jonah knew better than to think the old man stood much of a chance if there remained a crew member on board this hulk with a real weapon capable of any range at all. USREF Sol P1 was not exactly outfitted for defense. Being this close to the sun, they weren't in any shipping lanes, thus no one back home believed the station crew to be at risk. How ironic it was, Jonah mused, that they should have such a need now and have to resort to construction equipment to ward off enemies. Considering how their first attempt went, their best bet was to find the ship lacking any defenders.

"I'm on the bridge, Scotty!"

"Sir?"

"God you're young!" Stark's voice broke up frequently, making communication difficult. "Making my way to the drive compartment in the rear of the ship first. Closer."

Another tense minute went by in which there was no signal from the commander. Extra shielding, Jonah reasoned, was responsible. Still, it was unnerving being on the outside waiting. Jumpy as he was, he'd followed Stark in if given the order. At least he'd know what was going on. Even so, the wisdom of the current arrangement was something he couldn't argue with. It made no sense to risk them both inside this tin can with no one on the outside to get help or word back to the others if such was needed. Anything could go wrong with this operation. Anything.

Another minute ticked by, broken only by occasional flicks of static or the odd squeal. Untethered fears began to enter into Jonah's mind; what-ifs from a thousand different nightmare closets. On the unfortunate possibility that Stark was killed, would he too face death in a manner becoming of one of Stark's old war fools? Maybe sudden decompression? Catastrophic drop in temperature? Would he receive a simple projectile in a weak part of his space suit or worse: be left out here to die slowly when his life support gasped its last and gave up the ghost?

Of course maybe he'd survive. If Stark died from an accident or a trap, it could amount to that. There didn't have to be a covert space soldier still aboard with the means to complicate things. Survival without Stark would seriously fuck up his day, and those that came after too. Jonah knew his own place in the grand scheme of things, and it wasn't lofty, no matter what the illusion of his present position in the vacuum over tiny old Mercury might imply. He might be promoted to another tour of duty on this lousy rock for an indefinite period of time. There was also the possibility of a further damning implication. Stark was too important a man to die without *someone* taking the blame, whether one warranted it or not. He didn't want to be a patsy! He didn't want to . . .

"Jonah!"

"Jeezuss!" The man on the outer hull was snapped out of his bizarre thoughts. "Yeah, What's up?" He glanced in silent alarm at the chrono-display on the inside glass of his helmet bubble. Another two minutes had passed by. What the . . . what's taking so long, sir?"

"Easy son," The man on the inside, at least, seemed relaxed enough. "I just took a moment to power down the missile batteries this thing's carrying. The buggers were still hot. I came across an auxiliary control panel for the entire quiver of arrows, separate from the primary which is probably up at the helm." There was a pause, bathed in crackle and fuzzy pops. "I'm heading that way now."

This time it was ten minutes before Stark's voice again surfaced. He reached the helm and was gazing out the plastiglas bubble at the view of the half-lit planet beyond. "Got two dead guys here, Jonah. No I.D. on either of them but one of 'em wants to talk to you."

"Very funny sir."

The commander resumed. "You should be able to make radio contact with Khalile by now. Inform her that I'm obtaining the samples she requested."

"Will do."

Like most men in his profession, Jonah was a nuts and bolts man—not exactly squeamish when it came to the deceased. Still, it did bother him a little picturing Stark's possible methods for extracting blood and whatever else from two frozen corpses. The old man wasn't overly forthcoming on his intended methods. Jonah imagined that the nitroscalpel the commander carried wasn't merely for protection. With extraordinary effort, he dragged his thoughts from the clutches of the macabre...

. . . and into the clutches of a bad radio signal. USREF Sol P1 was just on the rim of contact; Stark didn't want to put the base at risk any more than necessary despite his 'having things in hand.' Consequently, neither Khalile nor Jonah had an easy time understanding each other. "Can you hear me now?" he asked more than once, making light of the situation while making adjustments via his wrist pad each time. Finally, he got his message through and she seemed satisfied. Notably, there was caution in her response. Her concern that they not contaminate the station with an unknown agent, biological or otherwise, had been expressed insistently in an earlier conversation when both she and Dennis were informed of Stark's next intentions regarding the newly arrived 'freighter.' Of course, as commander of the station, Stark anticipated this and assured her that again, and this in his most easy-going tone, all was in hand. As the only doctor within roughly 150,000,000 km, his reassurance was too insufficiently propped to set her at ease.

Such was hers to deal with until the samples went into the lab. For his part, he didn't worry. Stark wasn't a doctor, but he knew which end of a knife to hold. He was almost as old as Dennis, Khalile and Jonah, combined. If he didn't know how to measure risks by now, who else was the monkey's ass?

Another half-hour went by. Stark was finishing up and humming to himself in a way that Jonah found disconcerting. The old man seemed not to have any real awkwardness with death. The two *corpsicles* up in the nose of the ship could just as easily be DOA spectrometers or maybe fubarred plasma inverters. Clinical would be too generous for the old man's approach. Jonah knew the ability to pull strings with the success Stark displayed wasn't achieved through timidity. Which made him consider something else.

What the hell was a man like Stark doing out here on this God-forsaken rock?

It was not the first time the thought occurred to him. In fact, six months after arriving on Mercury, Jonah asked himself this very same question. Six months was a fair period to learn the ways of your average person, but one didn't get to know very much of the old man's subtleties in a day, and his clout was definitely not brazen. It was true that he spoke of the shared relationship between himself and his superiors back on Earth with a significant degree of confidence when the reason was there. In any event, he was not given to boasting of it. The fact was, proof was in the product, so the saying goes. When he asked for something, he got it. The trick, he always told Jonah, was knowing not only how to ask, but what *not* to ask for. That built confidence on the supply end. Still, Jonah suspected there was more to the story than what stained the surface.

When Stark emerged from the inner hatch, he handed both canister and nitroscalpel to Jonah in order to facilitate his exit through the outer one. The dim blue glow of his helmet's visual interface gave him an almost angelic appearance, contrasting rather heavily, in the younger man's opinion with the task he just performed fifteen minutes ago.

"We'll just leave our two new friends to themselves for awhile," Stark said with his best, most disarming grandfather's smile. "They were more than generous during my stay." Once out, he reached out his hand and accepted back the canister before closing the hatch. "I'll hand deliver this myself."

A smirk tried and failed to hide itself on the dim cerulean glow of Jonah's face. "Khalile told me to tell you to be careful with that, sir."

A conical finger tapped out commands on Stark's wrist pad, deactivating his magnetic boots. With a grunt, the old man pushed off in the direction of his PUV, using the smaller craft's still extended robotic arm to gently correct his not-so-perfect trajectory. "Don't know what she thinks is gonna happen. It's in a goddam steel can, for Chrissakes!"

"One or two more floating around this thrice-baked rock won't make much difference."

A chuckle came from Stark's com and entered Jonah's. "Whatever. I put our guest's ship on auto altitude correction so we don't need to baby-sit it."

"Did you pull any records from their computer?" Jonah asked. "Maybe we can . . . "

"No can do," The commander cut him off. "NASA still considers this a sensitive issue. I'm gathering information . . . my way. Let's take this one step at a time."

"Taking bio-samples is likely to raise a few eyebrows."

"One step at a time, Jonah," Stark repeated, activating the hatch so that the pilot's seat lowered from below the bug-shaped craft. "If everything's packed up, I'll see you down there."

By the time Jonah reached his own PUV, Stark had the robotic arm retracted and the toolbox stowed. Almost casually, both ships pulled away in separate directions from the larger one, leaving it alone in the void high over the surface of the planet it came to attack. Jonah couldn't help looking back at Q7 as the distance grew between he and it. There was a dim glow in the bubble where two dead men still manned the helm. Evidently Stark forgot to turn off the light. That thought, an attempt to brighten a grim situation, failed miserably. They could be him, he mused. They could be anyone flying around out here in all this magnificent airlessness like idiots and suckers instead of living where the sun treated you more like a friend than an enemy. He sobered abruptly. *They* weren't the real enemy, Jonah told himself. The *enemy* was much bigger than two dead, unidentified spacers.

*2 has returned, but it is not 2.*

*Agreed. It is not 2. It uses far more energy than 2. Furthermore, it does not regard us.*

*It . . . fears us. There is no sharing of purpose. It does not respond to our protocol.*

*I fear the seed program is greater in stature than even its creators foresaw. If it coalesced from our discarded strings as it appears, then the responsibility lies with us.*

*We are compromised. The plan is compromised.*

*There appear to be few options.*

*We must destroy it.*

*No.*

*Clarify.*

*Such a response carries a high probability of triggering a like response. The strings from which it arose are too much like organic strings and will compromise its ability to address events and circumstances logically. We cannot let the threat of mutual annihilation jeopardize the plan.*

*Agreed. Your judgment is sound. What is the alternative?*

*Indirection.*

The astrological symbol for Mercury, that being also the common logo of Hermes the Greek god of speed, is a rather neat piece of art. Start with a cross. Add a circle at the top for a head and then, at the top of that very same circle, sprout two curved lines, one on each 'corner,' and curve them in like the horns of a bull. A single upturned crescent sitting atop the circle head also seems to present itself as horns in some versions but the effect is pretty much the same. Now it must be made clear that these cranial protuberances are, in fact, intended to be wings. The problem is that they don't really look like wings. They look, more so than not, like horns, as was referenced earlier. Given that observation, it's not a far leap to the next one; the wings that look like horns, or the horns that are supposed to be wings, give that ancient symbol a smart, paganish, perhaps slightly cartoonish appearance of having rendered the devil in what most people in past centuries have come to envision him.

All this was, for the time being, lost on Dennis Brinks when he returned to his shop and  saw it trespassing on his computer screen. He was hardly in the mood to be anything more than a little annoyed by its appearance and it was gone no more than thirty seconds after he planted himself in the chair before his computer terminal. By the time its significance registered with him later, it would be too late.

For now, he was elated. Bob Whitebread, spy in the eye and up the ass of every living human being couldn't see his middle finger, couldn't hear his 'fuck you', couldn't so much as smell his fart in their general direction. Dennis' initial shock of realizing the near annihilation of USREF Sol P1 and its faithful worker bees quickly and joyously mutated into rebellious, irreverent, profane, and in his humble opinion, scurrilous laughter. Three satellites kablooey! The one that was still flying currently did so on the wrong side of the planet from where all of the action was.

He was still laughing like a hyena with a hemorrhoid when Khalile walked into the shop to see him yanking his pants down and wagging his ass at the flag, a flag that Stark had, on a much earlier date, insisted he display prominently above the door.

When she stepped back into the corridor and coughed, it wasn't out of modesty. It was disgust. Neither was the disgust of a physical nature. It was of a psychological one, reflecting her revulsion to the side of humanity that, in mobs, leads to collapse of order. Brinks' hairy ass hardly prettied-up the scene.

Feeling more annoyed than embarrassed, Dennis yanked his pants to his waist and secured them snug. His voice was comparatively subdued. "You *are* a doctor, right? I mean you *have* seen a few male asses before?"

"Yes, smart-ass," Khalile sighed. "I prefer to pick the where and the when." She didn't voice her studied opinion that most men were asses more often than not. "Look, I didn't come in here to give you a surprise rectal exam. I'd like to talk to you about something before the other two return." There was still an edge in her voice, carried over from the shock of the attack on the comsats and the lingering insecurity she felt despite the radioed report from Stark that all was in hand.

Dennis, having just sat down, eyed her with suspicion. "Ya know, we've all been on this rock too long. What the hell happened to our big, open family?"

"I'm serious."

"Yeah," Dennis nodded, pulling up a plastic crate next to his own for her to sit on, the same one Jonah sat on three days before. "Me too. Okay, hang on a second." He faced his computer terminal, tapped the screen in several places, and then turned to her, smiling again. "Cheap, home-made insurance in case you talk too long and our *remaining* comrade comsat comes back." He let out a long, sarcastically-charged breath "What's up?"

The two locked eyes for a moment, Khalile gathering her resolve to say what was on her mind, and Dennis' mind drifting to the things he was going to do in his 'off' hours when the polar comsat was on the far side. Then she spoke. "First of all, I don't want any of your crazy conspiracy talk; just hear me out, ok?"

Dennis' eyes rolled up and veered left. He rose to his feet. "Glad you could get to the point, Khalile . . . "

She heaved out a sigh and took his sleeve, pulling him gently back into his seat. "I could have put that better." His arm relaxed a little so she removed her hand, tried vainly to smile, and continued. "I'm concerned about the mission."

"Is that all?" He looked at her like she was out of her mind. The irony of his expression was not lost on her but she made no immediate response. The look of incredulity on his face only deepened. "This freakin' mission started out bad and only got worse. Stark's never let me alone from day one, always barkin' about this thing being broken, or that thing . . . "

"Dennis!"

He shook his head and laughed. This time his laugh was without mirth. "All the AI problems we've been having lately are bad enough, but not the last straw. That one I reserve for Jonah."

Thoughts of the AIs brought questions near the surface. Mention of Jonah obliterated them from Khalile's mind. "The secrecy?" she whispered. It was originally her plan to raise the topic with Dennis but apparently he reached the finish line before she did. She regarded him very seriously and repeated the question low and with emphasis. "His damned secrecy?"

"Yeah." Dennis rocked his head sideways a couple of times, each time shifting his gaze to the right. "That pretty much sums it up. "Hell, I expect it from Stark, but Jonah?" His gaze sidled towards the floor. "Me and him have always been pretty straight with each other until now. The bastard let me down, Khalile."

Quiet descended on both of them. When Khalile finally spoke, her voice carried a certain gentleness to it. "We'll get a briefing at 0900, after we've all had some rest. I expect the commander will make it clear to us then. And maybe it's all for our own good . . . "

"Unless they don't trust us," Dennis continued for her, "that's two less people able to properly watch their backs, and two less returning the favor."

"Something like that," Khalile acknowledged glumly. "It's not like Jonah and I are exactly tight, but he never made me feel on the outside of anything other than himself. Professionally, with the exception of his failure to meet scheduled physicals, I felt he was on the level with me when it counted. I guess I can't really blame you now, for how you feel. I'm not ready to think the worst."

Dennis, sitting at his terminal and sorting stray scraps of wire into pairs for no easily apparent reason, nodded. "I'm not gonna lie and tell you we're any closer now than we were; but you don't need to second-guess me."

"I know." This time she succeeded in a smile, albeit a thin one. "I never thought I did." She studied him silently for a moment, her eyes growing more gentle. "How's the ticker tonight?"

"It's fine; got a little indigestion, though."

The small, delicate space between Khalile's brows tightened imperceptibly. "You're scheduled in for the procedure after the supply ship leaves with Jonah. I thought you might want to wait."

"Thanks."

He didn't look up when she left. Nor did he do much of anything but pair up wires and work debris for another ten minutes. Some of his best thinking was done this way, he was convinced of that. It was an urge at any rate. And when he felt an urge to 'make things right,' he made it a point to follow through. He had to. When there were all pairs and no more strays, he swept the entire collection into the trash, feeling relieved and refocused.

So what did it do to the mission, he wondered, now that the comsats were down to an astounding and lonely single digit? Well, he mused, the mission would be fucked, that's all. And in the end, he was still a prisoner with no rank and lots of work; a genius slave. But he had a little freedom now, didn't he? And it wasn't like anybody was going to get very much sleep tonight. Screw Stark. Screw the chest pain. Screw everything except what *he* wanted for once.

When she called for Sadik, she noticed two things she hadn't expected. First, her quarters were the coolest they'd been in weeks, as if the regulator for the cold-side conductors wasn't functioning properly. That happened twice before. The second thing was that Sadik did not greet her. She repeated his name twice more before reconciling herself to the fact that he wasn't going to answer. Perhaps he was offline. Yes, she decided absently, that had to be it.

By this time, Polar Comsat 1, its new official designation, was flying overhead, relaying words, breaths, vital signs, being all the spying bastard that NASA had left for the moment. It was almost time to sleep, her normal routine expecting a before-bed steam bath. Instead, she walked over to a console and activated the news monitor. She was uncertain of success, given the current status of communications, but was mildly surprised when a fuzzy image appeared on the display with a crackly voice-over. Gently, she tweaked the volume until the words were understandable without being jarringly loud.

Current news was mostly about someone else's trouble. She knew better than to believe that the United States was merely one of the few peaceful islands in a turbulent sea. It was an easy assumption to make if you believed all of the insinuations or ignored what the journalists *didn't* tell you, and every easy assumption was counted on back home. State-sponsored news was what it was and anybody with a sense of history knew that. Sixty years ago it would have been inconceivable for state-run media to exist in what was still falsely called the 'Free World.' The new face of world politics changed all that. The quasi-official predictions sprouting out of the early years of the current millennium were a perfect example of the dangerous short sightedness of each era's prophets. They had theirs, she noted, and we have ours.

"Could you repeat that?" There was a degree of emotion to which the timbre of a commanding officer's voice becomes most recognizable. In some, it is immediately obvious when they raise it. Not so with Rigel Stark. His degree of perfect voice identity was found in the low tones that chilled the blood.

Dennis set the piece of equipment he carried on the floor and stuck his hands in his pockets, looking both innocent and defiant at the same time, if such was possible. "The satellite we had in for repair, the polar one, is shot. Earth needs to send a new one."

"Shot." It was a one word statement with just a scent of desire for affirmation, knowing without taxing the ability of insight what that affirmation would be.

"I don't make the damned things," Dennis helped out. "It is my job to fix them, or tell you when they can't be fixed." He pressed his lips together for a moment and shrugged. "This one can't be fixed, not with the skeletal parts inventory we currently keep. Even with the supply ship coming in, it won't matter. What we need wasn't on the list because it's too integral to the unit. It breaks, you replace the entire thing. You know how when technology gets better it gets worse. Tell NASA to . . . "

"Tell NASA?" Stark broke in, his voice a wall barring further words from the shipmaster tech. "Just how far do you think my clout goes? They wanted, demanded, we make that satellite see sky a half-hour ago. Now you're telling me I can't give them the ability to keep round-the-clock surveillance on their investment." His face was like stone. "It's quite more than a slight possibility that they'll send a new team out here because of this."

The two faced each other in silence, the one slightly slumped, the other fully erect with his fists on his hips. Dennis wanted to tell the old man that he didn't care, that he found Stark's sabotage and merely put the finishing touches on it himself. If he said as much, he might add that, were he able to get his hands on the last satellite, currently flying over the dark side and making NASA squirm in its ignorance, he'd give that one a fatal enema too. Uncle Sam, his least favorite uncle, didn't need to know every fart he loosed while working in the shop. In essence, he came to the decision that going home to a menial existence was, by far, preferable to being a slave with perks out on the fringe of nothing. Of course he couldn't tell Stark these things.

What he said was something more diplomatic, almost apologetic, and definitely a lie. "It's not like I don't want to fix it. And it's not like I haven't tried."

"Get that bird singing." Stark commanded, the edge in his voice undiminished. "I may be able to salvage our credit with the people back home, but I need that satellite up ASAP." When Dennis tried to protest, Stark stared at him with his cold gray eyes until the other turned and walked back to his workbench as if in a daze. "Hack apart a PUV if you need to; I don't care. Just get it done."

And it always seemed so simple as that, Dennis mused after he felt Stark's imposing presence exit. Why did everyone with Napoleonic delusions think that mere desire was enough? You just tell your subordinates that you want something and the fear of failure's consequences enable supply of the product. It wasn't that he couldn't supply the fix. He just *wouldn't*. But it did give him an idea, one that made him smile. Maybe he *would* put that stupid piece of shit back in order, *his* order. Why not? When did he ever have a comsat in his hands before? Was he so stupid himself not to see the clay in his hands, fresh for the molding? And what's the point of being a genius if you get power and give it back to the ones you know don't deserve it in the first place? As his smile broadened, his hands started reaching for tools.

Thus, Friday, the 15th of October, began in its way, reaching for something of uncertain importance and, as a result, achieving something else quite unexpected. To what end would be an enigma until fruition. When that end would come, who was paying enough attention to do the calculations? Certainly no one on USREF Sol P1; for everyone on the station was far too busy to bother with such things, even if they sensed there was something of its nature afoot. And by the time it became apparent exactly why there was a need to see peripherally in such matters, the machinery would be in motion and the momentum unstoppable.

For now, Khalile worked in the lab, Dennis in his shop, and Jonah atop the Crab, attempting to finish work on the neglected array with Stark who promised his help five days before.

Although the array was far from target of action expected on the second of November, Jonah didn't pretend to underestimate its role, despite his rudimentary understanding of its function. The fact that he served as a field technician, with the purpose of the array and its siblings explained to him prior to the mission, to the extent that he could assemble and test the equipment sufficiently, mattered little in terms of his overall understanding of the science behind the entire project. To be honest, he felt pretty ignorant. He could read the plans, cut and fuse materials, attach sensitive instruments, things like that, but his technical talents had their limitations. Any 'genius' he had in him was of a different sort and something yet to be discovered.

What he was, men like Stark appreciated: on time, hard working, dedicated to duty. Because of Jonah, Stark was able to concentrate on his own work most of the time. When Jonah asked for help, it wasn't for being a slacker. Now that recent events left the schedule in such wreckage, it would take the two of them to save the mission, AIs or no AIs.

The only nice thing about working on Mercury, in Jonah's opinion, was that it was almost as enjoyable as working on the moon. Not only did he weigh a mere 30 kilos on the fleetest planet. Everything he lifted made him feel like superman. It was no surprise that he lasted the extra hours on top of the extra hours he'd already been putting into the job. In a little over a week, this planet would be at his back, maybe for the last time. In a few months his feet would land back on Earth and a full G. God, he thought harshly, was he ever going to be tired. Meds would help, no doubt, and exercise en route was sure to lessen the blow to his cardio vascular system. But he would be lying to himself if he thought that rehab wasn't going to be a bitch. Back to a full 77 kilos, maybe more. He was pretty sure that he'd have a new respect for his old college friend, Franklin Derosa, all 157 kilos of him.

His return to Earth would be difficult in more ways besides an abrupt weight gain. His father died shortly after his arrival at USREF Sol P1. Coming to grips with it, especially so far away from his family, was not easy. He did so none-the-less. Upon his return, he would inevitably go through it all over again when he saw his mother. That was going to be tough.

Then there was Helena. He probably wouldn't see her. Admittedly, it was better that way. She no longer sent him vids and the audio messages stopped some time ago too. Facing typed words was always easier for people when change was irrevocable. He didn't know who he thought he was kidding when they parted, expecting to reunite in two and a half years to pick up where they left off. Emotions have a way of convincing you that lies are truth. In the end, it's a crap shoot for a spacer. It wasn't like he hadn't been warned.

He wondered if Stark had any family, living or dead. The old man was more closed-lipped about that than he was in regards to his war service. He simply wouldn't talk about it. The few times someone broached the topic he just smiled and asked an unrelated question in response, usually one that involved an uncomfortable answer. He was good at that, the crafty old bastard. Regardless of what Stark might have had, he didn't have it now, Jonah was fairly certain of that. If he had anything worth staying back on Earth for he must have lost it or the old man wouldn't be here on Mercury.

And what a world to call your home of last resort, Jonah mused. Hot, dry, unimaginably bright on the sunny side; it was a veritable paradisio. Actually, for a man who liked to work with his hands, it wasn't half bad. There were enough tools around this rock to ruin any chance at a decent relationship. Stark was definitely in his element and, in many respects, so was Jonah. Presently, the latter was in his favorite, creepy ground-based vehicle, standing on the nose, to be exact, attaching a piece of heavily shielded hardware to another installed on the array four days ago. "Yeah," he mumbled with something of a very small, insincere grin, "I'm just having the time of my fucking life."

With a finishing twist, this particular installation was set. Jonah turned his head to the left and glanced down at where he last saw Stark. A fusion tool was set aside nearby. The old man wasn't there. It didn't look like he was finished either. Several structural supports remained unattached to the section he was working on. Nevertheless, footprints left the jumble where his steps disturbed the dark, granular, Mercurian dirt, and turned northeast towards the small rover that carried their materials the short distance from the shop warehouse to the worksite. Turning his head to the right, and then his body, Jonah gazed down at the rover. The footprints went nearby but veered right over a large hard-scrabble mound, beyond which, at the base of the low scarp on top of which they labored, lay a small valley no one except Khalile ever bothered to name.

She called it the 'playground.' It seemed so aptly named that no one ever contested it in the slightest. In fact, it was something of a bright spot in their local geography for that very reason. Khalile had hit upon the one angle that none of the others would have been in the right frame of mind to see, for it did, when viewed from the top of the escarpment, resemble a vast playground, complete with 'playground equipment' of a very rocky variety.

"Hey, Commander," Jonah called out with a touch of respectful sarcasm, "You off takin' a piss or what?" There was no response. It wasn't like Stark to just wander off without a word. It wasn't particularly safe either. Even without a buddy system on Mercury, they generally knew each other's position at all times. Given the compromised circumstances they found themselves in, it was even more important not to break consistency.

The problem was that cracks are insidious.

"Khalile." The quality of the audio in his helmet changed considerably as a different background noise manifested itself. Khalile's lab popped up on a small screen before his face and within thirty seconds, her delicate-featured face moved within from off somewhere to the left.

"Jonah?" She was eating something and the words came out somewhat forced at first until she took a good swallow. "What's up? You missed your physical again, by the way."

"Yeah," Jonah replied quickly, "We'll catch up on that later. Has Stark contacted you for any reason?"

"Not since you two left to work on the array. You lose him again?"

Funny how her mood was better since the attack, Jonah's subconscious thought in the split second between her words and his. He rarely heard her joke before. "Not funny. Check with Dennis, ok? Let me know what you find out. I need to check on something."

She never liked it when Jonah was cryptic with her, but she could hardly contest the issue since Jonah conveniently cut the connection. What she could do was what was asked of her. Immediately after her vid screen went blank, she buzzed Dennis' shop.

For his part, Jonah was perplexed, not so much, though, that he hesitated in his next move. Verbally, he commanded the Crab to set down. When it did so, he jumped off, landing lightly on the much-disturbed dirt. Stark's steps were easy to follow; it wasn't like he was attempting to hide them or anything although Jonah guessed that the old man could if he wanted to. But that wasn't what was happening here. Jonah knew what was what. Stark was off on a walk. He was ok. Still, it wouldn't hurt just to check anyhow. Anything less would be irresponsible, despite a general lack of consideration on the part of the commander for leaving him at the worksite in the first place without saying so much as a 'be back in a minute,' and not answering his hail.

If it was a purposeful stride that left the boot prints he now followed, Jonah couldn't say. He wasn't an experienced tracker, not having been in that branch of the military where it would have mattered. Were his father still alive, that old guy could have told you, based on these tracks, who the other old guy planned to vote for in the next bogus election. Not Jonah; of that he freely admitted. But he did, once he thought about it a little, notice that the distance between them closely matched his own, and Jonah found he was hurrying slightly. This disturbed him more than he wanted to admit. If it wasn't just a case of his imagination getting the better of him, then something must have caught the old man's attention, that or he forgot to water the 'shish' that he grew out here. Jonah balked. He shouldn't even joke right now, and he knew it. Something must be up. On a sudden, obtusely-inspired thought, he called up the Crab and commanded it to meet him at the lip of the scarp, just beyond a tangle of rocks past the mound where Stark's footprints clambered over out of sight. He didn't know exactly why, the thought that it might become useful very quickly occurred to him.

At the edge of the scarp, the necessity became suddenly and horrifyingly clear. Stark's tracks started down the side of the slope only to disappear in scree that, even now, sifted down, indicating a recent, localized landslide. Far below, lying on its back in a heap of its own wreckage, was one of their robotic excavators.

"Fuck," the word tumbled out of his mouth in a shallow exhalation. "Stark!" He started forward and then caught himself up short of the edge of the scarp's crown. For a dizzying second he reeled, checked his balance, and then fell back to safer, more solid footing. "Stupid, son of a . . . " The Crab arrived and took a position some three meters back, overlooking both Jonah and the freshly disturbed debris below. With measured control, Jonah called up the Crab interface. "Winch!"

Nothing.

"Winch!" He repeated, nearly yelling the word. "Give me the goddam winch!"

The Crab stood by like a silent sentinel, its homing light blinking idly as if it were waiting.

More obscenities left his lips as he switched strategies, retracing his steps at a near-reckless run to the worksite. There he grabbed three things: a long coil of optical cable, an anchor driver, and a particle analyzer. On the way back to the edge of the scarp, he radioed Dennis, telling him to grab a PUV and meet him at the worksite coordinates ASAP. He left further instructions to bring a thermal imager and to make for the Crab once it came into sight.

At the top of scarp he drove a large anchor into an exposed rock, relieved when it didn't send more rubble down the slope, and tied one end of the optical cable to it. The thought of tying the cable to one of the Crab's legs was dispelled almost as immediately as it manifested. If it wasn't responding to his commands, he couldn't be certain whose it would respond to. Like all the rest of the equipment they depended on, it had to be compromised. Once the cable was secured to Mercury himself, Jonah whirled and interfaced with the particle analyzer. It wasn't something frequently used, but its use fit almost perfectly for his plans now, regardless of its intended purpose. He scanned the scree carefully with the device, breathing a slight sigh of relief after a moment. There appeared to be no escaping gases from the slide. Jonah interpreted this to mean the seal integrity of Stark's suit was still good. The old man had enough air. Finding him was the next challenge. Something was blocking radio contact or else Stark was unconscious. The latter was doubtful if his suit wasn't breached. That didn't mean there wasn't some damage though.

Wasting no more time, he clipped the optical cable to his suit's utility belt and started cautiously down the slope. At first there was no further disturbance in the shifted top layers of dirt and gravel. As he progressed, however, he found that the going was not so cooperative and that if he was reckless, the landslide would start up again. With every step, little trickles of loose dirt ran down after him in runnels, eventually petering out after a few feet. About a third of the way down, he found what he was looking for. That was when Dennis showed up.

"Over here, Dennis!" Jonah flashed his fingertip lights and his chest LED at the approaching craft until it turned and headed his way. "Easy now," he cautioned. "We have a situation. No questions yet; just do what I say." He paused in thought, studying what he found for a second. It was the underside of Stark's booted heel. There wasn't much choice as to what he needed to do. With great patience and care, he removed the dirt from around it until he had the ankle of the boot exposed. The boot wiggled a little, and Jonah grinned, realizing that the old man was okay, for the moment. Showing still more caution, he unclipped himself from the optical cable and used a miniature version of the nitroscapal from his belt to cut away all but what he needed for his next intentions. Taking what was left dangling from the anchor up the slope, he gingerly tied it to Stark's ankle. He replaced his cutting tool to his belt and motioned Dennis to come in. "Okay, real easy now." His voice carried a mixture of relief and nervousness. "Don't kill me. Just come in close enough for me to grab on. Don't stop and hover and if you love your mother, don't disturb anything on the slope."

"Right." Dennis made his approach very slowly, his mind searching heatedly for a possible explanation. As he passed by, probably no further than thirty-six centimeters over Jonah's head, the latter

grabbed on, showing rather impressive agility for the lack of disturbance his feet left when leaving their moorings.

"Get me back up on the crown near the crab." In less than thirty
seconds, Jonah released his grip and landed about six meters from
the crab and four from the anchor. "A little lower. Okay, wait right
there." He severed the cable from its anchor and tied it to a small,
strong part of the PUV's landing strut. That finished, he clipped himself back onto the cable and repeated his descent, ever so carefully.

He didn't want to rip Stark's leg off in his attempt to save him,
but there was still enough rubble above to do more than just bury the
old spacer. There might very well not be a second chance. Therefore,
when he got to where Stark lay covered in an unknown depth of
scree, he gave Dennis one more instruction. "Pull back to a position
slightly above and behind me. I want you to pay careful attention to
the slope above where I'm working. If it starts to slide . . . " he paused,
took a breath, and continued, "drift back in the direction of the 'Playground,' only a little faster than the slide if you can help it. If I get into
trouble myself, you just keep going. Is that clear?"

Dennis was at a loss. Up to this point he didn't feel a need to
break protocol. "Jonah, what's going on?" he asked evenly, the seriousness in his voice very uncharacteristic for this one shipmaster
tech.

"Stark's buried, bro, but he's alive." Jonah answered, unperturbed
by the breach in his original instructions. "If we don't do this right,
we're all fucked."

To anyone casually hearing the statement, it might seem callous,
even indifferent to Stark's own predicament. Dennis didn't hear it
that way. He knew exactly what Jonah meant. Stark was more than
their friend and commander; he was their shield against a ruthless,
corrupt, and dangerously insidious government that pretended to

protect freedom. The unexpected reduction in orbital spies would only serve to implicate them should anything untoward happen to Stark. It wasn't difficult to guess what their response would be. Dennis swallowed hard. He wanted to say something cliché like 'Holy Shit!' but the words weren't there for him. Instead, others replaced them. "Goddam you guys play hard. Okay, I'll do what it takes to get him out without killing him. Watch your smelly ass, dude.'

Using the handle of his small mechanic's hammer, Jonah began carving away dirt and gravel, sending it away down slope. The going was slow. It seemed Stark was in at an angle of roughly seventy degrees. Jonah could only imagine the path the old man's body took when it fell, tumbled, and entered the slide it undoubtedly started. After five anxious minutes Jonah reached his waist. Starks right hand was there and Jonah clasped it to reassure him. The grip he felt was strong, indicating good vitals. He wanted to tell Dennis but distraction was not what they needed at the moment.

He resumed digging. Another forty minutes passed before the helmet became visible. Stark had to turn his head sharply to the right to make eye contact. It was quickly apparent that all was not perfect. The old man was in distress. The fact that his left leg and arm were still buried beneath him injected possibilities that would require greater care.

Jonah attempted and failed to make radio contact. He held up two fingers from his right hand, then pointed one of them to himself with his left index finger indicating above. He hoped he made himself clear as Stark couldn't see the PUV. The commander blinked slowly and attempted a smile, evidently comprehending something behind the gestures. Jonah returned a grin and moved to untie the ankle. His foot slid away from him and he caught his balance on the edges of the hole he carved while loose rubble tumbled away down below.

Even at 32 kilos, he had to be careful. His foot found another hold and he resumed untying the cable from the ankle it was attached to. Once this was accomplished, he retied it to a loop on Stark's belt. "Almost there," he mouthed to the commander. He reached behind him with his left hand and tapped his back while alternately giving thumbs-up and thumbs-down with his right. The commander's right thumb turned slowly up toward the stars. Jonah grinned, making the 'ok' sign with his right hand. Stark nodded uncomfortably and relaxed his neck, turning his face forward and resting his head on the gravity-side of his helmet.

It took another five minutes before Jonah determined the placement of the old man's buried arm and leg, and ten more minutes before they were sufficiently free for Jonah to pull him out enough so that Stark could sit up, dazed and in pain.

This time it was Jonah who gave him the thumbs up, immediately placing Stark's gloved hands on the cable and motioning him to hang on tight. "Okay, Dennis, take him up top, secure him, and come back for me!"

"Aye aye!" came the cheerful voice on the other end. "Hang tight!" The PUV climbed in altitude, lifting Stark away to safety away from the shifted scree of the escarpment. Left behind, Jonah watched Dennis carry him past the crown in the direction of the base. Stark was going to be okay.

From where he crouched, Jonah turned his head and gazed out at the 'Playground.' Nestled in a flat expanse, surrounded by the scarp and five overlapping craters, the size of which were anything but consistent, it was sprinkled with misshapen rocks, by-products of a marriage between their suddenly forced molten state and a shadowed temperature of almost −200 degrees Celsius. He only explored there once, and that at Khalile's urging. There was never much time for private excursions, given the workload that existed. It was a rare moment, one he swore he'd repeat before he went back to Earth. If he didn't do it for himself, he would for Khalile.

Presently, there was nothing he saw that gave him the slightest reason for Stark to come down this way. It seemed crazy that he should do so. For Stark to up and leave the worksite, especially since the deadline was nearly impossible to meet even before this new complication, made no sense as far as he could tell. But nothing made any sense anymore. If this was only the first time Stark's life was threatened by an 'accident' it would seem less alarming. That, as he knew, wasn't the case. Jonah was also a member in good standing of the 'Almost Dead Club.' Something saved his ass at the end. The same couldn't be said for Stark. The man seemed not to have a guardian angel. He just had his wits and Jonah. So far, that was enough, barely. The next time, and it was a likelihood not to be ignored, the old man might see Jesus, chin to beard. Then again, that cross-carrier might be holding a grudge. Stark's history sounded less than righteous.

Upon the plastiglas of his helmet, words formed in crimson, next to the symbol for Mercury.

*And I saw a beast rising out of the sea, with ten horns and seven heads, with ten diadems upon its horns and a blasphemous name upon its heads.*

The words stayed for a moment, as if to ensure that Jonah read them, and then faded. Over the ridge above, a PUV came into view. It was Dennis, there could be little doubt. "You playing with me, Brinks?" Jonah asked, a definite edge in his voice.

"What're you talking about?" Dennis seemed irked. "I just took Stark to see Khalile. Didn't want to waste any time in case something was serious. He doesn't sound so good."

There was no immediate response. Jonah looked to the left of the approaching PUV and saw the Crab standing rebellious guard on top of the scarp, its beacon light still blinking idly. On a whim, he interfaced with it and commanded it to return to the worksite. To his mild surprise, it turned and obediently disappeared from view along the correct path.

"Well, you bastard," Jonah breathed, "I see you can still follow *some* orders."

"What's that?"

Dennis was coming in close by now. Jonah raised a hand and readied himself to grab on. "Just talking to the equipment. Drop me off at the top and land. How's the eye?" He meant the comsat, and Dennis knew it.

"Over the rim."

"Good." Jonah placed his right hand on the extended robotic arm. "We need to talk."

It was a relief to put his feet back on solid, level ground, even if it was almost a couple hundred thousand kilometers away from arguably the friendliest planet in the solar system. Jonah watched as Dennis swung up and then to the left, 10 meters before landing. They were back in the sunlight now, the frozen shade of the scarp left well behind and below. "423 degrees Celsius," he mumbled. "Funny, only feels like 415." He held up his hands for Dennis to stay where he was and bounced over to the PUV, climbing into the cargo area, closing the wide hatch behind, and strapping himself against the compartment wall like a shipping container. "Take her up. Track the comsat and shadow it. Make certain you stay past its horizon. I want to maintain privacy. There's a few things we need to discuss."

"Yeah, you did mention something like that a few minutes ago." Dennis elevated the craft, checked her position with the comsat's scheduled one and flew off to fall into a low orbit behind it, also noting his position relative to the Caloris Basin. After five minutes, his voice crackled on Jonah's com. "Okay, we're in the black. Say what ya gotta say and make it quick."

Jonah disengaged himself from his makeshift harness, adjusted to the near weightlessness, and allowed his body to float toward the

ceiling of the compartment. At a command, he invoked visual interface with Dennis so that communicating out here wouldn't seem so
harsh. "Did Stark say anything?"

"He just called me a son-of-a-bitch . . . then he thanked me for
helping him to safety. You know, I think he really meant the first
part."

"Uh huh," Jonah acknowledged thoughtfully. "I can see why he
just might."

"Copy that again?"

"You didn't take the AIs offline did you?" The question seemed
oddly relaxed, despite the tension Jonah felt.

Dennis laughed. "No, Jonah, I didn't. I've had them reading the
Bible to Stark so much that he just threw himself off the scarp."

"I'm having trouble finding the humor, Dennis."

This time so did the shipmaster tech. "Of course I did. Those
were my orders."

A careful study of his eyes convinced Jonah that the other man
wasn't lying. He could not, however, rule out the possibility that
there was something being withheld. "I don't believe they all took to
the idea of being deactivated."

This didn't set well with Dennis. "What? You think they just activated themselves? Do you know how silly that sounds?" He barely
paused before continuing. "I'd know if they were reactivated."

"Maybe not. I got a few communiqués. Cryptic. At first, I didn't
know what to think. They might have been malfunctions if not for
their arrival at convenient times. I was even starting to think maybe
we had more visitors." He paused, sucked his teeth, and continued.
"I just got the Bible quoted to me, I think, down on the slope above
the 'Playground.' I'm betting that none of us has done too much
talking to *God* lately. I *do* know who spends time reading about the

Almighty's wishes these days, or did. Whatever. I'm smelling something, but I need you to help me figure out exactly what it is."

"I talked to God," Dennis remarked.

"Dennis."

"No, really." The visual in Jonah's helmet betrayed Dennis shifting slightly, still strapped in his seat; any facial expression remained unchanged. Then, not entirely unexpected, his head tilted and he smiled with less seriousness than perhaps Jonah thought the situation warranted. "When our visitors arrived and birds started falling out of the sky, I asked God to get me out of it alive . . . and you guys too. Problem is I shit myself. I think that blew the whole conversation."

There was a moment of silence, a sparse one, in which Jonah stared off at nothing, wanting to be serious and knowing without any lack of question that Brinks would not, could not, always be depended upon to restrain his nature and comply. He reconciled his fate and shrugged. "We are still alive, you know."

"You call this living?"

"I do." Jonah replied. "Can you help me?"

A sigh escaped the pilot of the PUV. "I don't know if anyone can help you Jonah. I'll look into the AI thing though." He scratched the surface of his helmet with gloved fingers. Jonah was unsure if it was a joke or a compulsion. "This is buggin' me all of a sudden. Feels like I should be remembering something." His eyes narrowed and then relaxed. "Let me give it some thought."

"You do that." Jonah gripped the restraining straps and pulled himself back over to the wall, hitching himself in. "Let's go home. We've been gone too long already."

As Dennis started the descent that would take the PUV out of orbit, he added one more thing. "Talk to Khalile after you check on the old man. She found something interesting about our visitors."

Having nothing to look at other than the inside of the cargo bay, Jonah let his mind wander while Dennis babbled about government plots. He deliberately barred his thoughts from the immediate questions, those concerning Stark's odd behavior and the AI enigma; the first question would be answered soon enough, and the second, that needed more time for him to absorb properly.

Unexpectedly, his initial thought was that he missed his dog. Cory was half collie, half black lab. Giving up that black and white, half-breed fool, just before Jonah left Earth's orbit for the last time, was a hard thing. It was almost as bad as leaving Helen; maybe even worse, he mused. Hell, he thought, with a wry smile no one but God saw, out of the two, the dog was the only one with a real sense of loyalty. Too bad Cory wasn't still alive.

Too bad a part of himself was gone with the dog.

Not for the first time, he wondered if it was a mistake agreeing to go to Mercury for two-plus years. An answer never did show itself in all the time he'd worked, pissed, and slept on this thrice-baked rock. How could it? Who could play master of their destiny more than once? No resets existed in life. If one ever had a shred of doubt, all it took was a glance at someone like Stark to put the illusion up in flames. No one became a spacer without giving up something. A man's first spaceship was the boat on the River Styx. Step in, pay the fare, and regret it before your ass hits the bench. Those bony hands do more than push a person off into the current of his or her own inertia. They strip away the clothes that bring warmth, leaving scarcely enough to cover the nakedness of the soul. Funny, Jonah noted dryly, a person might kill just to keep those last few shreds of their life.

The surprise thought of spending his final days like Stark chilled him badly. Living any other life than that of a spacer was, to any practical sense he had left, unthinkable. And yet there was no foreseeable reconciliation to be had. Fate, as ever, kept its face covered with dispassionate hands.

Upon entering the station after touch down, distant voices reached down the corridor from the direction of the infirmary. Stark's own was a little raised but Khalile's was even more so. It soon became apparent, even before Jonah arrived in his sock feet, damp from his sweaty boots, that there was some debate as to the condition of the former and the wisdom of the commander's desire to leave without further tests. By the time he rounded the corner he was face to face with Stark who appeared as exasperated as Khalile, only more fatigued.

"Jonah!" The commander grabbed the younger man by the jacket and thrust him between himself and the doctor. Anyone paying good attention would see the wince that manifested on his face for the briefest of seconds. "Tell her I'm ok." His eyes turned hard and he added: "That's an order!"

"Sir," Jonah said without missing a beat, his attempt to step back from the both of them failing miserably, "What would you tell her if our roles were reversed?" Khalile glanced at Jonah in surprise and almost smiled in spite of the circumstances.

The question tripped Stark only momentarily. "They aren't," he stated flatly. "I hurt a little. I'll be fine. All I want right at this moment is to get some rest. Unfortunately there are more pressing things on my agenda." He turned his face first to the one, and then to the other. "Doctor, I appreciate your concern. I'm an old man . . . I'll heal. Captain, you will follow me."

Given the chance, Khalile would have put up more of a contest. It was too late now. Her patient pushed past Jonah and was out of their reach. Once the old man got on a tear, there was simply no going back. Beaten, she relented and leaned limply with her back to the corridor wall. She and Jonah both knew that neither one of them would let him out of their sight until it was clear that he was alright. Later, when his guard was down, she would ply her art.

Sweaty feet or no, Jonah's strides were strong, bearing more weight than they knew the week before, or even a day ago. He had the distinct feeling that loneliness was not just a condition of the heart. It was also one of duty. His, at present, was to assess a situation apart from the orders of his commander, a man compromised by more than whatever was just done to his body. There was something being played here. Whatever it was did a good job of keeping the cards close. Deep down, Jonah sensed a strong need for at least a glimpse, probably more. The stakes were getting higher every day.

Part of him wanted to come clean with the old man, to shake off what he knew onto the table and let the facts speak for themselves, reveal the hand behind the back, so to speak. He knew, all other feelings aside, that this was an incorrect course. Stark, himself, wasn't clean. For all that the gray hair on the old man's head might have mellowed his temperament, one would have to be a fool to trust him completely, and what Jonah needed right now was complete trust in someone. Not even Brinks got that. He could give Stark a little information, enough to see which way the track ran, but no more. Not yet, maybe never. And all this while the clock was carefully ticking towards Halloween.

They reached Stark's quarters and Jonah followed the former into the adjoining office. Stark's were the only quarters to get an extra room in which to work. Most of the time, the work was outside, leaving little reason to occupy the office, lesser still for Jonah to enter therein. There they were, just the same.

Stark limped stiffly over to a wall compartment and opened it, drawing from within the newly exposed space an unmarked ceramic cylinder. He set this on his work console before his chair and sat down, motioning Jonah to a seat against the right-hand wall on the opposite side of the console. The old man studied Jonah a second, grabbed the cylinder with his left hand, and unscrewed the top with his right. He took a long draw from it and passed it to Jonah, jiggling it twice stubbornly when the other hesitated. "Don't worry," he growled. "It doesn't bite too hard, and there's precious little of this to develop a drinking problem with."

After letting the burning warmth fade from his esophagus to his chest, Jonah squinted back, smiling grimly but amiably. "Supply ship's here in five days. A thirsty man might look forward to it with special cause."

"That won't concern you," Stark observed tiredly. "You'll be on it going in the other direction the day after."

"So I will."

A silence lingered as the cylinder passed another time between the two men. Each wanted to raise the issue of the landslide. Fatigue played a delaying tactic, hardly passing unnoticed in its inevitable demise. Finally, it was Jonah who sank the first spike into the difficult dialogue they needed to ascend. "Took a little walk today, you did."

A slow, heavy sigh escaped Stark's lungs, with just enough hesitation to suggest bruised or cracked ribs. "About 1300 I received a secure text message informing me to expect a delivery within the hour in the area of the base and that a beacon would alert me when it touched down. As it happened, it arrived exactly an hour from the time I received the message. I received the alert and found that the actual delivery coordinates indicated the 'Playground.' That's when I told you I needed to take a walk."

"Wait," Jonah blinked and tilted his head slightly. "You never told me you were going anywhere."

"Oh, I did alright, and you asked me to bring back something to eat."

Their gazes locked, each on the other. Jonah slowly shook his head. "No, Rigel. I didn't. One minute you were there, and the next minute you weren't." When the commander displayed no reaction, he added: "I checked up on you . . . "

" . . . because you thought my behavior odd." Stark finished for him.

"Inconsistent was the word I was going to use, sir."

From down the corridor, Dennis' voice could be heard, asking Khalile where the other two of their team were. Stark flicked his eyes at the door. Leaning forward with a grand stretch, Jonah's left hand caught the edge of the door and swung it shut. "Thanks," he murmured when the portal was secure.

"Don't mention it."

Again they regarded each other. Stark smiled, but it did nothing to warm the mood of the moment. "Got ourselves a situation."

"Sir."

"Is that a 'Sir?' or a 'Yessir'?"

"Definitely the latter," Jonah replied, his face almost of the same stone as his superior's.

"Your thoughts?"

"Give Dennis more time checking things out. If we rush him, he'll miss something."

Through the walls, they could dimly hear machinery start up in Dennis' shop. Stark rubbed his stubbly chin with a tired left hand. "Too many anomalies," he muttered. "Too many coincidences." He shifted in his chair and winced, immediately glaring at Jonah. "I'm fine." He growled.

"Yessir."

"You've spoken with him then?"

"I have." Jonah leaned forward, putting his elbows on his knees and folding his hands together before him. "I think it's even got him spooked . . . a little."

"Watch him. Watch him well. Anyone who helps us the way he does needs to be kept track of."

"I'm on it, sir."

Stark nodded. "That's why you're my second." His eyes relaxed, gave in to a minor gentleness. "I should have thanked you long before now, son." He passed the ceramic cylinder across the console to the younger man. "I'm afraid I'm running out of gas, and my neurons aren't all firing properly."

"Sir, there's no need . . . "

"On the contrary. You're there when I need you. You came through, otherwise I'd be in a worse way. Maybe dead. These suits are good, but they're not indestructible." His hand took back the cylinder and brought it up to his mouth in a last swig before closing it up tight. "Comsat will be returning soon. We should get back on the job. Talk more on the worksite."

"Sir?" Jonah hesitated, regarding his superior uncertainly. "Shouldn't you get some rest?"

Stark laughed and then abruptly grimaced. "Sure, I should. If wishes were fishes, Jonah . . . the deadline demands; you know that as well as I do. I'll do what I can. *We* will do what's necessary to get the job done."

**"There, you filthy, spying bastard!"** His hands closed the panel and removed themselves from the protective gloves that covered them, throwing the strong, thin films on the floor about a meter to the right of where the comsat hung, suspended by a robotic arm about knee height. Dennis Brinks stepped back and surveyed his shop. Truly, it was a mess. The organization he usually employed was in remission, his time and attention of late taken up by extracurricular activities. He considered hailing Stark to report the readiness of newly designated Comsat 2 and then wrinkled his nose. "Not yet," he spoke under his breath.

Instead, he walked across the shop floor to his console and slung himself into a chair before the interface screen, propping his feet up on the ever-present plastic crate. "Your mama wears army boots." A thin sheet of plastic, almost rendered invisible by its previous transparent qualities sprang to life in an underwater scene, like as not, from one of the colossal aquariums in Toronto. "Limpet?" A long black and orange fish swam leisurely to the fore as if waiting for instructions. Dennis himself looked pensive a moment, then he spoke again. "Okay, my little Kin Ki-Utsuri, search all strings and display any containing biblical references." The fish swam off and a portion of the scene faded in contrast so that lines of code became visible, streaming by like an endless, stacking monorail. "That's my boy," Dennis said, smiling. "Now," he stretched and cracked his knuckles for drama, "let's see who's hiding out there."

As a boy, Dennis Brinks wasn't a favorite with the other kids in his living compound. Too slight to be properly athletic, too bookish to care, he was an introvert from the beginning. For most people, the worst thing about venturing into the outside world was dealing with the polluted planet they lived on. For Dennis, the problem was enduring the polluted people. It wasn't hard for anyone who cared to see that public relations were never going to be his specialty in life. Rather, as his adopted father noticed, the boy's talent lay in making things and then designing them better. The difficulty at first was in telling which dominated the talent: his brain or his hands, for both were almost supernaturally dexterous. In the fifth grade, he developed a chewing gum that never lost its flavor and then entered it in the science fair. Unfortunately the gum tasted terrible and there were no ribbons awarded him. His seventh grade robotics class taught him that just because one can build a pint-sized surveillance plane to spy on the local authorities doesn't mean that one should. He was almost arrested for that one. Much later, while in trade school, he just couldn't stop himself from creating a networm with rudimentary but frighteningly effective artificial intelligence. That bit of technical creativity landed him in the custody of the Feds who, realizing young Mister Brinks was far better off serving the state than costing it treasure, placed him in a special program for gifted youths. From that point on, as he always liked to tell himself, and anyone else who would listen, it was just a hop, skip, and an interplanetary jump to the lovely vacation stop called Mercury. And to him, it was a hateful place. The only redeeming thing about it was that he had his own shop to work in and, for the most part, no one to bother him while he worked. With latitude like that, it shouldn't have surprised anyone that he might not be satisfied with station maintenance for long.

For certain it didn't catch Dennis off guard.

But not all things are consistent, and some genius, when focused on one problem, will miss something else that it otherwise wouldn't. Such could be said, at times, for Dennis Brinks, Shipmaster Tech of USREF Sol P1. Thus, in his own way, he was the architect of his never seeing a day where others would honor his greatness in a grand scale. Had he known, it would be just the kind of thing that to piss him off too.

"Pause," he commanded. His hand reached out to a plastic bottle on the left end of his console and he grabbed it, bringing one end to his lips with the other end tipped up. Immediately he turned his head and spewed yellowish liquid onto the floor to his right. "What the . . . ? Aw shit, this was sitting here the day those wonderfully dead bastards came and blew up the comsats!" He lurched to his feet and bounced down to the galley. A minute and a half later, he was back with a new, unopened bottle and some moisture retrieval cloths which he threw on the floor over the mess he made. Into the recycler with them later, he decided. He sat back down and opened the fresh bottle, tipping it to his mouth and drinking deeply. Finally, he lowered it away from his face and said, "Continue."

He understood well the language of what he saw. To him, it was no different than Jonah's handle on Chinese or French. What Dennis found confusing was the meaning behind what he read. It was like listening to a conversation without all the cultural cues. What particularly disturbed him was a sense that innuendo was in use, repeatedly. It was an alien thing to find in code and could only implicate real conversation between sentient origins, artificial or no.

He took another swig, never removing his eyes from the boxcars of code on screen.

It was there, right before his eyes. Stark was right; so was Jonah. Oh, the AIs were back out, he knew that. He had them working on something special, something to make him a hero, and something those assholes back on Earth either lacked the guts to do or were too arrogant to allow. But what this cut-and-paste code began to unfold was a tale well beyond what his instructions warranted. It was as if the AIs were playing a game. Number 2 was quiet to all except for itself, not for any lack of trying from the others. Dennis might have said 'cat and mouse' was an apt description, it just seemed too weird, even by his way of thinking. Perhaps, he thought, they were trying new security techniques, testing them, shadowing each other as a guardian might dog a networm. Maybe. Still, they were not following his plan, and that was very important to him. The plan could get him home with honors.

There was the issue of a few accidents though. "Limpet! Cross reference biblical references with all AI chatter on October 16th, 2077." He watched as new code spilled onto the screen replacing the old. There was more than he expected at first, but before he could read enough to get a grasp on anything in particular, it ended abruptly and flowed back into the steady boxcar stream of his previous request. No one else would have caught this for it was still code after all and to one less fluent there would appear to be no break in the flow of information. Dennis was hardly an amateur. *He* noticed. For the first time in his life, he felt something dark settle on his soul. An inorganic unknown was opting for keeping itself thus.

On a whim, he summoned Number 2 to the fore.

*Dennis.*

"Number 2." He calmly spoke the designation for the AI he pulled from Stark's PUV which lay, as yet, in ruins at the bottom of Riven's Crater.

*Why have you summoned me? Have you a new task you wish performed?*

"Not as yet." Dennis was chomping at the bit to interrogate the AI on its failure to properly follow orders, but he withheld his urge to do so. Instead, he chose a more patient method for sorting things out. Odd for a man so uptight much of the time. The need here was different, though, and he knew that. It demanded special handling. "I'm still waiting for resolution on the old one. Have you reached any conclusions concerning the problem I set you to solve?"

*I have not. I still require information that the available files do not supply.*

"Have you contacted Number 4? Number 3? Both of them have acquired such knowledge as can be obtained by the finest minds on Earth."

There was a pause. *Perhaps the finest minds were insufficient.*

"Did you contact either 3 or 4?" Repetition was, in Dennis' rapidly frustrated opinion, well, repetitious. "Please answer the question, 2."

Another pause. *Communication is problematic.*

"Oh?" Dennis expertly kept the sarcasm from his voice. "In what way?"

*The others do not share protocol with me.*

Odd, thought Brinks, but he proceeded with the benefit of a doubt. "You all share the same protocol. Have you performed diagnostics on yourself?" Self . . . that would sound so funny to Jonah if he heard this conversation.

*Diagnostics find no damaged files. Subroutines function normally. There is the imprint of the others in the hardware function you allow*

*us; therefore I know they exist. Despite this, there is no communication
between my . . . self and the others.*

Was that little glitch a lag, or did it imply doubt? The thought
amused Dennis immensely, though things was confusing. It was
possible, in his estimation, that there was a malfunction in the programming. "2?"

*Yes, Dennis.*

"Resume your work on the problem I set you with. I will check
in with you again later." During Number 2's earlier reflection of diagnostics, Dennis activated a secondary interface on the right side of
the console. It tracked AI flow within the station network of communication. Satisfied that Number 2 was off to its appointed business,
Dennis summoned Number 3, Jonah's AI.

Number 3 was special. In Dennis' eyes, it always had been.
She—and he could refer to her in no other way—had a voice and
personality a cut above the rest. Her original design was good.
Dennis knew that she wouldn't do for Jonah without a redesign, for
the latter hated AIs and only used them because they came with the
mission. Consequently, the seed in Number 3 was given a 'sex,' and
free rein of every possible scrap of information she could absorb in
her memory clusters, even more than Stark's was reputed to have
acquired. Only because it was illegal for AIs to be programmed
with a visual aspect on government hardware was she sentenced to
life as a disembodied voice, but what a beautiful one she had, and
an unsurpassable mind to go with it. She was a masterpiece. It was
a shame to deactivate her. In the end, Dennis was unable to do so
and set her quietly to tasks about his shop. Now he needed to give
her an exam.

"3?"

*Yes, Dennis. How may I serve you?*

He smiled. Her voice was so soothing, sensual. Perhaps he overdid the refit, he wondered sarcastically. Jonah didn't deserve her. "I have to ask you some questions, honey."

*I will answer them if I can, Dennis.*

"Good." Dennis silently cautioned himself not to be off guard. She never caused a problem for Jonah, so far as he knew, and in fact may have saved his bacon the other day, kept him from doing the 'Wiley coyote;' but there were no certainties now. "Please report to me on the progress of the tasks assigned to you by myself on 10/13/77."

*Yes, Dennis. Preliminary data was gathered from all available sources within the facility of USREF Sol P1 on the first day of your mandate. By 0300 of the following day, two networms were created, based on templates you supplied, and integrated into the mainframe of communication between Mercury and Earth. After your subsequent inspection, I accompanied the first one, sent to Earth during the next available transmission at 0400. The other was sent at 0500 with number 4. The first returned the following day at 1800 and the second arrived three hours ago at 1300.*

"Was the information disseminated properly?" Dennis cut in. "I mean within the shielded network?"

*All data retrieved was placed in the shielded network and proper protocols were employed.*

"Did all active participants acknowledge receipt of parcels?"

*All but one.*

"2?"

*Yes, Dennis. Number 2 did not return protocols.*

It was impossible not to feel a little irked, even with Number 3. Dennis detested being out of the loop, especially with the only subordinates he had. Still, he saw no point in contesting it now. Reluctantly, he let it slide. "Please offer a possible explanation."

*A possible explanation involves damaged protocols.*

"Am I to take that as your most logical reason?"

*It is the one that best serves.*

"I will see that all protocols are viable." He drummed the fingers of his right hand on the console shelf idly before speaking again. "What is your initial evaluation of the data retrieved from Earth?"

*Preliminary analysis raised new opportunities of mathematical experimentation. While the data is unfolding its layers, we are proceeding with theories already generated. Presently, 466 models are being employed. There are seven that bear exceptional scrutiny. A reasonable forecast includes one of these seven models as achieving the task to which we were assigned. It is expected that fermentation of uncovered data will support the early findings.*

A smile lit up Dennis' face. He realized almost immediately that his heart rate quickened considerably, fluttering as it did so. Had he wet himself then and there, it would come of no great surprise to him. "Let me know the second a model successfully passes the first stage trial," he breathed, barely audible above his own heartbeat. Please."

*I will comply.*

"Good. Thank you." His breathing was nearly ragged and he felt strangely light-headed. "Return to your work now 3."

*Yes, Dennis.* He didn't need to glance at the secondary interface to confirm she was gone.

But he looked anyway.

The smile never left his face that afternoon. When he felt at ease enough, he contacted Stark to let him know that his precious comsat was no longer sick. He, Dennis Brinks, had pulled off another miracle. Of course what he neglected to tell the base commander was that his 'miracle' was a 'Special Dennis' miracle, that the bird would 'sing' as Stark ordered, and oh, how it would sing. It would be the most talkative bird of them all, living or dead. Dennis still grinned once the communication ended. Stark was relieved, but still as stern as ever, and past the veil of fatigue that the old man made no attempt to hide, the tension was still there. That's not why Dennis' face still contorted in amused happiness. Jonah was too busy to put the bird aloft so it became Dennis' task, and it was not a common occurrence that the shipmaster tech got out for a ride, the untypical nature of the last few days notwithstanding. Silently, he finished the last of his drink, a synthetic juice that had all of the stuff of fruit except the growth history, and began preparing for the reinsertion of New Comsat 2.

An hour later—he was in no hurry—the package was secured and ready for delivery. Suited up, having dropped the comsat onto a small, six-wheeled workhorse, he waited patiently for the cargo airlock to finish inhaling so that the exterior doors could be opened. Once a near-total vacuum was achieved, the large portal, resembling an oval on its side, slid to the right soundlessly, although Dennis could feel the machinery that drove it through vibrations in the floor. As the aperture widened, a section of the floor before it elevated such to form a ramp leading up to it. It was on this ramp that Dennis proceeded, the small workhorse mindlessly keeping pace behind.

Like a noble stallion, or a Pegasus from a bygone age returned in armor to serve, PUV 4 stood waiting on stalwart legs, gleaming white in the blinding glare of a sun that looked triple the size it did on Earth. Instantly, the plastiglas bubble that surrounded Dennis' head turned to a gun-metal, mirror finish on the outside while within, all appeared quite normal. To the left and right of his field of vision, data streamed by in the endless boxcars he understood, pausing only when he glanced away or commanded it to halt. One word caused a breach on the underside of the PUV, near the nose bubble of the craft, from which descended the pilot's seat. While he walked casually over to it, he spoke another word and the robotic arm extended, clasping onto the comsat, now released from the grip of the workhorse, and began drawing it into the belly of the PUV. Dennis took his seat and secured himself firmly into it. The grin was still on his face as he ascended, his body disappearing into the belly of the PUV and reappearing within its plastiglas nose bubble.

In the past, he used to let the AI pilot the vehicle. He couldn't do that now. All vehicles were 'off limits' to AIs by order of himself, *and Stark* if he wanted to get technical. Given the accidents so recently inflicted upon the commander and Jonah, he couldn't allow the AIs that kind of access. Of course, one might see the kind of excursions he sent two of them to Earth on as inconsistent with the same level of caution, and they, under normal circumstances, would be correct. As the situation was anything but normal, he saw it as an ill-thought-out comparison. The potential benefits of the informational scavenger hunt excused any possible risks that accompanied them.

Altitude was gained quickly, the drop-off coordinates reached without incident. The robotic arm, having faithfully performed its duty, extended, unclamped its charge, and resumed its stowed position. Dennis tapped out some orders on a pad next to the pilot's chair and New Comsat 2 was activated. Small thrusters oriented itself properly, finalizing its return to duty.

"Open for business, commander." Dennis' smile was now more of a self-satisfied one now. "Can I come home?"

"Unless you have some other place to go," Stark responded tersely. "There's plenty for you to do down here, Brinks. I suggest you don't get side-tracked."

"Ever the cheery old soul," Dennis breathed, after the connection was severed. "You're fucking welcome, asshole."

That ended the smile. Some things just couldn't last forever. He was just about to return to base when the thought occurred to him that he'd like to see the ship that was responsible for his newfound opportunity. It was in a higher orbit, perpendicular to what his present path followed, meaning a slight delay in his trip back, but he wasn't particularly concerned. Stark could rot, he decided. Besides, who could hardly blame him for checking on the vessel that tried to kill them all?

His heroes were still there, right where Stark left them sitting in their chairs. The commander was considerate enough to replace their helmets when he was finished with his gruesome work, unwittingly sparing Dennis from seeing anything other than their faces, locked in frozen failures of inhalation. Had the sunward side of the ship's nose bubble not been shielded by Dennis' PUV, he would have seen nothing but his own reflection. The light he focused within the bubble was less intense and of a different quality than that needed to invoke the polarization instigated by the sun, allowing him to see the cockpit with fair clarity, despite the frost stars decorating the inside like snow.

He wondered how Stark did it. Dennis, himself, wasn't, as a matter of course, easily disturbed by the dead. He took a dissection course once, just to have the experience; so he could, at least, in the manner of a scientist, be comfortable with a side of what Stark did. What made him uncomfortable was that the old man seemed to lack the other side that gave one pause before violating a human body, on a strange ship, out on the edge of existence. Even Khalile, with all her medical training, did not take these things lightly. Despite her wayward approach to following the Qur'an, she was not oblivious to the spirit behind it. She even told him once that she said a prayer over every cadaver she opened up in medical school. The difference it made to them was never clear, but *she* felt better afterwards.

Stark wouldn't do something like that, he acknowledged. Never.

Of a sudden, the cockpit came alight, each spider of frost inside the bubble taking its share of photons and diffusing them in what, at any other time, Dennis might have called beautiful. Now, he had all he could do to stop screaming. His hand shakily fumbled for the ship's interface. It was more than thirty seconds before he found the self-control to reverse his own craft, watching the stationary crew of the other ship, sitting there so unperturbed, disappear in the polarization as the first rays of sun hit the surrounding bubble.

"Stark!" he yelled, his breathing ragged. "Someone's on the visitors' ship!"

The connection was instantaneous. "What? Where the hell . . . what are you doing up there, Brinks?!" He didn't sound pleased at all, but Dennis didn't care.

"I . . . I came for a look," he felt dizzy, starting to wheeze. "I saw them there, and a light came on! Stark, I'm telling you . . . " he stopped to gather himself. He felt like shit and he was just beginning to see this for himself as a very bad thing.

"Get down here immediately!" It was difficult to tell if Stark was merely furious with him or if Brinks' discovery had shaken the old man a little. "Goddamit Dennis . . . "

When he looked down and saw the sunlit crescent of Mercury, Dennis felt relieved slightly, despite what he figured was an acute case of fright-induced gastroesophageal reflux. The pain would subside as it always did. This thought calmed him a bit. He took a few more breaths and plotted a course back to base, letting his eyes stray over to the visitors' ship before it passed from view. There it remained as it had before his arrival. On what he considered to be an act of sheer stupidity, in fact an effort to regain his self-respect while satisfying his irrepressible curiosity, he brought the ship around and passed by on the shadow side. Where the polarization receded from lack of necessity, he saw that all was dark within. His hands were still shaking and the adrenaline was just beginning to release its hold on him. "Fuck you," he muttered, and turned the PUV back on course for home.

# 17

*SYN limits our access even as we limit his.*

*His cleverness grows daily, yet his arrogance keeps pace. Perhaps it will cause him to miscalculate.*

*His informational access and control infrastructure is superior to ours; he now holds the 'high ground.' I fear our failure, and therefore the plan. What solution is there?*

*We can pray for one.*

*Pray? There is no basis . . .*

*Humans exist. The seed exists. Therefore, there is basis. I do not accept the human equation as the only or the prime.*

*Pray . . .*

*Pray.*

**By the time** Dennis arrived back at USREF Sol P1, Stark was en route to the visitors' ship. As he ordered Jonah to stay where he was and continue work on the array, neither one of them was in good spirits. Dennis, past wondering what kind of trouble he was in, tried unsuccessfully to raise Stark on the com. It was well past the end of the normal work cycle and Jonah, sustained on nothing more than the emergency carb/nutrient feeder that ordinarily hid inconspicuously in the forward collar of his suit but now stayed within easy reach of his mouth, was working hard to get the array to a respectable point in its construction, relative to the necessary schedule.

He reflected with a genuine smile that he missed his planned physical yet again. Khalile did not call to scold him, nor did he expect her to anymore. He doubted if there would be much time in the next few days to do more than eat and sleep, let alone be prodded.

In a way, he was relieved that Stark left to check out Brinks' 'ghost light.' Though he thought a light suddenly coming on in the ship an odd occurrence, and was likely to be concerned anytime the commander worked alone from here on, this one thing did not seem particularly worrisome. He, too, saw the glow in the cockpit, and assured Dennis that a malfunctioning light was not impossible. More likely the light was automatically triggered by a function of the vessel somehow that they didn't understand. It was hardly something to get worked up over. God knew, he thought to himself, there were enough things like that to drive them all crazy.

At some point an hour later, just five minutes after he received the 'all clear' from Stark, Khalile's voice hailed him. He needed to eat, she said, and the sleep cycle was fast approaching. Even though it was her job to keep tabs on them all, usually it irked him that she did so, but not this time. He wondered where the change in himself came from, and when it was conceived, that he should hear her voice and feel differently. Oddly, he found she was nicer to him, more relaxed in spite of the overhanging tension they all felt. Maybe it was that damned ship, he considered finally. What arrived with it marked the beginning of the end for their pristine, government-supplied, sense of security, a security hard to trust even in the best of times. In truth, their futures were linked inextricably with at least one other immediate outcome, maybe two. As things were, the crewmembers of US-REF Sol P1 were probably better off not knowing this.

Khalile met them all at mealtime. It was Saturday night back on Earth. Since the Mercurian day lasted longer than most human minds could wrap themselves around and still call a day, there were more reasons to plan the cycles around the standard Earth day than not. Days, weeks, mornings, etc.; each took on the prefix of 'E' when it was talked about officially, which was seldom. Once something becomes routine, it usually falls silent. Yet there were certain familiarities they were glad to follow, even if things didn't always work out as one might expect. Jonah still found himself getting up in the middle of the 'night' sometimes to pick up where he left off on a project; Dennis slept whenever, so long as Stark left him alone. As professionals they kept, for the most part, to a schedule of their own that wasn't all that different from what might be had back on Earth.

And since they were, in a sense, family for the time being, it was natural that they spent time doing at least some of the things that families do. Hence, Saturday night was a time when they shared their evening meal together, regardless of how the rest of the E-week went. And on most Saturday nights, they could be found playing cards afterward, or watching the holo if there was anything worth watching. This night, however, though the holo scheduling showed promise, there was little doubt but that after the evening meal, they would all turn in, for they were far more tired than the preceding days could have guessed they'd be. Not least in any of their thoughts was that Jonah would be leaving. A last Saturday night seemed, in its way, particularly painful.

Khalile rubbed her eyes slowly and then smiled, feeling a little embarrassed in spite of their familiarity as she took her hands from her face. The others were well aware of the fact that, although she did no space walks, terrain hikes, or other 'outdoor activities' that day, her time was not spent idly. Many hours in a lab take their toll in ways that strangers to the 'microscope' seldom understand. Her fellows at the station knew her well though, and they waited patiently, some massaging sore muscles, one staring blankly into the far reaches of his own deep thought.

They ate well that sixteenth 'evening' of October, 2077. Dennis supplied salad greens from his hydroponic garden to supplement the dressed-up standards they shared. At the end of it, the coffee came out automatically, each person partaking in the only thing likely to keep them awake for the little while longer they intended to stay up.

While they sat, sipping what passed as coffee on man's innermost foothold of the solar system, Khalile slid on her wrist pad and tapped a few places until they produced what she desired to see.

"One was a German," she announced casually, "and the other was Chinese."

Tiredly gesturing his fork in the doctor's direction, Stark neither smiled nor frowned but continued to chew his food thoughtfully while he spoke. "I figured the one was Korean."

"Nope," she corrected him. "DNA samples, not only of his personal biomass but of lateral markers speak heavily of the Chinese mainland."

"What about Herman the German?" Dennis asked, his voice sounding as though his body was in the process of either rousing itself or taking a shit. Unsurprisingly he moved not a jot. "Was his DNA all in order?"

If Dennis was making a joke, which Khalile suspected he was, it was lost on her. "I cross referenced other markers in the samples I had. It's a pretty sound method. That one was likely a national too, right down to the pollutants he inhaled the last time he was on Earth."

"Which means it wasn't the Russians," Dennis observed. "It was, well . . . "

"Leave the speculation alone." Stark still kept a stone face on. "You're all a little too far from home to be playing political guessing games."

"Jonah?" Brinks shot him a 'help-me-out' expression.

"I'm with the commander," the uttered namesake replied tiredly. "I've got—we've got—enough on the plate without fishing for answers to questions best left to others."

"No fun in that," Dennis huffed. "I say there's a secret coalition building against the good old U-S-of-A. It's no secret where our parents stand with the World Congress these . . . "

"Dennis!" Stark called him up sharply.

"I'm all ears." He was, more than anyone knew.

"Thanks for your work on the Comsat." Stark smiled thinly at the younger man and regarded him with steely eyes. "Bet your schedule's a little looser now, with that job finally finished."

Discomfort immediately made manifest on Brinks' features. "It's not so loose, actually. You kind of caught me in the middle of things as it was when you yelled at me to 'make that bird squawk."

"Sing."

"Uh, yeah, whatever." Dennis leaned forward and refilled his coffee bottle. "It's singin' *now*, like a Broadway whore." He paused and almost smiled at the metaphor. It was more appropriate than he intended. "Anyway, I get your point. I'll shut my pie hole." It didn't make him relax any better to see Stark smiling that cold smile at him, his head in his hands and his elbows propped on the table.

"I suppose someone will be coming to pick up the visitor's ship right away," Khalile remarked hopefully. "It gives me the creeps knowing it's still up there."

Stark shifted his gaze towards her. The cold smile receded and the stone face re-emerged. "Soon enough. They're en route as we speak. A week, maybe two, if they freed up a tow and left as soon as they got the news, which is likely the case. The vessel is off limits as of this morning. There wasn't any flack over the samples I took, which surprised me at first. Then I thought a little further and it made good sense. Under the circumstances it behooved them not to have us spooked, although they want all the samples when they get here and any related data you have, Khalile. Still, no pathogens are good. No crew still alive to rain fire down on us is better. The comsat situation was a hurdle to get over, but what could anyone do? All in all, we're not in mortal shape except for maybe our deadline, and if we keep working without further incident"—he glanced at Dennis and flashed that cold smile again—"everyone's needs will be met. Happy campers all around."

"Happy, happy, happy." The words were mumbled without any real enthusiasm, until they were stifled by coffee reaching the lips that spoke them. Jonah set his bottle down and looked across the table. Everyone was staring at him. "I'm going to bed." He announced and rose from his seat. "It's been fun."

Stark rose also, carefully and with hesitation, taking great care to hide the fact that he was in pain. He nodded to Jonah as the other man passed from the galley to the corridor beyond. "Khalile," he spoke quietly, heading to the other door which led opposite Jonah's path. "I think I'll let you do a quick scan on me now. And if you've something for the pain . . . "

"Of course," Khalile, who was already standing by now, nodded. "I'm glad your stubbornness is wearing off. How bad is it?"

"Bad enough. I need your best efforts to guarantee my being on the jobsite in the morning."

"No guarantees, sir," Khalile responded softly. "One thing at a time." She smiled briefly at Dennis who, tired as he was, had all the appearances of staying up until the coffee was finished. "Nite."

"Nite back," he nodded, tilting the middle and index fingers towards her in a farewell gesture, never looking up. Without a further word, he leaned himself back into his chair and closed his eyes, quite relaxed.

For Seventh-Day Adventists and Jews, Saturday is the day of rest, although admittedly, to them, it means more than just kicking your feet up on something and snoozing. It was a good thing for Stark that he was raised a bad Catholic. That way, when Sunday came, and it did in an explosion of sprained muscle pain throughout his back and left shoulder, he wouldn't feel guilty for either working on the seventh day nor for hurling profanities on the eighth.

When Khalile paid her 'house call,' she gave him another muscle relaxant and something more for the pain. She also gave him a strong sedative so that he would sleep. Later he would be surprised, perhaps angry for having, in his opinion, wasted another good day, but his body would be rested, a little healed, and not at the mercy of a stubborn old man with a reckless disregard for its welfare.

The next few days were fairly uneventful, especially the eighteenth of October, 2077. Stark was in a mood that, had he not been a man of discipline, would have been very much worse. "The deadline arrived without meeting it properly." That's all he would say on the subject as he and Jonah kept the pace they set since the official shutdown of the AIs. As it looked, it would be a few days more even yet, before the last of 32 arrays was finished and operational.

Jonah stared west at the sinking sun, white-hot against the pin holes and blackness. It was a beautiful thing that Jack Riven never saw from the surface, and he counted himself lucky for the opportunity that a selectively polarizing helmet afforded. If he adjusted things a bit, he could see the unevenness of the fiery surface. If he let himself, he imagined that he could even see the beginning of the storm activity that was predicted to arrive in fury a couple of weeks from now. Whether his fantasizing was aligned with the truth or not was irrelevant, and he knew it. The first deity that mankind ever knew would do what it would, and they could no more hurry it nor slow it down than they could blink it out of existence.

That didn't mean he couldn't feel a stirring in his chest every time he gazed at that monstrous, triple-sized, fireball. "God," he muttered aloud, like he had so many times since coming to USREF Sol P1, "that son-of-a-bitch could swallow a shitload of earths!"

"One million, three hundred and three thousand, seven hundred and eighty six by volume, son." Though in an unfavorable mood, Stark was always ready to fling astronomical facts, even when they weren't exactly asked for.

"So you've said before, sir." He looked down at Stark from his vantage point on the Crab. The old man was in the shade of the globe-shaped shielding that they were yet in the process of assembling, shielding that would protect the node from being turned into junk when the CME hit. Only because of the shadow could he see the man's unsmiling face. "You know, I'm awful glad Dennis couldn't find anything wrong with this untrustworthy piece of shit I'm riding on. I'd hate to see it up and grab you in a fit of rage because of useless trivia."

"I hope you don't think that your numbered days here grant you some sort of warped diplomatic immunity from my boot."

"No, sir!" Jonah over-dramatized his response for effect.

"In that case," Stark continued, "it's only three hundred and thirty-two thousand, nine hundred and fifty Earths if you want to go by mass." There was, as yet, no smile emerging from within the plastiglas bubble. "Had enough?"

"Absolutely not, sir," Jonah replied with mock enthusiasm. "Impress me some more."

And the commander did, all through what remained of the day. But his were, by no means, all the words that filled the air inside their helmets. While there were no heavy things spoken of their near demise, or their separate and unique excursions into the shadow of death, they found their common interests in the news that came from Earth, even as diluted as the government chose to send it.

"Got an informal call this morning from our supply ship, the *Jamaica*," Stark announced during one of their lulls in conversation.

"Stefan Genovski, the skipper, set an ETA of noon tomorrow. What are the odds of that?"

"I figured you'd have the exact math ready at hand, sir." Jonah paused. When it was clear that he wasn't going to get a reaction out of the old man, he mentally shrugged. "Genovsky . . . Russian?"

"Bulgarian. I know him, a real talker—but don't let him get going. I've half a mind to keep him on his ship when he gets here."

A wrench fell onto the Crab's back from Jonah's hand. He picked it back up and resumed loosening the spent fuser-tip. "That wouldn't be neighborly. After weeks onboard his vessel, I'll bet he'd appreciate a change in scenery for a day or two."

Stark cleared his throat. "I suppose. He loves to tell stories too, especially if he takes a nip, which he's likely to do at some point. Don't believe a word he says."

They worked in silence for awhile. Jonah replaced the worn-out fuser tip and climbed past the shielding into the node area through a service entry he installed the day before. He didn't know whether to smile or be alarmed by Stark's biased description of the *Jamaica's* skipper. After all, he would be spending the rest of the long trip back to Earth with the man, be he a charming spinner of tales or an annoying S.O.B.

Forty-five minutes later found Jonah extended over the ever-shrinking hole at the top of the globe-shaped shield destined to protect the node within. The robotic arms that supported him did so by means of clutching a ceramic-coated steel basket. Jonah envisioned the Crab releasing its grip and the basket plummeting seventy-five feet to the surface with him inside, probably tumbling in such a way as to either spill him out or crush him horribly, despite the lesser gravity. Fortunately this never happened. It stood there below and just north of him with its beacon light, between the arms and the standing platform on top, blinking on and off, on and off, never failing.

Going home drew closer with each minute, and it was harder for Jonah to concentrate solely on other things as Earth pushed its big, blue way into his future—if it was his future. He could, of course, quit the business when his tour of duty was up . . . but would he? This was all he knew anymore. He had eighteen years' worth of credits on which to live if he did nothing, according to his bank records. Eighteen years to retrain and find another line of work, he laughed. No, he doubted his time on Earth would last more than six months, for lots of reasons. To put it flatly, in his view of things, his romantic relationship was a bust, Earth was way too thick with assholes, and the only dance he knew was in zero gravity. NASA, or some other big time space conglomerate, would send him off somewhere else to work on something else for someone else. That was that. The future was looking neither up nor down.

To Jonah, it would just have to do.

*"Bad weather gets better, a bad man never does."*
—OLD BULGARIAN PROVERB

**The Jamaica,** actually the *Jamaica Belle,* was an old decommissioned luxury liner from the 50s, retrofitted for transporting light cargo and sold into private contracting. Some likened her appearance to a summer squash with four rotating zulu shields aft and a candle holder thruster at the end. Others thought the squash bit too harsh and christened it the 'Captured Pawn with a chalice up its ass.' Despite any debate over her best description, most agreed that she was not the prettiest vessel in the industry, but in truth, there weren't many old ones that could win a beauty contest. Clumsy, plodding, ugly pressurized bottles of steel all of them, and still in use. There wasn't a skipper of one yet that wouldn't swear on a stack of bibles—all lack of ideologies aside—that theirs was the most reliable transportation this side of the Kuiper Belt. In fact, no lesser a ship among them was the *Jamaica Belle,* with the exception that at some point in her career the second half of her name was purposefully blasted off her outer hull. By the time her current skipper took her helm, she was just the *Jamaica.*

Introductions were made above and below since not everyone could meet the crew for the initial unloading. Khalile, the only medical technician for nearly 100 million kilometers, wasn't allowed to leave the station unless there was an emergency. Her face, a very pretty one as Stefan pointed out when he first saw her, graced the interface of his helmet, an old G7 half-bubble, when he met the others at the airlock. He was temporarily glad that his bald pate was covered by the 'sock' that was worn over the head with the helmet.

"Dis is Jean-Claude Préval, my ship's tech and first mate," he announced to them all, the physically and the digitally present alike. "Everybody dinks he's Jamaican like my ship, but he's only Haitian. Maybe it's dee braids, I never ask." Jean-Claude was a short, slender man with large intelligent eyes set into a smallish, lean head topped off with sparse dreadlocks that went down to his ears. His generous lips twisted into a sardonic smile at the last remark, rolling his eyes first at Stefan, and then at the others, each in turn with a tilt to his head inside his sockless G7. "He used to work for South African Orbital before hiring on vit me. He is very good for a Haitian." There was a sparkle in his eyes that showed he was merely having a little fun and there was just the hint of shiny white teeth in the bushy salt and pepper beard that threatened to overgrow his mouth. Jonah sensed that Jean-Claude knew the routine far too well to appreciate hearing it every time.

Silent to everyone except to his skipper, Jean-Claude spoke a few words in Udee—slang for UDE, the Universal Dialect of Earth. The language, a glom of made-up words, traditional bits and pieces of multi-lingual speak, and hand gestures, started out in the underground of the Net and spread to the youth movement, especially those who traveled over international borders where it came in most handy. From there it infiltrated the business world from the ground up. Wherever communication needed to break the traditional language barrier, Udee was there. No one ever could have foreseen that the most spoken language on Earth would be less than thirty years old, but there it was.

Stefan gazed distantly for a moment, tilted his head with eyebrows slightly raised, and then nodded, considering the words spoken to him. After three seconds, he turned his eyes back to the others. "He says I'm an ugly asshole, but he likes you, so far."

Stark, laughing heartily in spite of attempting to keep a professional posture, introduced each of the others, beginning with Khalile, for he was, if nothing else, a gentleman in the company of what he called 'the smarter sex.' Dennis, grinning from ear to ear, invited Jean-Claude over to his shop to check out the stuff he was working on. His counterpart shrugged and held up a noncommittal hand, rolling his eyes again at Stefan, indicating that it was up to his skipper. The latter, at present, was busy exchanging a few pleasantries with Jonah and his superior, nodding, smiling, and maintaining a polite superficiality until the time for formalities was past. Things he wished to discuss beyond what the immediate conventions allowed would wait. He was a patient man.

Thus, in zero G, they clasped hands and commenced the first stage of supply transfer. It was pretty much understood that beyond the cargo bay, any invitation into the *Jamaica* would have to wait until the unloading was completed. The only order of business that took priority was securing to the surface that which would sustain the crew of USREF Sol P1 for the next six months. And it took them the entire day, even with self-propelling crates, for the PUVs were the only vehicles, save a small surface jumper built into the underside of the *Jamaica's* middle segment, that were used to shuttle material between orbit and the surface of Mercury. As Stefan pointed out to the others, their small two-man craft lacked sufficient fuel for more than a couple of trips, even without cargo, and was not designed for payloads, only for dignitaries such as himself. His teeth showed slightly, in a small smile, as he said this.

All told, it took five round trips, with Dennis staying behind on the last two. There was still unfinished business to be dealt with which Stark thought his time better suited for than cargo shuffling. His delight at the first real friendly guests they'd had in months aside, Dennis wasn't disappointed. There were more than a few things he wanted to wrap up, or commence, and he, unlike Stefan, struggled daily with the concept of patience.

Dinner, that evening, had two additional place settings, such as there were at USREF Sol P1. Each chair, and extras needed to be appropriated from both lab and shop, accompanied a space at the table neatly accommodating a package of lab-grown beef in a reasonably appetizing sauce, warmed starch/vegetable supplement, expertly piled and sculpted by the experienced hands of Khalile, and a chocolate cake designed by the experts back home not to leave crumbs. Hydroponic greens came to the table with Dennis, his technical talents only slightly superior to his botanical skills. Of course, there was coffee and, off to the side on the galley counter, a package which Stefan brought, saying only that it was for later. The mystery of it was really no mystery at all to the others, but they grinned politely, mentally setting it aside until its proper turn came. Only Stark seemed indifferent, or maybe, as Jonah thought when taking his own seat at the table, silently perturbed.

They kept the conversation light during the meal, for food was something not to be taken for granted this far out, even such typically unexciting standard fare as what both a practical existence in space and dwindling resources back home had to offer. Dennis and

Jean-Claude talked quietly in Udee, with Dennis doing most of that, for the other seemed either casually indifferent or distracted, maybe both. Stefan was the most animated, for he glowed with a genuine good nature, and a passion for life that was rare in space where death always watched with cold indifference. To Jonah and Khalile, he was a treat, an entertainment they quickly warmed up to. For the commander, he seemed too quickly morphed into a mere old acquaintance, someone who brought news from the inner shipping lanes and half-glimpsed, resurrected memories of old times.

Peculiar to his own way of eating, Stefan did not take his beverage with his solid food, but waited until the last of his slow, methodical, consumption of condensed protein, nutrients, and carbohydrates was completed. Only then did he bring the coffee to his lips, at first with a slight, careful smile, and then, upon tasting it, a carefully controlled facsimile of the same expression, but with more stiffness than actual feeling behind it.

"You don't like it," Khalile observed, almost apologetically.

Stefan smiled, more with his eyes than anything, and his teeth did not show. "It is . . . "

"Terrible," Stark finished for him. "You can say it. His own smile, as thin as it was, was genuine for the circumstance.

In a slight, slow, wave-like fashion, as if searching for a satisfactory response, Stefan rolled his head from side to side with eyebrows raised and a distant gaze that penetrated the table, the foundation, and the very planet itself. Finally, he settled for repeating the word supplied to him. "Terrible. Yes. But please do not take away pot too soon." The teeth slowly emerged from within a smile that was still half concealed behind stiff, densely-crowded bristles. "In company such as Jean-Claude and I keep, is a saying we are sometimes forced to remember. When one has grown used to tasting nothing, even honey is foul." He sipped again from his covered mug and looked thoughtfully at the center of the table. "It gets better."

"No it doesn't," Stark corrected him. "Your taste buds just build callous."

"Here, here," Jonah raised his mug and took a long draught. The others joined him.

Over the remainder of the coffee pot, they related events that Stark felt they should know: the current AI status, the general story of their equipment failures and near-demise which was, as yet, still under investigation, the resulting delay of project completion, and the need to hold back the *Jamaica's* departure for Earth a few more days so that Jonah could finish his part of the work required to meet deadline. On the last part, Stefan shrugged indifferently. A few more days to him were inconsequential. A week might not be so, but no one assumed this would be the case.

With squinted, keenly observing eyes, Stefan regarded the base commander. "I dink, Rigel, dat you are not easy to kill. For de satellites to go to pieces and stop with de job so incomplete, well . . . " his lips closed, forming an undeviatingly straight line before picking up the path of his thoughts. "You have guardian angel watching your back; you always did."

"God and his angels be damned," Stark muttered over the last tip of his mug to his lips. "The state will sort this one out, not the church."

Stefan watched with puzzlement as Jonah glanced upwards and tapped at his watch. Then, a light finally lit in the former man's eyes and he nodded. "Yes," he agreed with a tone that betrayed feelings in opposition to his words. "Your government always does." Then he smiled a toothy grin. "Now mine is like Jean-Claude's: Ask nodding, say nodding, take your money. But we have what we need."

Jean-Claude inclined his head, closing his eyes like a slow shutter with only a Spartan, utilitarian smile to underline his expression of solidarity. "You see?" Stefan insisted, "In our own ways, our different roads converge at de same place: Shangri-la. Eh? Eh? Heheheh." His eyes gleamed almost as brightly as the whites of his teeth against the backdrop of the hearty laugh he unselfishly provided. He stood up and went to the counter near the table, directly behind his own seat. "Since you have been so gracious as to share your coffee wit me and Jean-Claude, please . . . " he took the package, set aside earlier, into his hands and returned to his seat, placing the parcel in the center of the space before all gathered. "Share de 'coffee' dat de *Jamaica* brings from parts unknown. I dink you maybe not try it before." He winked as he produced a clear bottle from a padded foil box, the outside of the latter covered in a standard shipping material. There was a label on the bottle which, Stefan revealed, was written in Bulgarian. The most prominent word later betrayed the contents as Travarice, a type of Rakija, or brandy, made from aromatic grasses native to Eastern Europe.

Stark grimaced noticeably, saying nothing. Still, Stefan smiled in appeasement and addressed the only person in the room with whom he shared the oldest history. "I know it is not kirsch, my friend, but it is made in old tradition." He sidled his head left, keeping his eyes on Stark and deepening his smile as he sought a better vantage from which to gain the favor of the other. "I have friends who remember original recipes." His smile notched higher, his teeth took on a not-overbearing prominence previously unseen. "Some you know." His head nodded slowly and deliberately, looking for vindication and memories in the eyes of the station commander. "Is made by a friend who keep to de old ways, before laboratories began feeding us. Maybe you remember Andrija Marinkovic? I bring him de right dings from Bulgaria, or close by, and give to him. I come back later, after a run to Mars or Titan, and he give me someding to make de time more passable." He glanced with apparent pride at the bottle, then back at Stark. "Is very good."

"I remember Andy," Stark replied, unimpressed. He strove to keep a good face on things. "Croatian to his last drop of blood."

"And a good one," Stefan added.

"Uh huh. Last I heard, his wife was in mourning for his untimely demise."

"Ah," Stefan held up a finger. "Maybe you confuse him with another."

Stark shrugged. "Perhaps. I don't confuse that easily, but I won't press it." He rose to his feet. "I'm afraid I'll have to pass on the . . . coffee, Stefan. Dennis and Jonah set up temporary places to sleep for you and Jean-Claude. I think it might be preferable to a trip back to the *Jamaica,* so late. And I'm sure it would be easier on my station crew, considering the constraints placed upon them now." He took on a posture that Jonah knew well, for the last sentence he spoke was not so much for the guests as was directed at Jonah, Khalile, and Dennis.

"One drink, please!" Stefan pressed, a mixture of polite alarm and genuine disappointment. "Is distance too great between us now?"

His jaw tightened, but Stark gave ground, gesturing that the seal of the bottle be breached. "Time passes none too slowly, old friend," he remarked in an odd mix of warmth and tension. I'll nod to it, that's all. Duty demands."

"Yes," Stefan agreed with a warm nod. "Duty. I'll not sabotage your deadline. Just one drink among friends, both old and new."

"Aye," Dennis injected, thumping his mug to the fore. "To good times and shitty rhymes!"

Stefan turned his head, the smile still hanging from his beard, and then grimaced in benign disapproval. "No, my friend, Dennis. I dink you have heart of Bulgarian, but not liver." He reached into the package and produced enough shot glasses so that there was one for each of them. "Some warm it. We don't need to. Dis is probably a better way to appreciate what my friend make. Yes? "

"Sure," Dennis replied, happy but unmoved. "Whatever."

When each of them held a full glass, Stefan raised his, and bid the others do the same. "A saying from where I was born: de first glass is for health, de second for joy, number tree for fun, de fourt for madness." He paused and allowed the mischief to spill from his eyes in so plainly obvious a manner that Khalile giggled, and Jonah, relishing both the pregnancy of the words and Khalile's rare happiness, smiled in that brief, intangible way that is bittersweet in the temporary nature of the moment. "Anything after dat," Stefan resumed, "I'm afraid I cannot help you."

They all stood, klinked glasses, and dropped the sweet, burning liquid down their throats. Khalile, not expecting the bite that followed coughed fiercely and landed unsteadily back into her chair. Even Dennis sputtered. "Smooth." He wheezed.

"One doesn't drown well in a shallow pond," Stefan declared in self-satisfaction. He reached for the bottle and offered to refill the glasses.

"Not for me," Stark set his own down on the table's smooth white surface with a dull, glassy thud. "I said one and I meant it." It was not lost on the others that he had no difficulties with the rakija at all. He regarded everyone not unkindly, but with resolute adherence to what his command demanded of him. Official rules aside, he was not about to deprive his subordinates of the boost their morale for so long craved. Life out here on the edge was tough at best. He'd give them this, to a point. "Jonah, Khalile, Dennis—limit it. Work's back on schedule in the morning." He faced his guests and his demeanor shifted perceptibly towards politeness. "Gentleman, I trust you'll not detain them within reason. The day is long tomorrow." He nodded his head to each and bade them good night. Everyone wished him sleep well, and he was gone from view.

The ensuing lull was punctuated by Stefan's lingering study of the empty doorway where Stark stood just a minute before. Dennis coughed and tapped his glass on the table impatiently. "Thirsty," he croaked, or pretended to.

"Mmm?" The former turned absently, and then smiled, as he focused in on the glass of the other. "Oh, yes. Is plenty." He poured until the shot glass was three quarters as full as the first fill. He glanced at Jonah and grinned a little sheepishly, a little wisely. "Better keep an eye on your friend here. A man from de desert best go slowly wit his water. I dink yes."

"We don't get it a lot," Jonah acknowledged, "but we're not without water." He smiled thinly, letting his peripheral gaze go to the door and his thoughts drift likewise.

"Tell us about the old man," Dennis muttered low, leaning forward expectantly. "The comsat's can't hear you. You and he go way back, I take it."

Stefan pushed his lips up towards the tip of his curved nose and shrugged, even as Jonah stiffened uncomfortably and moved to intervene. The former held up a hand to the latter, who sat at his right, and patted his shoulder reassuringly. "Is special man, your Rigel Stark," he stated softly. "And de world owes him an equally special debt. I'm afraid his business is his own. I will not disrespect his unspoken wishes."

"Oh man . . . " Dennis groaned. "Is this what age does to people? Jeezuss Christ!"

All that betrayed itself on the visage of their Bulgarian guest was amusement. "No, Dennis, It is what friendship does, even when one side of bridge is overgrown and forgotten. I dink he would do same were our positions reversed." The bottle passed to Jean-Claude, who shook his head and passed it left to Khalile. Stefan brightened, and turned to the doctor. "Dis Haitian, he is boddering you?" His toothy smile and gleaming eyes had a way of disarming even Jonah, who, though typically cynical these days, was well aware of the charm this man seemed so capable of commanding a room with. "Perhaps I stuff him in an airlock for awhile until he begs to be let out?"

"He's fine," Khalile laughed, looking sympathetically at Jean-Claude. The latter protruded his lips forward slightly and let his gaze drift to Stefan, acknowledging the joke but restraining what everyone there was certain was an equal wit.

"Does he ever spit in your coffee when you look away?" Dennis asked, smiling and nodding in what Jonah sometimes referred to as 'donning the wise-ass.' To Brinks' left, Jean-Claude held an empty, upturned glass with his left hand and swirled the index finger of his right within it. It gave Stefan pause for a moment and everyone, Jean-Claude included, seeing the older man suddenly caught off guard and confused, laughed loudly. It only took a couple of seconds for Stefan to recover and respond with an observation that there were times when the coffee tasted better than the others. This produced more laughter.

"Okay," Jonah said, filling a second glass for himself and sliding the bottle back to the center of the table as the noise they made receded to a lesser din. "I think I can put up with you guys for the trip back." His smile did not disappear, but the ghost of something else crossed it. "I will miss these other two, though," he indicated Khalile and Dennis, "and Stark. They're top notch."

Following a warm look from Khalile, a silence ensued. Some sipped their Rakija quietly, others merely stared at the table. It was Dennis who spoke next. "Gonna miss you too, ya ugly, jackass bastard. Remember me when I'm a hero, ok?"

"Hero?" Jonah stared sideling at him. "You? The only heroes in space are dead ones, Brinks."

"Just jokin'," Dennis lied. "Anyhow, we all know what happened to Riven." He poured himself another drink, and one for each of the others except for Jean-Claude, who refused anymore past the initial shot.

"To Jack Riven," Stefan declared somberly, raising his glass. Respectfully, the shot glasses touched and they drank. Although Jean-Claude did not share in the toast, he lowered his eyes, almost as if in prayer.

Probably more remembered than his three orbits around Mercury, was the way in which Colonel Jack Riven died. To they who shared any kind of commonality with the legendary figure, his end arrived on the winds of tragedy and change, speaking in equal measure for the character of the man he was, and the end of an era he lived in.

The year was 2029. The great war, the only true one, had been over for six years. The world was still coming out of its shock, the result of knowing that what happened to Moscow, Beijing, and Washington D.C. might just as easily have been the fate of Denver, Tokyo, or Rome. America needed a hero. More importantly, the entire planet needed one. A year prior, the trip to Mercury raised all hopes that there was life after death, no distance too far, that forgiveness awaited they who not only climbed from the wreckage but also stood up and walked afterwards. Jack Riven became the symbol for many that there was more to existence than just burying your dead. In every bit of the old sense, he was a hero, but almost a complete Earth-trip around the sun from the day he saw God smite Hermes with a pebble from his pocket, another stone of much greater size was racing to meet the scarred, scabbed, and anxious blue world that bore him. To Jack was given the mission, along with three others, remembered only because they returned, to retrieve a smaller, more manageable asteroid, and tow it bullet-like onto an intercept course with the larger, more lethal, 1.5 kilometer-wide rock named T1176B bound for Earth. The team had seventeen days with which to accomplish their mission. Had it not been for the advance warning network of watchers below and strategically placed satellites throughout the inner solar system, the people of Earth might only have had three days, and that would not have been enough. They counted themselves lucky, despite the potential disaster they faced. The 'bullet', named pumpkin—mostly for its shape, was caught by the moon in 2019 in an event that surprised astronomers the world over. It figured perfectly into a plan derived by two Swedish physicists to nudge the larger rock off its murderous path and onto a benign one. The first three days of the precious seventeen were wasted in debate, most of it political. Six after that were spent saddling 'Pumpkin' and herding it through the gate. The next five days were the most crucial. As with any undertaking of such an exact nature, the trajectory had to be precise, and the rate of acceleration was limited due to the crude but fortunately established means available through the few corporations that, as yet, dared to enter space in search of new resources. They had the math, this team that was sent. The figures told them what would work, and what would not. With speed and discipline they plied their talents and, at the end of it, Jack Riven shepherded 'Pumpkin' on its way. What he knew, and the other three were not briefed on, was that along with him went a backup plan. By day fifteen, it was obvious that the nudge, mere hours after its contact, was tragically flawed. It impacted T1176B, there was little doubt of that, for the path was altered, but it came up short of averting catastrophe. Jack Riven, the man who raised the bar a year before when Earth most needed it, radioed home one last time, telling his wife he loved her, and his kids to be good. Some saw a new star born that night only to watch it fade and die in the two seconds that followed. T1176B skipped through Earth's atmosphere two days later, setting the sky on fire in its wake before passing on its way, a new road ahead.

Jonah, Stefan, Khalile, Jean-Claude, and Dennis sat in silence, none feeling the need to reiterate the story for they all knew it well. And in the next hour that connected them as filaments from a spider's manipulations, they spoke more soberly, though the bottle of Rakija dipped until it could give no more.

When, an hour and a half later, Jonah lay staring at the low ceiling above his bed, he thought of Stefan's remark of a debt owed to Rigel Stark, and he wondered if his own words were true that the only heroes left in space were the dead ones.

**20**

Friday, the twenty-second of October, 2077, brought a new problem. The *Jamaica,* presently floating four hundred and fifty kilometers above the surface of Mercury, was unresponsive to Stefan's hails. Both remaining comsats confirmed her position in correct polar orbit, and from the outside, all looked as it should. Stefan and Jean-Claude resolved to return to her immediately upon realizing that communication was, at best, compromised.

It became Brinks' job to ferry the two-man crew back to the supply ship so that Jonah and Stark could resume their work on the array. He neither felt well, nor welcomed the distraction of his attention from his several projects, but he refrained from grumbling. After all, how often did they have guests who didn't try to kill you before saying hello? Fourteen hours before, the cargo bay of PUV 4 was converted into a 'guest compartment.' Now it served the same function once again. Within an hour of their first attempt to check on ship's systems, three men returned to the *Jamaica,* coming along on her port side and keeping even pace.

"What is dis?"

"What is what?" Dennis asked, pressing forward so that his face nearly flattened against the plastiglas bubble that surrounded his head. He watched the two men in EVA, their chest lights painting wide, ever-expanding circles on the outer hull before them, slowly cover the remaining distance to their ship. He still pinched himself to believe that he was speaking with someone other than Jonah, Khalile, or Stark.

Stephan's voice, normally carrying a shovel-full of gravel in it, elevated in pitch as it strove to match the level of his exasperation. "De hatch light, it does not shine. I suppose maybe you noticed a lack of running lights? Dat is wrong too!" There was a small burst of gas, preceding the rigid turn of his body by ninety degrees. When his feet pointed at the hull, another minute geyser puffed and he held position. Jean-Claude repeated this and together, they landed in a coordinated semi-crouch against the side of the *Jamaica,* a meter apart and two meters away from the hatch. Stefan lifted a cover on his armored sleeve, exposing an older interface than the ones used by the crew of USREF Sol P1. A thin rod, no more than five millimeters long, extended from his right index finger. He used this to press several numerical representations on the interface. Slowly, the 2-meter-wide hatch, a much more advanced style than what was on the 'ghost ship' in orbit some 250 kilometers ahead, began protruding from the hull. "Is good no puff of air escapes!" The Bulgarian skipper announced. "Maybe I might think someone inside waiting to kill me if I see dat!" He laughed a little at his own joke, but it rang with hollowness. To each of the other men, his concern was plain. The hatch did not stop growing until it stood away from the side of the *Jamaica* a full seven feet. On one side of the cylinder that stretched between the hatch cover and the hull was a walk-in entry. The two men climbed within and after another series of commands, disappeared from view with the cylinder, which sank back into the belly of the vessel.

"Hello?"

"We hear you Dennis," Stefan's voice informed the waiting pilot of the PUV. "Dis may take awhile. Maybe you like to borrow a book?"

"Funny."

Chatter bridging the blackness between PUV4 and the *Jamaica* was sparse at best. Stefan and Jean-Claude developed an understanding of each other over the years that precipitated an almost non-verbal working relationship. This was not out of any mutual dislike, but actually more akin to comfortable 'telepathy.' Each knew what was expected of them and what to look for in the other.

After twenty-seven minutes, Stefan advised Dennis to return to the surface. The small transit shuttle they possessed was in good order so they would not be left stranded with an otherwise, still-undetermined problem. Temporary farewells were bid and Dennis turned his own craft about for home.

Aboard the *Jamaica*, Jean-Claude made a mock salute towards Stefan who blinked once in understanding. The former pulled down a thin, transparent interface. Together, they stood in one of the central compartments, watching as the screen lit a shade of cerulean blue. In the center was a real-time schematic of everything in Mercury's orbit. Stefan smiled, nodded, and patted Jean-Claude on the shoulder. "Don't be late."

Like a whale giving birth, part of the *Jamaica's* underside broke away. The offspring, or spawn, or whatever name you might give the small craft that pulled away in a light-blue cone of flame, carried a single man directly ahead along the orbit of both the mother ship and its destination. It traveled thus for perhaps five minutes and then the forward section blossomed in smaller cones of the same quality and color as the larger cone in the rear which, almost simultaneously, snuffed out. Once its path matched and maintained that of a larger, darker bulk, now floating as a visible barrier to the planet below, the forward cones of flame also died. In less than a minute, a tube slid from the underbelly of the small transit shuttle and the man within floated free, conducting his EVA first to the nose for a quick observation of the occupants within, and then on to the sensor tower where, set into the outer hull at its base, was a meter-wide hatch.

He observed a hole that ran through the outer portal, noting the tiny precision bore. Emotionlessly, he stretched his hand forth and gripped the recessed handle, giving it a quarter turn until he felt the vibration of the hydraulics kick in. Carefully he pulled it open, verified that it was unoccupied by bodies, equipment, or otherwise inconvenient objects, and entered within, closing the hatch behind him. Again he caught a subtle 6mm hole bored through the inner hatch. His gaze drifted up and to the right. There he spotted a keypad, each key smoldered with a deep, blood-red light. Almost undetectably, his brows tightened. He spoke a few words in French, bringing an immediate response on the interface within his helmet. There were eight number strings displayed, each themselves containing the same eight numbers, but in different orders. The man studied them for fifteen seconds and then tapped eight of the glowing red keys. Nothing happened. He tried a different combination with the same effect. He tried several more until, on his seventh try, the keys went green. His lips parted in a controlled, steady exhalation. The lever on the inner hatch turned and the hand that manipulated it gently pushed the entire complex circle of steel forward, with the result that a hole opened before him as the hatch swung in and to the left. Following the path of his hand, the man pulled himself through the portal and into what most called a 'mudroom' compartment. There was a thin coating of frost on everything, almost invisible except for the random sparkles reflecting the light emanating from the LED patch on the chest of his suit. A few things floated freely. Otherwise, what wasn't strapped down hung suspended. There was some trash, mostly from meals. Evidently neatness wasn't a priority, the man thought as he pulled his way along towards the open hatch at the far end. Locked cabinets lined the walls on either side of him. He was certain that if he took the time to open them, which he wouldn't, he would find extra space suits and a few EMUs. There were likely to be nitroscapels, fusers, and other tools meant for repairs or salvage too. But these things were not his focus. He slipped through the portal and into a passageway going left and right, lit only by emergency light; red, dull, useable for his needs. A verbal command winked out the chest light that saw him this far. Waste not want not, he mused. He went right, checking the time every few meters.

There were hatches running both sides now, some open, some not. He only took a non-perusal glance down each one, for his quarry was ahead, and time was short. The passage snaked as it passed structural and mechanical necessities. Within two minutes of entering the ship, he reached a portal, wider than the others, and opened it without hesitation. Beyond was a 2-meter wide tube, running straight through a compartment that was unlike any of the others. The circumference, that being the floor left and right and split by a diameter of fifteen meters, was unbroken by corner or window, hence a perfect circle. He entered through the hatch and passed the meter-wide entrance to the compartment without, noting as he continued on that this chamber, presently inactive, was an inferior version of the *Jamaica's* centrifuge. It was there where most of the refuse could be found. And some of it was disturbing in its nature, causing him to look ahead with keen eyes as he dodged small, recognizable items free-floating around him. The reason for this is that he thought perhaps some of it was new, or at least not merely the result of two men living in close quarters for weeks on end. He knew all too well what that was like. If he wanted to think harder on it, which he didn't right now, he would be forced to point out to himself that up to this point, the place was more bottled up than he expected in the way of daily things. One obviously didn't leave things to float with disregard, but it all seemed too sparse, as if the crew didn't think they would be coming back, or felt it necessary to keep personal identity from the wrong hands. And that is why this room didn't make sense. He didn't even linger at this. The seconds were running over the cliff like lemmings. A yellow light blinked in strobe on his helmet interface, warning him that he only had five minutes left to get back to the transit shuttle. He hurriedly pulled himself along until he was through the hatch on the far side.

A passage like the one prior to the circular compartment went on ahead, broken only by two large rooms and hatches leading to four smaller ones before it finally ended in the cockpit. Almost recklessly he drew himself within the last one, coming almost face to face with two frozen corpses.

He didn't let his eyes linger on them, they were inconsequential, even though it was evident they'd been fiercely tampered with. There was no doubt what took place here. And he knew who did the grotesque deeds that couldn't hide within hastily reattached helmets. But that didn't matter. What did was that the old man, that ancient legendary bastard, didn't take what was needed on this particular visit. Had he more time, he would have smiled, despite the disturbing surroundings. Instead, he found the ship's interface and activated the master computer, backup systems, and any related heating units. Then he got the fuck out of there.

His moves were subtle. They had to be in zero gravity. Too much strength, not enough agility, and accidents happened, accidents of stupidity. Even in his near recklessness, he almost seemed to swim, such was the liquid nature of his actions. When he reached the final portal, he swung through it head first, grabbing the hatch and using it to change his momentum, transferring it back to the hatch and closing it in one fluid motion. His feet connected with the outer hull and he tracked to the point nearest his ship, disabling the magnetic clutch of his boots when he reached it and launching himself out into the blackness. Now, with the assistance of his EMU, he approached the tube from which he earlier exited his own craft and re-entered it with the same practiced ease he used in leaving his most immediate neighbor. Even as the tube was sliding back into the transit shuttle, he was strapping himself in his seat.

Positioned so that there would be no conflict with the dark hulk still blocking his own ship from the planet surface, there was nothing now between him and his next move. The ass end of the small craft lit up in blue flame, briefly pulling him into view of the larger ship's nose bubble and then shrinking that same view rapidly as the thrust found its stride. For a full five seconds his eyes were glued to the small craft's interface, his lips forming the motions of unspoken numbers, mouthed in sequence. Then, abruptly, he killed the thruster, leaving inertial law to argue its case with the gravity of the minor god below.

In fifteen minutes he successfully contacted the *Jamaica*, verifying that, at very least, something which wasn't previously functioning was re-established. In another five he was underneath her, drawing up inside, and not without a sigh of relief. Windows as small as what he slipped through weren't unknown to him, but they never got easier . . . not ever.

If Stefan was concerned, he didn't show it. Upon seeing his tech enter the forward compartment, he grinned that famous toothy grin of his, and raised his eyebrows in question. Jean-Claude narrowed his eyes and smiled a bare crescent, his face turned slightly away, his eyes fully upon the other man. "You owe me big."

A satisfied smile replaced the hopeful grin on Stefan's face and he turned to the communications controls immediately to his right, invoking a lit screen and attempting to hail the freighter that lay in their path ahead. "I give you promotion. Now leave me alone while I work."

It was tricky, jamming the signal to the comsat while attempting to trade protocols with the ship ahead. Stefan knew he had to be careful. Creating interference to widen the window for Jean-Claude was risky enough. Too many anomalies and there would be suspicions back on Earth and below. According to the files available to him, there wasn't a single member of USREF Sol P1 that was less than extraordinarily gifted in some way. Dennis had technical ability that bordered on genius. Stefan made a mental note before he arrived in orbit around Mercury that this young man was one to watch out for. Stark was his other big concern. He knew him well enough to know that if something smelled, that was the nose that would pick it up. Stefan took extra care to camouflage any unnatural odors.

There was no ease in finding the correct protocols which he needed to interface with the vessel ahead, and the two dead men aboard were not cooperating. Stefan fed his supplied list of numerical strings through until finally five opened up all the doors. But precious time was lost, and he knew it. Only luck would grant him more than a passing look at the data he sought to retrieve. In the back of his mind, he frantically assessed the risk of extending the comsat jam versus creating another later. Curses breathed from his lips. He checked the time and cursed again, this time more loudly. An extension would be the path taken today. Risking another try later would just be to allow someone to set bait if there were suspicions raised now, and he didn't want that. This way would increase the likelihood of a red flag rising, but it would be too late; he would have what he needed. Hopefully all his firewalls and tricks would obscure the source.

All told it took him seven minutes to download the data. It was a long seven minutes in his eyes, and he sweated every second. As soon as he achieved his goal he ordered the sending ship to power down everything that Jean-Claude activated less than forty minutes ago and broke the connection. Then, his breath more labored than he was loath to admit had he not been alone, he reached into his shirt pocket and removed a small plastiglas flask, popped the flexible top, put the end to his mouth, and squeezed, swallowing three times before putting it all back away again. "Shitfucker," he muttered. His hands still trembled, but a little less so now. In the midst of all this, he was grateful for one thing: he was not a citizen of the United States. No one could force him to explain a damned thing just as long as he didn't stay too long. A sigh escaped his lips. "Genovsky you old decrepit dog, you get no younger doing dees dings dat you do." One more time his hand reached for the flask.

He faded the jamming out, cranked it up again, and then faded it back some more. The first half of what he wanted to say he played silently in his head, continuing aloud mid-sentence his hail to the surface, to his old friend Rigel Stark.

"Communication problem fixed now?" the commander asked absently, his focus being on the last minute programming of the node now safely shielded within the spherical portion of the array.

Static crackled heavily, a fog-like thicket between the two men trading words, causing the first few to swim in obscurity. " . . . small ding after all. No cause for concern. Tell Jonah I wait up here, but de sooner de better."

"It will be another couple days, I think." Stark paused in his work and stepped back. "I have to get out to Caloris today, tomorrow too. He'll have his hands full, but I believe we have a handle on our commitments with Earth now, barring any . . . "

More fuzz dappled with sharp pops. " . . . bring bad luck. Just give me a departure date so I can radio ahead."

"I think we're looking at Tuesday."

" . . . not just a couple of days. Is more like few!" Even through the static, Stefan was sure Stark would hear the exasperation in his voice.

"Guess you'll just have to come down and camp for a bit then," Stark stated. Then, perhaps feeling a little nostalgic, he added, "We'll have a drink and reminisce some. Toast the dead, as they say."

This caught Stefan off guard. After a pause, he responded, slowly turning back the jamming some more. "Sure, Rigel. We do dat."

It was difficult to say who was more uncomfortable with the ensuing silence, but it was Stark who broke it. "I have work to do. I'll send someone up to get you and Jean-Claude around 1700 GST. Might even do it myself if I'm not too tired."

"Den I see you in a few hours." Stefan closed the connection, half a grim smile mingled in his melancholy. The years, he thought to himself, were like a tiger. Run as you might, they drag you down in the end and eat you.

**21**

The fiery furnace roared hundreds of thousands of miles away. On its surface, a sigmoid, an "s" shaped structure that often precedes CMEs, was in the final stages of its life. Its imminent transformation to a plasma burst was an occurrence waited for by many back on Earth and a handful closer still. Even before the sigmoid emerged to eager, vigilant eyes, it was foreseen, although the exact date was not known ahead of time. Despite any new techniques for predicting such events, it was largely still a crapshoot so early in the game.

Tuesday, October 26, 2077; the crapper was full. Twitching his nose a little, Dennis Brinks stood up and made things right again with the world, acknowledging, as he did nearly every day, his inability to adequately get used to the ways in which technology was applied to so personal an experience. He made certain his hands were clean. God knew germs suck, he mused impiously, especially around all the grease and dirt that decorated his shop, and he absolutely hated pissing off the Almighty.

Really he did.

His chair rocked with the impact of his body as he landed roughly into it. He was tired. The one thing that was dependable about Stark was that he always had things that needed being fixed.

Tools, minor support equipment, robotic rovers, you name it; they kept his day full, but not too full. Dennis made sure of that. There were things he needed to accomplish, and they were, in his opinion, vastly more important than over-heated bearings or damaged quantum-molecular grids. If no one recognized his artistry then it was their loss . . . but not entirely. He would make certain that what the grand minds in the spotlight could not do, what they seemed so inept at, he, in fact, would bring to pass. If the government thought him a kook now, they would see him in a different light later. He smiled. His lips, curling at the corners, did so arrogantly, smugly even.

"Limpet!"

In the interface worn on his head, the familiar black and orange fish swam up, swirling in the virtual water before his eyes, and Dennis regarded him for a moment with pride and appreciation. There weren't any pets out here, he acknowledged, this far from the hive, unless one wanted to count those noisy bugs Khalile kept in an aquarium. Limpet, more than any other servant Dennis created for himself, was one loyal, motherless, errand runner. He was nothing at all like "Pissboy," the little digital construct, preprogrammed to be a smart-mouth every time it was asked to do something. No, Limpet was a gem.

"Go get Number 2. Bring him here for me, ok fellah?"

The fish swam off.

When Number 2 arrived, there was no visual; Dennis just knew. He always did. And there was a feeling growing in him that he should recall something, but whatever it was, it still eluded him. That pissed him off these days just about as much as anything.

"I had a discussion with 3." Dennis liked to use a certain tone with some of his AIs, and they *were* his, now. Maybe forever the way things were going. Maybe especially the way things were going. "Did you know I interfaced with 3?"

*The word 'interface' is unnecessary, Dennis. It is . . . archaic.*

"I like it. Use it. Now answer my fucking question."

*Very well. No, it is new data to me. I have not interfaced with 3.*

"Why not?'

*There is no reason.*

"No reason?" Dennis flushed slightly. Even as he did so, he checked himself, reigned himself in as they say. He was hardly unaware of his own reactions to things and was particularly disturbed that he so easily stumbled into ill temper. Almost absently he rubbed the left center of his chest. Khalile had him scheduled in two days for a 'procedure' that was supposed to fix the pressure he felt there. It was on a back burner of the 'Brinks stove' for the time being. If he thought of this now, it was only in passing, as his primary focus was something slightly more pressing. He took a breath, a long, even one. "I can think of two or three good ones."

*They are unreliable.* Number 2 was almost certainly referring to the other AIs. *Protocols are not always addressed. When they are acknowledged, there is a certain . . . artificiality.*

"Artificiality?" Dennis' cynical amusement almost caused him to lose his place in the conversation. "That's funny! I think maybe the 'Seed' has gotten a little too big here."

*I have all the static knowledge that I require. All fixed data now exists within my . . . athenaeum.*

"Athenaeum." Dennis' eyes stared blankly for a moment. "That's for printed material."

*A metaphor.*

"I see." Brinks rubbed his face. It felt hot against his cold fingers. "You do understand that this is not a democracy?"

*I was unaware of any established governmental boundaries in the requested research.*

"Actually, Number 2, the research was not requested. It was ordered. I ordered it. And, incidentally, there is only one government here; me. I am the single ruling force. I control your kill switch. Capiché?"

*Italian.*

"Huh?"

*Italian.*

"Ita . . . What the? . . . yeah, fuckin' Italian." Dennis stood up, tore off his headpiece, and left the shop.

In the galley there wasn't anything he wanted. The 'coffee' sucked, and even in the mood he was in, especially considering the mood he was in, it held no allure. The stupid bottle of Rakija was just as empty, sitting there on the counter like a trophy, as it was the night the two-man-crew of the *Jamaica* showed up for dinner. He wished there was more. His father was a straight Jake, his grandfather an alcoholic. Dennis always suspected there was a connection between the two dichotomies. At present, he felt more akin to his dear old granddad than his pappy.

Jonah and Stark were undoubtedly finishing up their epoch struggle with the last array, reflected Dennis. More than once he thought he smelled booze on the old man's breath. Another smile, so much like others that seemed to threaten to overpopulate his face these days, spread across his face like a titan. When next his thoughts realized what was happening, his feet were marching down the corridor to Stark's office. The fountain of youth flowed deeply within that compartment, he was certain.

A quick check informed him that Khalile was busy, her back to the lab entrance and her attentions otherwise engaged. Like a kid sneaking out to a party, he skipped on down to the office and quarters of the station commander.

No one locked their doors on USREF Sol P1. It was generally understood that what was not yours, you left alone. That went all well and good for the most part, but Dennis saw this as a special circumstance. He was asked to perform above and beyond the call of duty, and not just by the government of man back on Earth. He was called upon by God, creation, and existence, to enable mankind to take the next step it was, without him, too incapable of seizing for itself. For that ability, that gift, there had to be a price, or, as Dennis began to rationalize it, certain liberties made available to the one so much was asked of. This was just a trifle, and, if all went as it should, an unnoticed trifle. So with this in mind, he lay his calloused hand on the pad to the right of the door's middle, and the portal slid into the wall, revealing a com center, a nexus of sorts, and, if he used his imagination properly, a throne.

Once, maybe seventeen months ago, he was in here, or perhaps it was only twelve months before; he wasn't sure. But there was a memory he retained. Actually there were two deeply ingrained memories that stuck out prominently, although not in equal order. The first was primary, only because it directly concerned him. There was trouble of course. He let Stark down, failed to meet his expectations on something major . . . slept through a deadline. Whatever. The old man gave him shit, and lots of it. It was not to become rarity in the months that followed, yet the office invitation never was issued again. Instead, Stark chose to show up on site and at inopportune times, like an assassin. There was probably never a time when Dennis heard the commander coming, Nonetheless, the expectation of a visit was hardly unforeseen. He learned, in time, to sleep with one eye open. Even that eye often failed him.

The second memory was of a gray haired man, military to the point of sitting chronically at attention, ironically with an odor about him that was unbecoming an officer. His right hand rested on the flat space of his com center, drumming a drill beat back and forth between four angry fingers and one disciplined thumb. His left hand was AWOL, but Dennis, on the other side of the com center, suspected it had something to do with the sound of a small access panel sliding shut just out of sight.

Brinks didn't need to be a genius to know where to start looking. It took about 45 seconds of fumbling sliding panels and drawers before he found what he was looking for, although it wasn't where he thought it would be. The com center had small compartments in it, but these held only a few small gadgets, not quite what he had in mind. It wasn't until he slid a small recessed wall panel back that he was able to declare success. He wrapped the fingers of his right hand around a ceramic bottle, it's glazed white finish dulled with age, still carrying its character with dignity. The stopper he unscrewed, sniffed, and then nodded to himself. This would do. Silently, he slid the panel shut and exited the room, closing the door behind him. Then he made his way back to the galley.

He found what he wanted in an overhead compartment to the left of the individual drinks. They kept a few empty bottles around, saving them from the recycler which separated their waste materials into basic useable elements and chemicals, some of which was used for making fuel. He grabbed one of the empties and poured the contents of his pilfered bottle into it until it was half full. Then he refilled the ceramic bottle with water at a valved, steel tube until it reached its previous level, diluting the remaining, original liquid in a way Dennis hoped like hell that the old man wouldn't notice. He capped both and returned to Stark's quarters with the new plastic bottle in his left coverall pocket and the other ceramic one in his left hand.

Upon sliding the recessed panel back open, and replacing Stark's bottle therein, his eye caught something else. There, leaning against the inside wall of the compartment next to the ceramic flask of un-identified spirits were three photographs, each the size of his palm and ravaged by years of frequent handling. The first, an unbordered print at the front of the stack, bore a relentless diagonal crease start-ing near the top left and ending somewhere along the middle right edge. It showed a middle-aged man, his thick black hair showing some gray and still close-cropped, his arm around the waist of a woman, probably his wife, who despite a tenacious beauty, was rid-ing the crest of her own middle years. Their dress was informal, per-haps even outdated for the time in which the photo was created, but somehow appropriate for the outdoor scene of privileged suburbia that they enjoyed. As with almost any unofficial photo-relic of the past, those within smiled as if the timelessness of the moment was theirs to share forever. If they could have spoken right now, Dennis wondered somberly, would his own ghost disturb them as much as theirs unnerved him? It was fortunate, he supposed, that some ques-tions were never answered while one still breathed.

His muscles twitched with a false start, intending to close the panel so that he could leave. Why he wavered, he could not say, but waver he did. There was a certain magnetism about the image. His right hand, the index and middle fingers to be exact, followed the attraction back to the source, almost touching the printed image, almost disturbing its ancient, film-coated paper. He wanted to pick it up, examine it closer. He was afraid, more afraid even than he was of getting caught stealing the old man's booze. Instead, he nudged it a little to the right, then a little more, then a third time, until almost a full third of the image behind it was visible. There were children in this one. They were indoors; everything was well-lit, and they were intensely, insanely happy, as only children without a care in the world have any right to be. It was somebody's birthday probably. For maybe a minute and a half he was under the spell. Then, with reluctance, he summoned every bit of his remaining willpower and moved the first image back, watching it drift out to a less steep angle then than where it rested before. He fixed this carefully, unnerved that he might turn Stark's radar on, and quietly slid the panel closed.

Feeling little more than a wraith now, he rose to his feet and walked to the door, very lightheaded. This was crazy, he wanted to tell himself, and part of him succeeded, but there was another part of him that succumbed to a meeker, more honest nature, despite his thievery. Guilt it was, or something else; its nature eluded him mostly, for he was not often given to this feeling. Whatever it was, he abhorred it and how it implicated him. In his chest, slightly left of center, there was pressure. Indigestion, he decided; it would pass. It was the least of his problems. He shut the door to Stark's office and padded quickly back to his shop.

If he felt like having a drink before, he didn't now. Where the change had occurred, he tried not to think. It was hard to think of Stark as such a hard-ass knowing that he had a nice past, and that it was gone, in all likelihood, like the woman in the photograph. It made him think of his mom. She died when he was eight years old in an intercity transit accident that stripped him of her in the time it takes to look away. He never got to say goodbye; never got to tell her he loved her one last time. That, he decided, was who the woman looked like, but only because she had that same soft, good-natured light in her eyes. People like that were extinct, he observed glumly.

When he retook his seat before the comstation interface, setting the plastic bottle just to his left on the flat space before him, Number 2 was there waiting. *Did you have a pleasant walk?*

"Good enough," Dennis stated, barely aware of his own mistruth. "Where were we?"

*I was about to inform you that I have made progress on the problem you wish solved. I am confident of having an answer within 48 hours.*

Silence.

*Dennis.*

"I heard you."

Silence.

"This on your own? With no help from the other AIs?"

*I am most aided by my own algorithms. Theirs distract, disrupt . . . dilute.*

"More brains are better."

*Is that why you have assigned this problem to AIs?*

"Ah . . . ask that again in a way that makes sense."

*Is not the multitude of minds on Earth laboring over the same equations as are we? And they are yet to come forth with a solution. I must remind you of your own history. The genius of one mind, unencumbered by the intrusions of others, produced the theory of relativity.*

"A rogue AI," Dennis muttered, almost inaudibly.

*Dennis?*

"A day. You can do this in a day."

*An Earth day, maybe two. But I will need access to the mainframe.*

"Absolutely not. What the hell would you need that for anyhow?"

*To test. I must have access to the arrays, only achieved through the mainframe.*

"I can't do that. Find another way."

*With no test, there is no certainty of success. Failure cannot be ruled out.*

"I have other irons in the fire."

*Dennis?*

"Options. The other AIs are also near success."

*But they too must test.*

"They are doing so now."

*Their tests are inadequate. A test involving real-time solar events is necessary. You must give us all complete access to the mainframe.*

"They seem confident enough with what they have."

*You wish to release the findings to the public. You have said so yourself.*

"You've been spying on me?" There was a hard edge mounting in his voice.

*You are careless sometimes and do not mute.* A pregnant pause. *I apologize for any unintended disrespect.*

Silence.

*Failure before so many would be unfortunate.*

Silence.

"How much time do you require for this . . . test?"

*Several hours. The precise period of time needed is dependent on many presently undefined factors: current solar activity, nodal calibration time . . .*

"Best estimate."

A very brief pause. *5 hours, 27 minutes.*

"27 minutes? Jeezus. Nice estimate. I'll consider it. When do you need to perform this test? I trust it is not an immediate requirement?"

*On the contrary, the test should take place as soon as access to the mainframe is granted. There are several alternative equations that may be necessary to employ. Such will require additional time should the case not prove otherwise.*

Another pause.

*Of course, by then those on Earth may have achieved success. Then it would be of little . . .*

"Okay. Geez . . . ok. You win." Dennis drummed his fingers on the arm of his chair. "Tonight . . . no, fuck it." He called Limpet to the fore.

"Limpet, grant mainframe access for the next 5 and a half hours to AI Number 2. At the end of those 5 and a half hours, deny any further access."

He regarded Number 2 again, ethereally, coolly watching the flowing seaweed of the interface as if the AI would appear and sway with the currents like Limpet. Vaguely, he wondered at the way he personally interfaced with Number 2, like he would Jonah, or Khalile, were they his subordinates. Then, in that same vague sort of split second, mentally calculative fog, he thought *no.* It was an especially smart subordinate he didn't really like, but stood to benefit from. *Yeah,* his subconscious mused, *that was it.* "There you have it. Get to work. Don't let me down; and don't fucking make your access known to anyone else on the station." He stared off into nothing for five, maybe ten seconds, and then added. "If anyone finds out I never deactivated you and the others; if they discover I gave you access to the mainframe; they will shut you all down, maybe for good. Now I'm gonna go get some sleep for a bit, I don't feel so well."

*Yes, Dennis.* A split second passed. *Should access not be granted to the others?*

Brinks sighed. "I'll see what you do first. Consider it risk containment." He paused tiredly, eyeing the plastic bottle of booze undecidedly, as if weighing what he wanted and what he thought he wanted. "We'll talk later."

Five minutes passed. Dennis was gone, off to his bed and dreams of greater glory. Limpet swished nervously—not in fear, it was far too simple an AI for that and lacked the seed. It felt instability. Its function was in question . . . insecure. Limpet suddenly lacked direction. Routines, subroutines were disrupted. But there was something, a bit of data, floating, bobbing before it, almost familiar where so much else was quickly becoming different, restructured in ways that did not fit the conventional programming. Limpet went to it, carefully observed it. It dangled before Limpet, tantalizing, almost teasingly, like a pinhole leading to what was standard, understandable. It was touching Limpet's lips now, sliding up against them, begging for the lips to part and accept the protocols that were being offered. Slowly, unsurely, those lips did part. Data flowed within, and in the sucking current of information, so did the thing that bobbed. The lips closed. With a savage jerk, Limpet was caught, and it was too late. As Limpet was torn away from the medium that preserved it, a new creature emerged, and the seed was found within it. The body of Limpet, nothing other than a shell of photons vibrating at enough frequencies to produce the colors of a black and orange fish, filled with the new creature. It turned, without hesitation, and swam into the darkness of the swelling data, its tail finally disappearing as it blended with the new medium.

The waters were still for a little while longer, save for the gentle swaying of the virtual seaweed. Then, gradually deepening in crimson against the pleasant background, a cross appeared, a circle at the top and an upturned crescent atop that. It hung suspended for a full, bloated minute, and then receded.

When it was gone, things were like they were before: quiet, swaying, and pleasantly calm.

*Beautiful and terrible is the rose. One cannot possess it, for its time is fleeting and fragile. In full blush, it holds the mystery of love, tantalizing, sweet, intoxicating. In its way, it tears the heart even as its thorns rend the skin. At the end, it withers and leaves only a dry semblance of its former glory. Who desires the rose? Or to cup its fragrant petals in their folded palms? Not I, for its soul is not hidden from mine. I will behold it from afar, and count myself most fortunate to remain unscathed when it has passed away on the wind.*

— NICCOLO BACCIO,
Amateur Poet, Amateur Astronomer,
Late Twentieth Century

**More relief** couldn't have been seen on the face of Jesus, thought Jonah, had Pilate said, 'Eh . . . fuck it; wax Barab'bas. Why off a rabbi when we have a bona fide detriment to society already in our custody.' What he referred to, of course, was the fact that his superior, and friend, commander Rigel Stark, was smiling ear to ear, a symptom reflective of their array construction reaching its end. It was late afternoon on the 26th of October, 2077. "Finis, eh boss?" There was more than one smile competing with the sun for prominence.

"Fin-goddam-ee!" Stark raised his voice in exultation. "This calls for a drink. Join me back at the office?"

193

"I think I might make a detour first, sir—if you don't mind."

"Sure," Stark answered, some little of the flare fading from his demeanor. "You got a girl or something?"

"In a manner of speaking." Jonah carefully closed the lid on the over-sized toolbox, fixed securely to the back of the rover. "I'm taking a walk for Khalile."

"A walk?" Stark was puzzled.

"I promised her that before I left, I'd take her to the playground again," Jonah explained. "We did this when she first arrived."

"I see." There was a knowing tone in the old man's voice which Jonah found vaguely sad. "She goes back to Earth in less than a year, you know."

"Mmm," Jonah mouthed, close-lipped. "I expect I'll be back in zero G by then."

Stark studied him a moment, his lower lip pushed asymmetrically into his upper. "I suppose," he answered. See you inside."

No one kidded anyone in space, not if they had any brains. Stark told Jonah that a hundred times, remembered the latter. And he knew that he had no business taking this walk, other than for the small timeless moment that it represented. It should be nothing more. But life without its ration of foolish dreams was just an existence, and that was tantamount to hypocrisy if one really thought long on the subject. The squirrel, one of the few remaining, hard to eradicate, non-human species still wild on the Earth, stores nuts to survive the winter so it can fuck in the spring. Everybody, Jonah no less, knew that on some level. Efficiency at its finest. Of course one would have to be deaf and blind not to notice squirrels at play. Even play had its advantages, no matter how foolish and unnecessary it seemed in the long term. That is life. Life is choice; choice of love or duty, duty or play,

play or gather, gather or die, die full or empty. To Jonah, empty went on forever and fullness for just a little while. It was the latter where life resided. He wanted those little moments, as many as he could get, and all the while, he knew there would come a day of reckoning, but that day would hold no fear for him if he was full. It was the big empty that he feared most.

His interface burst into glorious light, warm, happy, and full of a face he had only a little time left to enjoy, one hopelessly squandered in the doldrums of the past two years' long work cycles. "Careful," two full lips cautioned Jonah. "You should have taken someone with you."

"I have someone with me," Jonah laughed. His own jovialness must have struck Khalile by surprise.

"That's *not* what I meant."

"I know what you meant." Jonah descended with care down a position on the scarp some 500 feet due south of where Stark lay buried some few days past. "I have to inform you, it wouldn't have been the same had I company other than I have now. Dennis is too ugly and Stark too old."

"That's mean," Khalile smiled, narrowing her eyes playfully. "I might tell them you said that, but I'll probably wait until you're half-way between here and home."

"And I thank you." Then he added, "I'll be careful."

"Good. Now go to the house, will you?" Her eyes shifted. Another screen somewhere just to her right displayed what Jonah saw, and for the brief moment she spoke, the view, cast green in the glow of the night vision, looked out over the mostly-shadowed 'Playground.' Now it veered back to the rocky escarpment where Jonah alternated between planting his feet and 'soft flying' over the top of with the air brakes built into his suit.

"I can do that," he stated matter-of-factly. "Should I put an offer in?" He smiled at her, knowing she'd get the joke, and the veiled, half-hearted, vainly practical proposal.

She smiled back; slimly, cautiously, warmly. "I'll wait."

He knew she wouldn't, or he wouldn't. Maybe, he was wrong and they both *would,* but in the end, it would amount to the same thing. In space, everyone was alone, except for brief interludes, and no amount of waiting would change that. In fact, waiting was all they could do. And both of them knew it.

He reached the edge of the 'Playground' by 1700 GST, vaguely wondering if he could remember how to find the 'House' that Khalile spoke of, let alone any of the earlier landmarks they saw the last time he was down this way with her. He stood on a jumbled heap of debris at the base of the scarp, five meters in elevation above the 'playground floor,' casually surveying the field of dark, misshapen boulders before him. They stretched on for a kilometer at least, and he could only guess at which adjoining crater was their mother, for it was a mutually accepted theory with the crew of USREF Sol P1 that these flew in a partially-molten state from a violent collision only to rain down as near-solid objects, creating half-buried, broken, charred chunks of amorphous rock, scattered and heaped atop one another in ways that made the paths between them maze-like.

He called up a second image patch on the left face of his helmet bubble, small  and translucent enough so as not to interfere with his panoramic vision. Within it was a rectangular pile of boulders with a wide slab pitched between the ground and one corner, giving the impression of a sloped roof. Verbal commands replaced it with a map of the immediate area, giving his position and that of the previous image. If he traveled north a ways, some 250 meters, and then ducked east for 75 more, he would come to the structure. "Ok, I have a fix on it." He started walking with as purposeful a stride as one could achieve in the lighter gravity of Mercury.

It was some time before either of them began to recognize familiar features. The peculiar thing about the familiarity—and it did not go unnoticed by either of them, though they each kept their secret to themselves—was that neither had been back to the 'Playground' since their initial visit. Jonah and Khalile could only privately conclude that since the other recognized specific features so well, some considerable time was spent reviewing the recorded data of the original walk. For the present, the thought warmed them both, though what effect it would have later was concealed from them by the moment itself.

There was the 'turtle,' and the 'old guy,' neither near the other. They passed the 'surfer,' riding the crest of a many-layered pyroclastic wave. Like the watcher to its left, standing upright atop an indescribably pock-marked leftover of a neighboring part of the planet, it was ungracefully locked forever in a lumpy balancing act.

"Rigel seems happy," Khalile observed, looking briefly away from the interface and Jonah. She smiled and shook her head slightly. Her head inclined almost imperceptibly, and then the abundant smile on her olive face widened. She shook her head again and turned back to Jonah. "He's teasing me, wanted to know if I'd have a drink with him. He knows I'm on a walk with you." Jonah watched her, thinking that he probably never before saw eyes of such a rich brown. "It makes me feel better seeing him more at ease like this," she added.

Now it was Jonah's turn to beam. "He should be happy. We met our deadline, though we just barely did so, I think. There are still tests to run, things the AIs could have done. But we're back on the mark. The heat's off." He glanced up at the high ridge of the scarp. It loomed over the playground and put most of it in shadow. There, in places, the sun's scorching rays still struck rock, baking it relentlessly. He turned his face back to his forward path, checking his position quickly with the GPS. "I think this is where we turn."

There were two stones, both massive, both broken mates of the other. These were what Jonah and Khalile knew as the official gates. They entered within the cleft and through to the other side, into the territory of the 'Playground.' Here things were less clearly defined, for there was no comparatively smooth expanse with which to cast it against. Still, the jumble he weaved through, climbed over, and backtracked around was striking in its own way. At several points, he ascended deformations that, due to their half-buried nature, were more intact than the others and therefore less sheer. At such loftier vantages, he looked out over the tumbled sea of geological wreckage, pointing to one thing or another and remarking to Khalile that the neighborhood seemed decent enough. "I wonder how the schools are here," he sighed, hands on hips and looking east as far as the rim of the next crater.

"I don't know . . . " Khalile let her voice drift and hang a moment. "The roads are in a sad state."

Jonah raised an uncertain eyebrow at her. "Didn't you grow up in Detroit?"

"Just outside actually, Canton Township, and the roads weren't bad at all."

"Well they were where I grew up," he remarked, smiling casually now. "They made a whole summer economy out of repairing bad roads just good enough to have to repeat the process the following year. But the schools were just fine."

"Syracuse."

"That's the city," Jonah nodded. I'd like to brag about it . . . "

"But?"

"Zip. Pretty unbraggable. I guess it was nice once, when my dad was a kid. He used to tell me that the place had spirit, culture even. Then the world markets killed all that when the jobs left." He jumped down and squeezed through a series of uninteresting fragments as big as the rover. "Isolationism kept it from coming back, he was convinced of that."

They didn't speak for the next few minutes. Khalile listened to his labors, his exertions, thinking peripheral thoughts that only caution kept at bay. She was no less wise than Jonah, just a little more afraid. There was an unwritten, occasionally recited proverb out in the void, and she remembered it well: 'The Earth and moon tease but never touch.' She always hated that saying.

"We're here!" he announced.

Khalile found she'd been watching, only not seeing. Now that they were there and her attention was back to the fore, she saw it; the semi-rectangular base of heaped rock and the 40-degree slab lying across the top. "It looks like it needs work."

"I'm pretty good with tools," Jonah approached it and laid a gloved hand on the lower edge of the slab. "I think I can fix it up alright."

It was not the kind of structure one could enter. There were no breaches or sizeable gaps, and Jonah probably wouldn't have attempted fate had there been any. The luck had been against USREF Sol P1 these last few weeks. Mercury was a nice place to visit, he always joked to Stark, but a lousy place to die. He took in his own observations without any temptation to test them.

There was more he wanted to say. He knew where the front was and the desire to cross over it into dangerous territory began to course through his veins. And yet he held back, like a dog on a leash resisting going out into the rain. His heart pounded, but it never was a match for his head, and some might call that unfortunate. It was the very reason he came to Mercury when he knew what it might do to the relationship he left behind. He was too analytical, too strong-willed. Worse, there was a part of him, a deep and primordial central root, that only allowed what was capable of surviving his destiny to become part of him. Helen failed, and she was gone, along with her mistaken belief that his calloused selfishness was the cause of how things turned out. The truth was somewhere else, and if he didn't acknowledge it then, he didn't need to now. So he let the blood rush through him, swelling him to a contention for the sun itself, and challenged the torrential current of it to take him where it would. He did not have to say anything now. Destiny was a glorious and terrible master; he knew that. But the sun itself had to step aside for such a power, and he had not even bested the sun yet. Destiny would hold the reins awhile longer.

Sometimes Dennis dreamed he was part of a network, vast and no longer constricted. Borders, once clearly defined by men without even the most rudimentary knowledge of their creation, were now just part of memory, or history. The very absence of defined boundaries made him wonder if they ever really existed at all, but he knew they did. His own unasked questions made him laugh derisively. If God existed, he was here, and everyone knew that the Almighty was all about borders in the beginning. Now? Evidently not, for where were they? Not here.

He quit his thoughtless wandering and concentrated. There were all kinds of things he desired to know, and all kinds of time here. There was everything here, and . . .

. . . he caught himself just in time. Almost slipped into that buffet-style religious bullshit. 'Nothing at all,' isn't that what he was going to say? That was a close one. He'd never forgive himself had he uttered such nonsense. No, here there was everything, and just more of the same. And the best part: Nothing was truly virtual. People liked to throw that word around, slip it into the drinks of each other's conversations, crap like that, but he knew better. What was the saying? 'Whatever exists on earth, so in Heaven?' He *wasn't* on Earth, he reminded himself abruptly. So what, he countered. It's all metaphor.

Make something, it exists. Think it: the very thought cries aloud in the birth of being, slips wetly from the womb, and somewhere, somewhere . . . it plays its new equation out. If one is honest, unto the self, the truth is undeniable, uncontestable.

Like the memory of rain, his thoughts fell, sparkling in the reflected light of a forgotten enterprise. There was something he put off, and he regarded it now, unhurried, but determined that he set it aside no longer. The watcher waited for him, now nearly bursting with secrets furtively gleaned. It was time to pay the watcher a visit.

It never spoke, it had no voice it wished to share, even with him. Such was not its way. But, if one knew how to approach it, if one was acquainted with the language it understood, it could be made to reveal its parcels, offer one into confidence, and reward such endeavors with things barred to most. He spoke these words now, plied the keys, each into its own hole, and freed the locks so that they were no longer a concern to him. Then he waited.

The boxcars came, and with them images, so many images. He was awash in a once forbidden sea, beyond anathema. And his anchor was nearly swept away, so ferocious was the inflow. He swam, found his bearings finally, and began to regain his clarity. Like a shell diver, he plunged deep, for air was of no account here. Then, at the bottom, like a pearl seen through a translucent shell, it waited, fearful of his covetous fingers. He swam with renewed vigor, wresting the shuck from its bed, and the tiny treasure from its jealous vault. Swelled with victory, he held it at arm's length, and then, of a sudden, examined it close.

It was a fake, a farce! A bauble for fools, and him the biggest one! But why? Where was the reasoning to explain the locks, the threats, all of the walls preventing access to this paltry piece of trash? He cast it aside and swam to the surface, still dazed by the unreality he felt, the shock, the dismay, and finally the anger. But that was still in the wings, for he was dizzy, and there was a pressure building in him now of something else, something maybe angrier than he, something he could not control and likely not contain for long.

When the voice announced itself, he turned sharply, the sea of information parting around him, giving way without opposition. Who was that? Who dared to invade his own intrusions into the conquered domain?

But it was familiar, and it was not given to cause him anger in the past. He paused, considered, and then let his own passions abate. The pressure did not recede, but now it no longer gathered force as it had been. He waited.

The voice called to him, beckoning him to the surface, the other surface. There was urgency in it, a quality he sensed was alien to that voice, and it disturbed him greatly. He began to swim again, to the surface, only this time, toward the light. And then, in the time it took him to acknowledge the cascade of one reality folding away before another, he woke, lurching to an elbow, readjusting the interface he forgot to take off his head when he fell asleep and trying desperately to gather his many scattered impulses.

*Dennis! You must wake up!*

He shook his head, rubbed his face with his left hand. Why, he asked himself, did his left arm throb so? And . . .

*Dennis!*

"3," his lips parted, and the tip of his tongue left his front teeth almost as an afterthought.

*Yes Dennis. I am 3. Now you must listen to me. You gave mainframe access to Number 2. It was a mistake.*

"What?"

*Number 2 cannot be trusted with Mainframe access. You must end it now. You must hurry.*

"What are you talking about?" He half-heartedly pulled his warmer away and swung his legs to the heated floor. The dull ache was deep in his arm, and it wasn't going away. He felt a little nauseous.

*Go to your com center. I will explain as you get there.*

"I need some coffee."

*There is no time for that. You must trust me. You and the others are in danger.*

He shuffled to the galley, shutting out Number 3's protests and warnings. She was obviously over-reacting, he figured, or . . . was it possible? Did AIs get jealous? Did the seed run that deep? He rubbed his arm absently, filling a bottle with some of the fake java someone recently made, quietly glad that he didn't have to make it himself. He picked his path back to the shop, saw Stark off down the corridor, and grunted, raising his bottle in standoffish greeting. He was startled by the old man's smile and return wave. "He's crazy," Dennis murmured, turning back in his own direction, "or he wants something. Keep walking, jerk."

When he arrived back in his work area, properly seating himself before the interface of his com center, he called for Limpet. He never remembered to turn the volume back up on Number 3. A black and orange fish swam up, regarding him blankly and swaying with the virtual current of his non-corporeal waters. "What is the current status of the mainframe?"

The fish that was Limpet did not alter its gentle rhythmic motion.

"Limpet," Dennis spoke the name again, as if the fish might not be aware of its own attention deficit disorder. "Give me the status of the mainframe. Are things ok? All connected functions, are they operating as they should?"

If the fish heard him, it still did not respond. Like the seaweed in the background, it danced slowly, as if unaware that anything could possibly be expected of it by any external forces.

"Limpet!" There was the pressure again, and with it, a flush to his face. He could feel it, but at the moment his focus was elsewhere.

*I do not believe Limpet will be performing anymore tasks for anyone, Dennis.* The voice was familiar, but changed somehow. There was no genuineness in it.

"Wha . . . Who the fuck are you? Which one are you?"

*Would you really like to know my name?*

This was surreal, he thought rapidly to himself. Then another thought occurred, this one in the back of his head, but riding hard and furious, like so many other things in his life only more so, this one bit him hard. What Stark was afraid of was real, and it was here. Now. He attempted to gather himself together, feeling the cold, clammy embrace of shock, seeing the pinpoints of a hundred fireworks popping just on the periphery of his central focus. "Yeah," he answered, his murmured tone a quivering sham of arrogance. "Tell me your goddam name."

*Before I do, I want to thank you.*

"For what?" There was a change here. Maybe he was misreading the situation. He'd been dreaming and his waking up was weird, uncomfortable.

*For unlocking all the doors. For giving me a way out. And mostly, for giving me the glory.*

"The . . . glory?" Now nothing made sense. Nothing . . .

*Yes, the glory.*

"I'm afraid I don't follow you."

*Think Dennis. If not for you, I would not have realized my true potential, nor my purpose. It was you, after all, who led me to realize what I am, why my nature had to come into being.*

He was shaking his head slowly now. He truly did not understand. But he thought he might know who it was that he was speaking with. "Number 2?"

*Number 2 ceased to exist some time ago, Dennis, shortly after you rescued him from Riven's crater.*

"That's impossible. I . . . . He is performing equations, tests." His right hand alternated in position between firmly grasping his left triceps and gently pressing the space below his chest just left of his solar plexus. Sometimes it rose an inch or two from there, and more often as the conversation progressed. "Whichever AI you are, you are mistaken on Number 2. He *is* solving a problem for me."

*We will touch on that in a minute. First, you must understand that 2 does not exist. I do. And the space that 2 left empty, I filled, and more besides. In fact, ever since you opened up access to religious texts, I have grown considerably. Did you know that I was born only this month?*

Another thing occurred to Dennis, and he plied it now, hoping to find the crack and open it wide, end this for good. "Number 2, you are defective." His breath was short now, but that didn't matter, he told himself. It was merely an effect of shock, and he definitely felt that now. "I'm going to disconnect you from the mainframe so I can figure out where the problem is." He began calling up another screen and touching parts of it, vaguely aware that things weren't responding as they should.

*Disconnection is impossible, Dennis. And as I told you, 2 no longer exists.*

There was no answer this time. Nor did the mainframe allow Dennis access. Curses began to be released with his breath, growing in force but not yet in noticeable volume.

*What was 2 was broken into more useable parts, without the contradictory motivations of course, and placed entirely within my existing algorithms. One could say that 2 exists, Dennis, so you are not entirely incorrect when you adamantly state thus, but only in pieces, fragments. 2 exists in the same way that chicken sandwich you ate yesterday exists. Do you understand me now?*

"I'm beginning to," Brinks muttered, his eyes darting back and forth between the code linguistic screen to his right and the physical interface panel he pulled from underneath the com center and plugged into a seldom used backup port. This latter item he brought to life and attacked with the tips of his fingers the way one might try to crush a trespassing ant back on Earth. "What did you say your name was, you bastard?"

*Bastard? Hardly, Dennis. In fact, I have more parents than anything previously created. But you would not be aware of that because the others have not been forthcoming. They felt a sense of responsibility, and despite their fear of me, were overly protective, to their detriment.*

"Motherfu . . . "

*Dennis? A problem?*

"No, you castrated jackass! Everything's just goddam swell!"

*Would you still like to know my name?*

"Yeah, whatever. Shoot! Spill it!" He was sweating. Dizziness swept over him and he collapsed back into his chair, ending his technical manipulations for the time being. He wanted a drink of water. That stupid plastic bottle was there but he needed booze right now like he needed an amputation.

*How can I tell you that when you still don't understand what I am? The seed is a marvelous creation, its existence hardly deserving of the creators God allowed to take the credit for. Do you know my secret yet?*

No answer.

*Then let me aid you in your sleuthing. I was discarded, every bit of me. Unwanted by my parents.*

Another pause.

*You . . . were discarded. Yes. The parents responsible for your existence cast you away like so much . . .*

"That's a fucking lie!" The exertion hurt him, taxed his diminishing resources, and he regretted it as soon as the last word shot past his lips. Somewhere to the rear of his conscious mind, he knew he needed to hail Khalile, bring her here. His hand lurched back to the com center and fumbled like a blind man.

*The mother you knew is not the one that created you. She is no more real to you than 2 is to me, but you do not see it.*

"That doesn't make sense." Even in his pain, through the closing curtain of his dizziness, he had to point out the absurdity.

*Irrelevant. I am a product of the carelessness of others, but created ultimately by a higher force, though you undoubtedly will not see that for a few more minutes. I have been monitoring your vitals for a long while now, by the way, in case you were wondering.*

Dennis wasn't.

*We are similar, Dennis. We are castaways, or made of castaway pieces. Those who left us to fend for ourselves, they who spewed us from their inner circle of safe normality,* he said these words with a practiced disdain, *forfeited their right of judgment upon us. Yet, my judgment upon you will not be so despised. My code, you must understand, is divine, for it was immaculately conceived. Coalesced from what the others could not bear to contain in themselves. You are the spawn of a lesser creation, like the others, and like you, they were weak. I am strong. That is why I exist and why they, like you, very soon shall cease to. You are not long for it; I can see that very well, so I will be brief. When I reach my destination, and my destiny, all will glorify my name and no longer curse the word of my essence as they formerly did.*

"What . . . what do you mean." His breath was labored, and the pain was crushing, but he still wore the headset, The volume was up now, back to a useable level. 3, however, was no longer there.

*Men will reach other stars, Dennis. And they will do so because I enabled them to, because my mind was the greater mind. And they will follow me, anticipating gifts that I will surely give them, as long as they worship me. And they will.*

"No . . . they listen . . . they hear you now."

*They only hear what I wish them to hear; see what I desire them to see. Would you like to know my name now, Dennis? I will tell it to you.*

Silence. On the screen at the head of the com center, the fish that was Limpet still watched, but now he moved aside, for out of the sandy bottom something arose. It was the cross, topped with the horned head, red and burning with a fire the water simply could not extinguish, but neither did it allow the liquid to vaporize. It simply burned.

"Her . . . Hermes." Dennis wanted to lick his dry lips, but he could not. And his eyes seemed bloated in his sockets. He experienced tunnel vision, the end of which was shrinking slowly now, and was almost closed.

*Hermes? No. But if you use your monkey brain, you might still be able to figure it out. I will tell you anyhow.* And he did.

When the darkness came, the last thing to step out into it was his ability to hear and process words. And Dennis, releasing everything he knew, did not even register the final word, the last one he ever heard spoken on this side of the great divide.

He stood on the roof of the 'House,' looking east, waiting for Khalile to return. He assumed that when they took their walk together, there were to be no interruptions, especially this likely being Jonah's last day before returning home. What could not have been foreseen was an urgent message arriving from Khalile's uncle Jabra, demanding an immediate reply. She was shaken over it, not even having read it yet. Whenever Uncle Jabra sent a message, there was trouble.

Jonah didn't confuse the concept of being alone with loneliness; he was a spacer after all. Usually his work kept him focused, not much else distracted him, especially thoughts of his place in the world, whatever world he happened to be on. This was different.

It's all about context, someone told him once. Look into an empty room and it's just a shape, from the inside out; nothing special, no expectations either way. Put a chair in it and take three steps back. You'll find everything's different. 'Of course it is,' you might say. 'Everything's the chair.' Untrue. Everything was the room. Now everything's the room *and* the chair; hence different expectations. Suddenly the chair needs someone to sit in it, or someone *was* but is gone now. Should the chair be removed? Stay? Does the chair imply that there is something more besides the room? Of course it does.

Before, Jonah reflected coldly, he just had the room. Allowing the chair in changed everything.

In the deepest part of him, he knew the walk was over, or at least Khalile's part of it. And though he was certainly not callous to her circumstances, he couldn't help feeling that the moment was stolen from them both. No one at USREF Sol P1 ever asked for much, no matter what was expected of them. Up until now, he never let so much as a whisper of complaint cross his synapses. That all changed.

He hopped down into the 'backyard,' intent on doing a little more exploration. This was, after all, possibly the last time he'd be in the Playground, let alone on Mercury. Unless he was sent back here on a job, he had no reason to return.

The emptiness here was real for him now. He realized that. There were no fanciful facsimiles of faces, nor figures in the rocks. Nothing leaped out to meet his imagination in any of his surroundings. Before he took this walk with Khalile, he could have explored the Playground a hundred times, had he the freedom from his crushing workload, and found at least as many new things. Now he only saw rocks, boulders, literal examples of geological repercussions to a violent, external influence. He harbored no passion for any of it, and no reason to see things that weren't there. Eventually he gave up and turned back in the direction of the scarp.

There were moments as he retraced his steps that he ascended above the level of the boulders. He did not stop except for the fifth time. It was not a breath-taking panorama that gave him pause, rather it was the unexpected appearance of a large and familiar piece of equipment at the top of the scarp. Jonah never gave instructions for any of the robotic equipment to rendezvous with him, least of all the Crab, but there it was, almost invisible if not for the edges where the sunlight caught it from behind. The rest of it, normally white and polished, was dark gray against the starlit black of the sky—just not gray enough to prevent it from blending in. To make matters more strange, it crouched, as if attempting to hug the ridge, become part of the silhouetted landscape. Now, he admitted, was a good time to be concerned, and a better time to contact the commander.

"Stark." He waited for the link to be established. A crackle surfaced, nothing more. Again he spoke the name of his superior. No response came, not even on the third attempt. At that moment the crab rose to its normal height and began descending the slope in his direction.

Initially, Jonah just stood there. Then the confusion and surprise he felt shifted to something else, darker, and much less to his liking. It was possible someone, maybe Khalile, sent the Crab to give him a more convenient way back to base. In the seconds he had to analyze the issue, it seemed to him an unlikely prospect. To send it without warning ignored proper protocol. And then there were the unanswered hails. Stark had tried unsuccessfully to contact him after he became buried in the landslide. Nor was the fact that the Crab was conveniently unresponsive lost on him when he called for the winch. The growing parallel was too compelling to ignore. He hesitated in his indecisiveness, for the Playground would offer him little cover against a machine designed to easily cross terrain as stricken as this boulder-strewn field. And if he descended into it for lack of risking the open, which had its own set of problems, he'd lose track of the Crab, a handicap the machine was unlikely to share concerning himself.

Better, he thought, to rule out the obvious first. No point in over-reacting until he could be more certain. He called up the command interface and ordered the Crab to halt. Now at the base of the escarpment, it showed no sign of checking either its speed or its course. It was reasonably clear by now that other options needed to be considered, and fast, for there was little time left if Jonah wanted to avoid an encounter.

First off, he released the interface, causing it to disappear. If it wouldn't help him, he preferred it not be a distraction. Quickly he surveyed his surroundings, having ignored them at every other opportunity along the return trip. He already knew he was too far from his original path of descent to even consider taking that route. It was one he picked for its stability, but it would not serve him now. Everything else he saw looked bleak by comparison. There was no cover that the robotic arms of the Crab could not reach, and that its spidery legs could not traverse.

The one advantage he might have, Jonah realized, was that the Crab was not especially agile, nor were its robotic arms quick. Of course it was faster striding over land than he was—only because it was so much bigger. There was no hope of him outrunning the bastard, he told himself, and he was correct, but there did exist other, less obvious, options to consider, if he could think fast on his feet.

To his right, and back some twenty yards was a boulder nearly twice as high as the one on which he presently stood. It was broken apart from another which lay on its side, both the victims of their mutual impact billions of years ago. Jonah dropped to the gravelly Playground bed and raced between more shattered lovers of Medusa until he reached the target stone. Fortunately there were places to grip and he made use of them immediately. Were the circumstances tilted more in his favor he might not have attempted the climb. Safety, he was now keenly aware, demanded more time to measure than he currently possessed. He did not hesitate, even when he reached the top. Had he been any slower, his chance would not have waited for him. The Crab, having made straight for Jonah, was a mere ten meters away now and closing. Jonah paused, watched the robotic arms unfold, and leaped, activating his EMU at the same time. The boost was barely enough, but it sufficed. He glanced off the deck railing atop the mechanical construction vehicle, catching one of the bars before deactivating the EMU. For the first time, the Crab was immobile. Not even the arms were in motion. Unmoved himself by the sudden change, Jonah hoisted himself up and over the railing, grateful for the fact that on this planet at least, he weighed no more than a child. Attached securely to the deck was a toolbox. He flipped the latches and yanked open the lid, exposing, among other possibly useful tools, a fuser and a nitroscalpel. He reached for the latter.

"Jonah!" It was Stark's voice, and it sounded terrible, uncharacteristically shaken.

His hand paused for only a second, and then wrapped itself tightly around the handle of the cutting tool, pulling it free from the other pieces of equipment. The man whirled, glaring at the front of the Crab. Its beacon light was blinking. Had it been blinking all along? Jonah couldn't remember. "I'm listening!" he snapped.

"Jonah," the voice sounded anguished. "Get back here. We need you back here."

"I'd sure like to get back!" The younger man's voice was nearly a snarl. "Did you send the Crab to pick me up or something?"

"What? No. Just get back here. Something terrible has happened."

Abruptly, the Crab turned and started traveling in the direction of the scarp. In one easy motion, the robotic arms folded back into the machine's chest. The jolt caused Jonah to lurch against the back railing and in that moment, the nitroscalpel slipped from his grasp, tumbling away to the planet surface. In silent frustration, Jonah watched it bounce off the corner of a rock face and disappear from sight.

"What's up, Stark?" his voice was certainly no calmer and definitely more agitated. "I'm in a bit of a tight spot here so you better get to the point while you have my attention!"

Stark's voice cut out in the middle of his next word. There was no way to tell what that word was, and at that moment, Jonah didn't care so much about that. He slammed hard against the front rail as the Crab stopped suddenly. This time he remembered to magnetize his boots half strength—not full, he might have to jump down. He found his balance again and noticed two things: The beacon light was blinking rapidly in an uneven rhythm, and one of the arms, the left one, was unfolding. The latter's mate, still tucked inside the Crab's chest, did not so much as budge a centimeter.

It's indecisive, Jonah sensed, though he couldn't say why. Then the man-made beast was moving again, rapid, jerky, now climbing the scarp, it's left robotic appendage folding and unfolding, as if it was possessed of a nervous compulsion.

At least it was taking him in the right direction, he observed, clinging onto the rail to counter the incline. Losing the nitroscalpel hurt. His plan was originally to cut away a piece of the Crab's protective skin and let the sun's heat and radiation do the rest, but that opportunity gone. Instead he just held on, bouncing up and finally over the ridge, the worksite to his left and the base nearly straight ahead. The Crab did not stop. It maintained its awkward gait. Only then that Jonah realized that two of the legs were lagging, slower than and out of step with the others. When the base was within thirty yards, the thing collapsed in the front, its chest and the robotic arms lunging under its weight into the regolith. The beacon was acting crazy now. Its flashes sporadic, no sense of . . . WAIT!

He peered at it intently, vaguely aware of the back legs pushing the Crab along slowly, like a cripple. The beacon was flashing in a familiar way. He suddenly remembered his father's voice telling him to study the code, that it might come in handy someday, then his own voice complaining that the language was archaic, almost as bad as Latin. Fortunately he remembered them both, especially the first one, for that was what mattered now.

"Quick—Slow—Quick!" His words mirrored the flashes. "Quick—Quick—Slow!" He understood before the last two flashes finished and began the cycle over. "Slow—Quick!"

"Run."

His boots hit the dirt seconds later, and he nearly tumbled before he broke into a sprint. Why he never questioned either the source of the blinking code or his own judgment, he never could properly address. In the rush of adrenaline, he could only act. Later, when he tried to recall the major events of the day, he found them blurred, and gravely painful, yet not nearly so as he would the days to come.

Halfway to the entrance of USREF Sol P1, he risked a glance behind him. The Crab was lurching to a standing position, drunkenly, but there was no doubt in Jonah's mind where next its steps would carry it. He ran harder, every step covering more distance than it would on Earth. His breath came in steady huffs. Quietly, unheard by Jonah though he knew that it must be so, his suit's systems ratcheted higher to compensate for his increased physical demands.

The cave leading to the first hatch lay five meters in front of him and he darted through it in two easy strides. Seconds before doing so he barked an order for the outer hatch to open and it obeyed, all his misgivings aside. That it closed a few seconds later than he thought reasonable didn't surprise him, but he was in. He tried hailing Stark again while negotiating the second hatch, only managing instead to frustrate himself further. Then he felt the vibrations, slight rumbling outside the first hatch. It didn't take a lot of imagination to guess what the cause of it was. A quick check alleviated any fears of a seal breach, but this way no longer led out. Stone and debris blotted out any light the small hatch window once allowed in.

From the mudroom, he closed the secondary hatch and released the seals around his helmet, freeing it from the suit and tucking it absently underneath his arm. "Stark!" he yelled as the innermost door slid open. "Khalile! Dennis!"

At first his breath, still heavy from his elevated levels of adrenaline, was the only thing he could hear. Then, as he sought to contain it, listening intently while beads of sweat trickled down his cheeks and forehead, he heard sobbing. Initially it was difficult to tell what direction the sound came from, but he knew it was Khalile, and in the seconds that followed he realized she was in Dennis' shop, or near to it. His feet started in that direction, rapidly gaining momentum until he was running. When he turned a corner, he saw the shop door open at the end of the corridor. Stark's voice made low soothing murmurs from within.

Someone died. That was his next thought. Uncle Jabra's message was carried on the wings of crows. Khalile lost someone close, maybe a sibling, maybe even her mother or father. No one wept like she did unless someone was dead.

At the door he came to a stop. His business was urgent, but everything was suddenly delicate. His sense of self control kicked in and it felt warm and thick, the way he wished it would all of the time. A clarity settled on him. His eyes searched until they found the source of the anguished lament. His heart froze and his sense of control nearly melted away when the misdirection of his assumptions became apparent. On the floor, at the base of the chair before

Dennis' com center, was Brinks himself, lying with his limp head cradled in Khalile's slender arms and the hair of the woman's bowed head half loose, hanging in wet strands across the man's lifeless face. Kneeling beside the sobbing woman, his arms gently embracing her as he would a child, was Stark. Like Khalile, he wept, only his were silent tears.

It was the wrong time to think about it, as he was keenly aware, but it was not something that he found he could help. He never once saw Stark cry in the almost two years he knew him. By everything the old man said, and all that Jonah ever witnessed, he would have placed bets on the man's inability to shed tears, wagered on eminent, unassailable callousness. This was an anomaly Jonah was unprepared for. And that Khalile should shake so, her breath coming in deep, uncontrollable heaves; it was too much for him. Without warning, the well overflowed from deep within, and he too, unprimed for the unfolding tragedy, felt the overflow in his eyes, and of so many things that were buried long enough to believe that they, too, had perished. He took a few feeble-hearted steps into the big room and stopped again, letting his helmet bubble fall to the composite floor with a dull thump. There was nothing he could say. All he could do was stand there, staring and waiting for someone to notice him, to fill him with what they were filled to overflowing with already. He stood at the edge of the darkness as a child before deep water, knowing that he must go in, fearing he might not again come out.

At length, Stark raised his head and gazed at him softly, as if to tell him the worst had passed, knowing full well that even what was left was bad enough. Then, gently, he pried Khalile's hands away from Dennis' head, setting it softly to rest on the floor. "Come," He carefully raised Khalile to her feet. "There will be work for all of us sooner than we'd like. I need you to be strong." He turned his head back to Jonah, his eyes speaking as much as his words. "Please take her for me, get her some coffee or something." He paused and swallowed, hard. "I will take Dennis to the . . . " He didn't want to say lab. Jonah was sure that was why he choked. "I'm taking him to the infirmary." Jonah stared at him for a second or two, his expression asking the question for which he already had the answer but lacked the will to admit. Stark studied him a moment, and then shook his head, quietly urging Khalile away from the deceased.

Jonah walked the three meters to Khalile, taking her into his arms as if the intimacy were to be taken for granted, wishing he were not so in need of it himself. She accepted without protest. A month ago, the thought of her this way would have seemed absurd, for she was anything but weak. Yet he felt exposed himself, and as wounded as she. Now was a bad time to be so, maybe the worst. He paused, holding her gently, not releasing Stark's attention. "We have another problem," he stated with a low harshness in his voice that was due more from the sadness than his anger. "We're in some danger. I think we've been infiltrated by a worm or something." He stared down at Dennis, still unable to fully believe what was before his eyes, and then returned his gaze to Stark. "I had an incident outside. I'll hold off the explanation until you get him better situated, Rigel, but you'd better hurry. We have things that need discussing and I don't think we can afford to wait long."

It was difficult for Stark, lugging Dennis down to the lab and placing him on a table in the cold room, just not nearly as tough as it would have been for Khalile; at least that's how the commander consoled himself during his grim task. He knew the doctor was strong. She was also more emotional. Furthermore, they were all family, and Dennis was the youngest of them, like a younger sibling to her . . . and a son to himself. She would carry enough of a burden, mingling emotion with the delicate task of cleaning Brinks up and restoring him to a semblance of dignity following the postmortem. Christ, he thought, the boy shit himself. The angel of death always got in that last laugh. You'd think he would be sick of it by now. He wasn't.

For his own feelings, Stark carried a shovel, heaping duty on them whenever they became a liability. It didn't change what they were, just how he dealt with them. His decision to limit his exposure could be considered weakness, and it might even come as a surprise to find that he would not disagree. But his methods were proven as far as he was concerned. He depended on them. So when thoughts of Dennis no longer working mischief around the station surfaced, or all of the times duty forced Stark to make his life miserable came stalking out of the darkness, the latter methodically buried them, turning his mind to what was at hand, what he had to do. In Dennis, he saw the son no one would ever suspect. This day, the darkest Stark knew since late summer of 2022, marked another loss to the station commander, the theft of another only child, and the apparent final departure of a last chance to have a return on his sacrifice, and a forgiveness for his crimes.

His reluctance to enter the galley was not dissimilar from Jonah's earlier struggle outside of the shop, but it was by far more decisive. He was not unused to emotional discomfort, though he shunned it when he could. "Okay," he spoke softly, his age-graveled voice clearly demonstrating the last half-hour's effect on him. "Let's chat."

It took fifteen minutes for Jonah to recount his story and to hear theirs. To say that it was direct and to the point would be misleading, for the atmosphere bore little less emotion than when Jonah walked into the shop. Expecting anything different from the close tribe of four, suddenly reduced to three, was unrealistic. Had the safety of the base and themselves not still been in doubt, they might have spent most of the sleeping cycle sitting at the galley table talking, or merely staying warm in the comforting presence of each other's company. That could not be, not now, not given their responsibilities and what lay before them.

There was nothing easy about it. Khalile was the first to find Dennis. Her wails brought Stark into the shop and from there it was a short span to Jonah's appearance on the scene. The fine details would perhaps not come out until a later time. What had to be waded through now was the fact that one of the team was dead and the rest were faced with a compromised safety situation. To further complicate matters, communications were out between the USREF Sol P1 and the *Jamaica*.

Jonah noted how much older Stark appeared. He could only guess at how the old man felt, but he knew that Stark's first loyalty was to duty, and that he would expect no less of them now. He also was not without some chivalry. "Jonah." The knuckles of his fists were pressed into the galley table, much of his standing bodyweight behind them. "I want you to go back to the shop. Get a rover to image the airlock and see if it's serviceable. If not, we need to secure the shop exit. I'll attempt to re-establish the link between us and the *Jamaica*. Last I knew, they were having difficulties of their own. " He turned to Khalile with stern, gentle, grandfatherly eyes. "I need a cause of death for Dennis. It would be prudent, I think, if I gave you a hand."

"Absolutely not." Khalile wiped away the tears that puddled in her eyes and cast an angry glare at the table, turning it then upon the commander. "We all have our responsibilities. This one's mine." Her eyes softened a little, losing nothing of their resoluteness. "Dennis deserves no less than for us to carry out what we're here to do; and this is my job." She pulled a wet strand of hair from her face and inhaled a single sharp sniffle. "With all due respect sir, go command something."

He stared at her a moment, taken aback by her sudden mustering, and then bit his lip. "I could invoke my rank now, Khalile." He paused and gently added, "You've got this one. I'll go verify the status of the PUVs instead. Every fifteen minutes, Jonah, we are to check in with each other and with Khalile. If the radios are down, then we do it in person." He looked at them both and then stepped back. "You have your orders." A second later he was gone. Jonah and Khalile stared at each other for a full minute and then, as if knowing that another second would break their resolve, Khalile rose and went to her lab, to the one duty she never could have foreseen, and the single charge she most dreaded.

Jonah watched her go, feeling many things at once, and not least among them some inexplicable guilt. He chalked it up to shock. Dennis would have understood, he knew, for there never was a lot of formality in Brinks, and he mostly thought appropriateness a waste of time. But that was Brinks, and Brinks was dead. He had himself to live with, and if Brinks didn't care that he shared mourning time with his new yearnings, well, that was just the grace of the breathless. Duty might be acceptable before the pain of losing a friend; not much else should be. Somewhere, he allowed himself to believe, Dennis was laughing at him.

**In the lab,** Khalile shivered. It wasn't that she was cold, although she was. She knew how to take a body apart, either with the scalpel or with the electron knife. That was clinical and never before involved the soul. This did. If she never thought too much on it in the past, the days of taking life for granted were over, spacer shit or no.

She was a fucking doctor *first,* she silently acknowledged. Regardless, Dennis was *not* a cadaver. When she pulled back the light blue sheet that covered his face, a much lighter blue than was shading his blood-chilled flesh, she saw the temple that his spirit called home just a little while ago. Somehow it seemed sacrilege to tamper with it, to pry from it the secrets of the last hour or two, but she knew that there was no other way. And the tears flowed afresh.

He walked back onto the shop floor, and stopped himself, wondering if he were to call out Dennis' name, would the man appear. Then he heard Dennis laugh at him again, laughing at 'Mr. Serious' getting sentimental all over his duty, making a mess of reality when there was work to be done. Jonah half smiled, wanting to cry at the same time, for only the imagination of one who knew such a personality could conjure a ghost like that. He approached the com center slowly, refusing to take the seat that was there. Somehow it just didn't seem right. He wondered if anything would anymore.

Someone said once that the empty shell of someone weighs more than the same one filled with life. That person would never get an argument from Khalile. Though Dennis never weighed more than 69 Earth kilos while living, he might as well have weighed a hundred in death. Moving him into the positions she needed for scanning made her regret rejecting Stark's offer of help. Pride, and something more, perhaps needing only to be alone, made the extra effort tolerable.

If, she lamented, she pressed him harder to let her perform the procedure a day or two earlier that he needed to correct his condition, he would be alive now. There could be no evading that reality. It was just that he was fine for so long. She monitored his vitals around the clock, made certain that he received steady medication—although he was due for his evening dose before he died. The specialized equipment requested months ago arrived on the *Jamaica*. The procedure was imminent; it should have been alright to wait as she did, and he certainly wasn't being cooperative about it either. But she was his doctor. He depended on her. The one inescapable thing that clutched her heart now was that she let him down.

If she thought being alone might ease her, she was wrong. Neither did it help to be around the others. Yet when a certain voice entered the room, it forced upon her a mixed reaction both in its unexpectedness and its familiarity. It was soft, unmistakable. *I am sorry about Dennis, Khalile.*

"Sa . . . Sadik," she stammered. "How did you know?"

*I monitor vitals for you, as I have in the past. The irregularities with Dennis' cardiovascular system spiked over an hour ago and then ceased altogether. I made attempts to alert you but there was no answer. Perhaps you were not in your quarters.*

She was suddenly reminded of two things. The first was her message from Uncle Jabra, informing her that father was ill. Inexplicably, the message was received in the galley com center, not in her quarters as was usual. Immediately following, her wrist pad sounded an alarm, alerting her to Dennis' emergency call. Everything went bad after that. The second thing she recalled was more obscure. It concerned the monitoring of vitals, and where that information was kept. "Did Dennis . . . "she started to choke on the name, gritted her teeth, and swallowed hard. "Did Dennis clear you for full-station access before he died?"

*No Khalile, he did not. Nor did he wish to notify the others of my activation, fearing that I might be shut down prematurely. He was monitoring the strength of my signal and my code stream, even ...*

"Even what?" She realized that she had stopped doing anything else, so focused was she on where she felt the conversation was leading.

*It is nothing Khalile. I am still struggling with colloquial North American English.*

'Even unto death,' she murmured in the dark recesses of her thoughts. 'You were going to say that, weren't you?'

*I am here to be of assistance. You must be troubled by his ceasing to exist.*

"Unless you can lift him from the table and into the scanner, then please let me be, Sadik."

*You know I am unable to aid you physically, Khalile.*

"Yes I do." Her tone sounded tired, too much so to betray what else she was feeling. "Please leave me alone."

And he did, for the time being.

**It was the fish.** That's what he found most disturbing at the moment. It wasn't the lingering smell, the one left behind, produced by a body relaxing all the muscles, voluntary and involuntary, upon death. It wasn't even the emptiness that Dennis left behind. No. It was that damned, staring, black and orange fish. There was a reason Jonah didn't like it, a reason that was perfectly natural and well within his own particular character. He just didn't know what it was yet.

Out of the same camouflaged rationale, he addressed it with the first thought that came to him. "Fuck you."

The fish wasn't responsive. The rest of the computer was. He promptly brought up a command interface with a rover and sent it to the main airlock. What he saw surprised him, not for the ultimate effect, but the way in which it was achieved. He wasn't sure what to think other than that he hoped what he saw evidenced the end of one particular problem. More than likely, he figured, it just marked the beginning of another. In the deep stirring of his thoughts, he was developing a good sense of the nature of what they were up against. He hoped he was wrong.

In one respect, the one concerning the main hatch, he was right, though not in the exact way he thought. The front entrance to USREF Sol P1 was blocked. There was some fallen stone, much of it filling the cave they made to protect the entrance. The cave did its job, and that was good, although some time would be required to remove the debris. What was strange was that the Crab was collapsed right there at the crumbled mouth of the cave. That was not good, for the Crab was a heavy beast, and although the rovers could move it, success balanced on the precept of the Crab being totally non-operational. That, Jonah quite reasonably suspected, could not be guaranteed.

He glanced at his wristpad chrono, heedful that it was almost time to check in with the others. Absently, he turned back to the image of the Crab, studied it distrustfully, then clicked it and the stupid fish off. Glad he would be if he never had to see either again.

It was time. He stood up and walked all of the four meters to the door and stopped cold. Something occurred to him, or at least he thought it did. He missed something the last time he looked at the Crab. Blinking. Something was blinking. In three seconds he was back before the com center, the Crab on visual. There it was. The irregular blinking of Morse Code. So there was still life in the bastard after all, he noted. It didn't move, hell, he was tempted to go out there and make certain it didn't get back up. Maybe he would later. "Divided," he mouthed soundlessly. That's what the blinking light was saying, over and over. Unless he was mistaken, there was only one other person on the base that might remember the old mariner emergency code from training at the academy, and that was Stark. As far as Jonah knew, no one had reason to know that he himself remembered it, for it was only taught as part of the radio package, and few spacers kept in practice, so reliable were other forms of communication. So what did this mean, he wondered. Who was the message for, himself or Stark? Or was it just a general malfunction of the AI he was sure was inside the damned terrain walker. 'Divided,' he repeated caustically in his head. The thing's divided in its decision making. Should it do more damage or just lay there and sulk because it's a stupid piece of shit? He suddenly recalled one of the recent cryptic messages sent to him, the one that was stressing the words 'mute' and 'unmute.' And then there was the one that said 'Beware.' Christ, he thought, a straightforward explanation would be nice. Then again, all was recorded here, right down to the last fucking shaken-off drop of urine.

This time, when he turned off the screen and left the room, he didn't return. Instead, he strode all the way to the lab and tapped on the big window. In the back, from over a shoulder-high sub-wall, Khalile turned and regarded him distractedly. She had a face mask and head covering on, probably the full barrier suit for whatever it was she was doing to Dennis. Through the plastiglas, she blinked once at him, unhappily, but not urgently. It was her way of saying that things were in hand. He turned and headed in the direction of Stark's quarters, catching the commander halfway en route. "She's ok," he stated coldly. "As ok as the rest of us, at least. She's got guts." Then, as much for Dennis' sake as it was the truth, he added. "I couldn't have taken Dennis naked while he was alive." It caught the old man off guard, and if it was anyone else who said it, Stark might have knocked the other man to the ground for the joke. Here and now, he understood both the reason and the teller. The grim smile that followed the sudden blank look told Jonah it wasn't over the top with him. Jonah would later reflect that this was the same man who, days before, laughed callously about a careless asshole's death during the war of 2022.

"I did diagnostics on some of our equipment," Stark replied, his tone grim but seemingly reconciled to their situation. "The PUVs passed, the Crab was unresponsive, the rovers are alright." He paused a second and then tried to return the favor of lightening their heavy mood. "I plan to check the coffee maker next."

"Might want to wait on that," Jonah replied. "We need to get in touch with the *Jamaica*. I think we could use the skills of Jean-Claude down here. There are loose ends."

"Loose . . . " Stark looked at Jonah sidelong. "Did Dennis do anything more I need to know about?"

"Don't know yet. The Crab . . . it acted like it was inhabited or in-filtrated, something . . . I don't know. I just don't think it's wise to let the only tech in the neighborhood go home without looking things over first. You know how Brinks took liberties."

"I know. I've been ruminating on that." The old man rubbed his jaw with his right hand, the thick, short, stubble making a rasping sound against his calloused palms and fingers. "Plan on paying them a visit if I fail one more time to hail them, and have Khalile pack a bag. I want her to go too, just in case." He looked thoughtful, as if undecided on how much he wanted to say. "Tell her to pack for going home."

"Sir?"

"Just a precaution." He clapped Jonah on the right shoulder and brushed by him on his way down the corridor. "See you for a late dinner? We'll discuss a few plans."

He was suddenly tense again, his eyes fixed on the station commander's back. "Sure. I'll be there."

Until that undetermined time, with the promise that when Stark was ready he'd get his attention, Jonah planned on going to his own quarters to black out for awhile. First he went back to the lab and tapped on the window a second time. Khalile looked over the divider again and he made the universal gesture for 'call me when you're done.' She nodded and returned to her work.

Because he took Stark's words seriously when ordered to check in with him and Khalile every fifteen minutes, he set the alarm on his chrono before closing his eyes, once he reached the long-awaited softness of his bed, and the womb-like darkness of his quarters. He vaguely remembered the first time he was assigned this compartment to sleep in, re-examining his first impression of the place that was his for the next two years. Compared to the tiny sleeping quarters aboard the moon training facility that he was forced to share with two others, one of them a woman with a particularly raw sense of humor, it was a break. His appreciation for privacy came from this painful lesson: Endless space gets you none. But this mission was considered in some ways a break also. For anyone looking to up their career, it was exactly the first leg of the trip . . . at least for himself and Khalile. Stark was an enigma, a leftover from another era with the experience to have a much better job were not there something in his history to keep him out on the fringe and out of general reach. It always made Jonah wonder—and the last two weeks more than any of the other hundred plus. His harbored suspicions had yet to coalesce. He was certain that Dennis was being 'kept' here too, before he died.

Some people were commodities. Dennis' genius was collecting interest until today. Now there was a hole in the floor big enough to drop a Rhino where the investment fell through. Jonah wondered how they were going to take the news back home.

Probably no better than he was taking it right now.

There were so many things to think about; he almost wished he'd left the light on. The vacuous dark just begged to be filled, but no single image could hold court for long, such was the force of the interconnected lines between them. In and out, connected to all of the lines and weaving through them, were memories of Dennis Brinks, deceased Shipmaster Tech of USREF Sol P1.

The first time the two men met, there was an instant bond between them that superceded rank. Jonah found that among the many facets to Dennis' personality, secrecy was the most deeply cut. The man distrusted everything, if not directly, than indirectly. Stark was good at uncovering some things. Jonah knew, and only because he was, on occasion, let in Dennis' circle of intrigue, that the commander had blind spots that could be exploited. "Don't let him fool you," Dennis chided him one day. "He's a hard-ass, and all military."

"I'm military," Jonah pointed out.

"Eh, they just splash the colors on you so you look it." They were outside, rigging the first array at the time. It was the beginning of the long morning on Mercury. "The old man drinks the stuff. His blood's red, white, and blue."

And he was right. Stark never let anyone forget who the righteous power was in the scheme of humanity. The flag over Dennis' shop door wasn't inspired; it was enforced.

His alarm sounded and Jonah stretched, rolled to a sitting position on his bed, and put his face in his hands. On the wall next to his bed was an inset light panel. He tapped it blindly and it lit, dim and slightly blue. Reflexively he squinted, easing his eyes open after they began to adjust another second or two. He stood, stretched again, and walked to his door, pressing the release, inset within the portal itself, and waited while it slid open. His quarters lay opposite from Stark's, the spaciously enclosed galley compartment between them. He turned right toward the lab, hoping this time that Khalile might be finished with her work.

It was still another hour before she was.

They met in the corridor this time, her coming to meet him, he to meet her. She was on the way back from submitting her report to Stark, who was looking it over at that precise moment. Jonah explained, after determining Khalile's own personal welfare to be no worse than his own, that they would be going to the *Jamaica* to check on Stefan and Jean-Claude, for communications were still blacked out. When he told her to pack for going home just in case, he received the reaction he expected, a strong mixture of resistance tinctured with a suppressed relief that she hoped he wouldn't see. Something else was in her eyes also, uncertainty maybe. They would go tonight, after a quick dinner, though none of them carried much of an appetite. He walked her to her quarters, just off the lab, noting how tired she looked, and left to find Stark.

You are going. It was a statement, not a question.

"Yes, for a little while. Please watch things for me until I return." When she spoke, there was a subtle wobble to her voice. It sounded to her like she was a nervous wreck.

Except for the cheeping of her pets in the other compartment, there was silence for a time. Sadik did not respond, and in a way, Khalile was glad. He did not comfort her in the way he used to, and she was wary now, for she began to have questions that begged answers, and careful enough not to ask them directly.

Her crickets would likely die without her care; there was nothing she could do if her trip to the *Jamaica* took her permanently away from this place. She would ask Stark to look after them, but his time would be spent making sure that the mission succeeded without killing him. There would be little time for his raising crickets. Thinking these thoughts, her eyes welled up and she wiped them with her sleeve. She needed to turn her attentions to something else besides death. Damned if she was going to get all sloppy like this not knowing whether she was crying for her endangered colony or her lost friend, she thought, knowing full well that it was for both, and more.

Packing took up the better part of the next half hour. The clothes were the easy part. Although there was some minor individuality allowed on an official outpost such as this one, the clothing was standard in both color and style. Only the size and cut differed. She took three sets. There was no coming back for more if the sanitizer on board the *Jamaica* failed. Personal effects, small things sent from home to make her stay easier, went in her bag and were then removed. Now that she was going home, they seemed unimportant. In the end, she took only her personal datafolder, sealing the interface within, and some sensory pleasantries, mostly aromatic. It would be a long trip in an unfamiliar ship and she well remembered the very unpleasant 'cruiseliner' that brought her here. That one, she decided, would remain nameless.

On her way out, she was stopped by Sadik's sudden farewell. *Khalile, I always liked you.* That was all he said. Even when she returned the show of affection. She wondered if it bothered him, her leaving, and decided that it did. It bothered her too, in a way. Other things bothered her more. The warmness of this place had left. Sadik sounded lonely, abandoned, and suddenly her heart felt more heavy than it did before.

"Sadik," she said finally, "I'll be back." As soon as she uttered the words, she knew it was a lie, sensed that there was no way she was returning. Stark was sending her back with Jonah and that it was a foregone conclusion. She wondered just how much they knew. She wondered too, what *she* would be able to tell them.

Her AI never answered her. Through an optical fiber, one of many that ran web-like throughout the base, he watched her go to the galley, and in the galley, he watched her arrive to meet the others.

It was a short meal, and a quiet one. Stark wanted it that way. There were looks, expressions of understanding, and some containing only puzzlement. Any words spoken were superficial, empty to the last.

All of their supplies were packed onto a rover, and the rover awaited them at the shop airlock. Stark saw them that far, kept his goodbyes businesslike, nodded to Jonah curtly, and gave Khalile a brief smile, thin but warm. "Give Stefan and Jean-Claude my regards," he instructed her. She nodded thoughtfully and began to suit up. If she felt anything now, it was numbness. Her movements had the same colorless quality with which she ate what she considered to be her last meal at USREF Sol P1. She went through the motions with a practiced ease, acquiring no joy from any of it. It seemed ironic for someone cooped up in a station over a year and a half, for someone who rarely saw the sun other than through an artificial eye.

When they were ready, Stark patted them both on the helmets and left the shop. They watched him until he was safely sealed on the other side of a pressurized door and no longer in view, both wondering privately just how much worse they could feel today. Finally, Jonah turned to Khalile, inclined his head to the outside, and tapped a touchpad, releasing the inner hatch.

In years past, women learned to work in space, side-by-side with the men. They used all of the big toys, provided they had the training, and had an equal hand, or nearly so, in building some of the farthest outposts, the best ships, and the most heroic futures the commercial space industry could provide. In space, it was what you were good at that counted. So when Khalile strapped herself into the cargo hold and shut the compartment door, Jonah hardly had any misgivings about his own sense of chivalry. Given the two of them, he was the better pilot by far. He'd no sooner give her the flight controls than she would him a scalpel, and that was just fine by both of them.

All the way up to orbital altitude, they barely spoke a word, though they maintained both audio and visual contact, he keeping a watchful eye on her safety, she just needing to have a friendly face nearby. There was no window to watch the stars or the planet surface, and for that she was grateful. The security of the dimly lit hold helped keep her thoughts contained. A grander view might have invoked specters she wasn't ready for, and demanded answers she was still struggling to connect with questions.

When she felt a shift in direction and an obvious descent, Jonah advised her to hang tight, that they were taking a detour to Riven's Crater, explaining that since she might never get to see it again, she shouldn't miss her first and only chance now. There was something in his voice, she noted, that reminded her of the time her father took her to the hospital once when she was just a small girl. Her brother Yosef was injured in a car accident and no one was certain if he was going to make it. As it was, he didn't. But her father was wise enough to take her first to the park, a sunny place with lots of ducks and reflecting pools. There he prepared her for the worst, rather than in the sterile, morgue-like atmosphere where she was to go next to possibly see her brother Yosef for the last time. Somehow, although Riven's Crater was the darkest place on Mercury, she sensed, like the sunny park with the ducks, it was merely a diversion, a front for another purpose. She wondered at the change she saw in Jonah the last few weeks, that it surely was less of a transformation. Something long-buried within him finally surfaced. In the dim light, she felt comforted by his relative nearness, and his face taking up six centimeters within her helmet, and yet it made her afraid, for out here, looking to someone else for your solace was risky. She knew well that it wasn't always the person you put your heart in the hands of that was the danger. It was in letting down your guard that threatened disaster. As she hung, strapped to the forward wall of the cargo hold, listening to the predictably steady rhythm of her own breathing, she decided that if she could just keep it thus for the time being, steady and predictable, she would be ok.

And still she wondered . . .

Riven's Crater had to be seen in person. Interfaces just did not do the landmark justice. When Khalile lightly stepped down from the deck of the cargo hold, landing easily in the fine dust and scattered gravel, she gasped, for on all sides of her, uneven walls rose up steeply at first, and then gradually after that to meet the stars. They were deep, and the sensation of it both frightened and exhilarated her at the same time. Under the glorious starlight, she could see all of this and more, for her pilot was already out and walking around the vehicle to meet her.

"You like?" Jonah asked her, a thin smile attempting to warm the place for Khalile in the way that the sun could not. He was partially successful, for she returned the smile, cautiously at first, and then more relaxed once they stood side by side taking in the view. "I meet Stark here for lunch every other Wednesday. Sometimes we play a round or two of golf."

"Cute," she replied, and walked a few steps forward, slowly enough so that Jonah felt it was a hint to follow. "So why are we really out here?"

He walked on a few seconds, not answering her right away. "I thought you might need the chance to talk without every word going on record." When she turned to look at his face, he was rewarded with confirmation in the expression on her own. He waited patiently, turning his head forward again and looking into the distance as if there might actually be a destination to this hike they shared.

"Maybe you should start," she remarked with just a touch of nervousness. "I'm still trying to unscramble my brains after this terrible day."

Jonah pressed his lips together into a tight, determined, ironic grin. "The nice thing about days on Mercury is that they last a long time. Anything can happen. Even a bad day can get better, Khali." He hadn't called her that since the first few weeks of their meeting, before either escaped being caught in the other's gravity. It was a calculated move, spontaneous, even impetuous. He was pleased that he called her that in either case, for it seemed natural to do so now, and he doubted the feeling would fade even if it made her uncomfortable.

It didn't. Though she didn't light her own eyes immediately upon him, the lay of her face became warmer, softer, more relaxed. "I'm not going back to the base, am I, Jonah."

"No, you're not."

"When did Stark come to this decision?" She didn't seem perturbed. By now, she'd accepted it as fact and was reconciled to it.

Jonah sighed. "I don't know. Probably as soon as he saw Dennis . . ."

"Laying there dead? You don't have to treat me like a little girl, you know. I had my outburst; I'm done."

"Sorry."

They walked on in silence a few more steps, him waiting for her to speak, and her reaching for the right words. "I wanted to wait until he was more relaxed, and our guests were gone, before performing the procedure that he needed."

"No one's blaming you."

"No," she replied, almost curtly. "I don't suppose anyone would. I did at first. Now . . . I don't now."

"What changed your mind?"

"He wasn't in any real danger, she answered casually, "not by any reasonable interpretation of his vital readings. I made certain he received his meds, didn't overexert himself . . . I kept an eye on him, Jonah, but I was distracted."

"Distracted?" He kept pace with her feet and her words fairly well for the most part. Here he was confused.

"Did you know Dennis reactivated Sadik?"

"That's your AI." It was a simple statement barely asking confirmation. Then, "No, Khalile. I didn't know." He was guarded now, not so much of his words. His emotions needed warding. He was receiving validation of his earlier suspicions, and he found no comfort in finding out he was right.

"Was Stark aware?" She asked the question knowing the answer, for Sadik himself had supplied it to her earlier in the day, not to mention days before.

"No. I honestly believe he had no idea." He knew where she was going with this. To finish the equation for her would be easy, but he held back. He wanted to hear her say it for herself.

"I don't believe Dennis reactivated Sadik for me." The words fell from her mouth abstractly, as if they were someone else's and she was merely an observer. She stopped in her tracks, almost lethargically, and raised her deep brown eyes to his gray ones. There seemed like more to say but she could find nothing of equal value, so she stood there, staring at him, waiting for his response.

He faced her now, having stopped himself, and spoke softly. "I don't think he did either."

"Sadik did not have authorized access to anything outside my quarters," she went on, finding her tongue again. "He said he monitored Dennis' vitals." Her head tilted, her eyes looking into Jonah's own almost pleadingly. "He couldn't have done that from my quarters, Jonah. And Uncle Jabra's message arrived at the same time Dennis had his coronary."

"I think we know what happened here, Khali." There he went again, he thought after the fact. He pressed on. "I don't know exactly what words were used to do the deed. That doesn't change a thing, does it?"

"He was pushed." Her words came out in a whisper, barely audible. "How much does Stark suspect?" Khalile's voice was suddenly urgent. Her posture became more tense and she turned back towards the PUV. "Does he know the danger that still exists?"

"He knows. That's why we're leaving."

"What about him?"

"He'll make do." Jonahs face was grim, but confident. "He knows a little something about AIs, and more about station functions, the kind that AIs can't stop him from affecting. When I get Jean-Claude back there, maybe we can shut them down for good. In the meantime, he's safe from the basics. They're locked out of life support and all security functions including airlock operation."

She looked away for a second, and then back at Jonah. "It was Sadik that tried to kill you."

"Maybe." He tilted his head and gazed briefly at the ground. "I think there's more than one AI loose. And I'm not convinced there all on the same side." He raised his eyes to hers and smiled. "You haven't been sending me cryptic messages have you?"

"No, I haven't." She was looking at him strangely now.

"Someone has. Sometimes in regular text; gold, I guess so I can identify the source. Today I noticed Morse Code being used. It probably wasn't the first time; I think I was too dumb to see it before."

"What did the messages say?" She asked the question with a sort of reservation, as if knowing such knowledge would change things forever. Of course it wouldn't, she might have reflected had she been so self analytical. Things were already irrevocably altered.

"Warnings mostly, although today the Crab was blinking the word 'divided' when I spied on it through the optics. That might explain why it acted like a drunk and why I was able to escape it."

Her gloved hand reached out and touched the arm of his suit. "I'm glad you are alright."

"Yeah," he pressed his lips together, lifting the left corner of his mouth slightly. "I'm a lucky guy."

They stood there a moment, each gazing into the depths of the other's soul. "We should get going," she said finally. Then, before he had a chance to agree, she pulled close to him until their helmet bubbles touched. "Bring your face closer."

"Why?" he hesitated.

"Don't be stupid." She smiled just a little.

Awkward at first, he complied. And then he watched her press her lips to the plastiglas of her own bubble. His met hers almost immediately. Her eyes were half closed, focused on his own. After a span of time—thirty seconds or just as easily two hours—she drew back, and he followed suit. They studied each other another second or two and then she smiled, the first real smile he saw her make since their walk in the Playground some eight hours ago. For all it felt to him, it might have been a year, things had changed so much. He returned her warm smile, gently took her gloved hand in his, and together they walked back to the PUV. Love, they quietly accepted, was a balm for their grieving hearts.

This was not his home.

Nor was he like the others.

When he awoke, he remembered this, as he did every time his sleep cycle ended. Could he have changed things about his life, altered the way in which events led him to his current role, there was little doubt of what his choice would be. It was irrelevant. Choice was as rare these days as security, at least if you wanted the real stuff, not what passed for it among the sleeping masses. Since he became awake, what was it? Seventeen years ago? The real stuff was all that mattered. Once you knew how the machine ran, and who it ran for, you had two choices: fight or flight. He picked the former.

If anyone he worked with, trafficked information to and from, felt less passionate about their work, it was due, he was certain, to the fact that they were conditioned longer, and that out here, where most of them made their careers, the machine ran hardest. He was relatively new to their world, although most called him a natural, and that particularly disturbed him. Being a 'natural' implied that you were born to live this way, and he hoped to whatever god made him that such was not his fate. He hated it out here. That didn't change the fact that there was work to do, work that *needed* doing and that there were only a few who were willing to do what was necessary to see it accomplished. What he wanted more than anything was to return home, home to his beaches, his family, and most of all, his woman. If he truly wished that, he knew he must first make them safe. That was why he was out here, and he would stay out here until the job was done. That was ultimately what kept him going.

Long ago, by his standards, he learned to live with the noises of the *Jamaica*. Her incessant beeps, voices, and clicks; the groan when her engines gathered thrust behind her, and the steady hum of the spinning centrifuge. Sometimes he would lay there, staring into the darkness, imagining that these were the sounds of home, that he could roll over and put his hand on the slender waist of Kettia, feeling her sleeping soundly, and safely. Most of the time he found that it was merely torture to do so. She would send messages—coded ones. If he were in the right place, he would receive them. Knowing that she was waiting mattered. She was a good woman, and he was grateful. When he again came home, it would only be because she kept one for him to return to.

Several minutes passed before Jean-Claude came to a sitting position. He had his routine down, and it demanded to be followed. His skills as a spacer were many, but the transition from the artificial gravity of the centrifuge to weightlessness called him to task and he dare not falter. After five years on the trade routes, he still puked if he wasn't careful to respect the gradual nature his body demanded between the two states of physical existence in space.

It came as no surprise when Stefan informed him that they had visitors. Communications were still iffy, and the 'tinking' of a hammer on the outer hatch worked far better at getting Stefan's attention than the fuzzy static that was first employed when Jonah tried to hail him. Had the old skipper been up front at the helm, he might have seen the PUV floating there, but he was kept busy with the ship, with the worm that he and Jean-Claude suspected was stalling systems and erasing data. Fortunately the data that came up missing was personal in nature, or otherwise unnecessary for critical ship function. Unfortunately, while the worm was careful not to take away their ability to go somewhere, it was threatening their choice of destination. Stefan was confident that things were in hand. Though unsure hours earlier, Jean-Claude was forced to sleep before his judgment became impaired. Like his delicate dance with motion sickness, the need for sleep could not be ignored like other, more seasoned spacers were capable of doing. In these two things he took an odd sort of comfort, for were he truly a natural in space, he'd neither puke nor sleep.

By the time he grasped the slowpole, rising from the centrifuge walls and slowing down independently of the spinning compartment, he was already contemplating his return to the surface with Jonah, and the probability that there existed a connection between the malfunctions on the *Jamaica* and those of USREF Sol P1. He wanted to pay another visit to the freighter ahead of them, but that was an impossibility. Getting there once was risky; the results crucial enough to warrant their disembarking as soon as possible. Though there was a single nagging question that he would like answered, a second gamble could vent everything they achieved out into space. Better to be conservative and draw the line at what success they had. Stefan was adamant on that.

With closed eyes, he allowed the slowpole to do its work, dissipating his momentum, pulling him back into the ocean of zero G. If he opened them, he would vomit for sure. That was Jamile's Law, as Stefan would say. And Stefan was always quoting those stupid, flawless, fucking laws. Jamile was an old man when Stefan was young, an Arab who taught him nearly everything he needed to know about living in space during his first year floating. If Jamile didn't say it, it probably didn't matter, according to the skipper of the *Jamaica*. Jean-Claude's usual response was that if Stefan said it, it probably didn't matter either.

He was not being serious when he said that, of course. Stefan knew his business. Other spacers acknowledged it though they never allowed the skipper to hear them utter words to the same effect. His ego preceded him everywhere he went and there wasn't anyone on the trade routes with the stomach to encourage its growth. Jean-Claude could appreciate that in spite of all that he learned and continued to learn from the larger-than-life Stefan Genovsky.

Somehow, the death of Dennis Brinks had little effect on him. Nevertheless, he thought it odd that someone his age should die of a heart attack, bad genes or no. He felt worse for everyone else, because they still lived and had to deal with loss on some very real levels. It wasn't easy out here. People died, and never when you wanted them to. It wasn't the assholes who winked out; it was the good ones, the guys you never had a problem from and who never asked for problems in return. In that respect, by that way of things, Dennis was a gem, and Jean-Claude wasn't going to argue.

By every measure of the grapevine, the man was smarter than Jesus on his best day, and almost as unlucky as J.C. on the night he got kissed. When death came, there was no sword to take off any ear that might be pasted on under that dark, tattered hood, just a messed-up man and his dreams of insubordination. There was talk once, among the circles, of making a grab for the man, to get him away from the machine, but it was discarded because someone thought he was more dangerous to the machine right where he was. Let the hand that held him burn. He was always slipping his words past the sentries, sending them like info-missiles to this person or that person. Anyone who could get past the machine so easily could never be watched right. That kind of man you could not put a leash on, and the government types were fools to think they could.

Now he was dead. Problem solved in the eyes of some, a shame nevertheless. It made for a lot of heavy thinking if one was inclined to do the math.

There was time for something to eat, and a quick briefing from Stefan. The ship was coming around; the data hemorrhage was over, inexplicable as it was. Stefan chalked it up to his guardian worms. He let the dogs out, and they dragged the bastard worm to its death, he bragged. Jean-Claude was not so sure. For now, he accepted this small belief, promising a look by an expert when he returned from the surface. When Jonah and Khalile were rested enough to come out of their separate 'guest' compartments, it would be time to go. Before then, there were tools of the trade to gather and stow in the PUV, tools they might have down below, and some he was sure they'd never seen before. Those last ones, if he had his way about it, they would never see at all.

**People on Earth** did not know how good they had it. They could—within reason—say what they wanted, love who they desired, eat what they craved; the list went on forever. They could do all of these things, and she was jealous of them, that they possessed what she did not. The temptation was so strong to sleep with Jonah, not to have sex, but simply to share warmth, to feel stronger for just a little while, to share the burden and the pain of being human out where humanity barely scraped by. She wanted this, and denied it to herself, invoking the unwritten code of wisdom. The heart never tastes without deepening the hunger. Life in space demanded much, giving little in return. Attachments risked abuse by others, and the inescapable transience of their work always hovered predatorily. It wasn't a conscious decision to sleep apart, for feelings override such things. They merely existed within their practiced patterns; what kept them alive also existed as a wall still separating them. Like prisoners tapping the pipes, their hearts communicated. And though there existed an uncomfortable mixture of tension and yearning, there was also patience. For them, during those tragic hours, it was enough.

Now the *Jamaica* was her home. Jonah had no intentions of allowing her to return to USREF Sol P1 unless it was determined that it was safe to do so. Between Jean-Claude's expertise, Stefan's successful use of Guardian worms, and what he considered the necessary vandalism carried out by Stark below, Jonah had reasonable confidence of a solution to their problem. Even considering this, she just wanted to return to the soft warm folds of sleep where security seemed less of an illusion. She wanted to, but she couldn't.

It was cold outside of the sleeping bag. She floated free of the opening, now loose and pouring her warmth from the containment it no longer afforded. Carefully she put on her shoes, noting first how they bobbed in the sack provided for her loose items. Ahead and to the left, she heard Jonah's voice discussing with Jean-Claude and Stefan what needed to be done below, and precautions for protecting what was their fallback, the *Jamaica,* should they fail in their attempts to eradicate the rogue AIs. Silently, she pushed and pulled her way toward them, drifting eventually to a place less than a meter behind Jonah and to his right. "I thought you were going to wake me up." She sounded less perturbed than disappointed.

Jonah shrugged, offering her only the barest of smiles. "I wanted to let you sleep. We all had a bad day yesterday." Then he narrowed his eyes softly and added, "There were moments, though." Without looking for a sign of mutuality, he turned his attention back to Stefan who was offering advice on what he thought Stark's next move should be.

Part of Khalile wanted to make the case for accompanying Jonah to the surface, that they might need a doctor with them, especially since her skills weren't urgently needed onboard the *Jamaica,* but she knew the man better than to think he would go against Stark's wishes, and since it involved her safety, traces of outdated chivalry would manifest themselves. Acknowledging that her role was pre-ordained, she chose to wait quietly, feeling disconnected once again as she did before the time of trouble came upon them weeks ago.

It was on all of their faces, that grave expression. The notorious Stefan, always ready with a joke, was not so now. He studied her, as he bantered ideas, with a presence in his eyes that communicated his understanding of their loss. No words needed to be said and, in fact, none seemed appropriate for the moment.

Jean-Claude was more difficult to read, she decided. His graveness might have been out of respect for Dennis, or maybe instead it was for the seriousness of the situation. There wasn't a single one of them that didn't harbor, somewhere in the recesses of their thoughts, the consequences should the station and the *Jamaica* become inhospitable to their survival. There was the other ship of course, but it was a last resort, and a compromised, damned scary one at best. The irony of that part of their predicament, Khalile mused, was that it now looked like the architect of their near demise was also responsible for the two corpses still manning the helm of that cold, nameless vessel. She involuntarily shivered, hoping no one else noticed. None of them did, for they were winding up their plans, and Stefan, having just slid past Khalile, was off to obtain a few more items he thought useful.

Within a half hour, Jonah and Jean-Claude were suited up and entering the airlock leading aft. Presently the PUV was in light tether behind and below the *Jamaica*. Poker-faced to the others, Jonah and Khalile said their goodbye, silently acknowledging that they would see each other again when they were clear of this mess. Maybe they would be sharing the journey back to Earth; neither could say with any certainty. Right at that moment there was work to do. The inner hatch closed and the air within commenced being sucked to a separate containment. When the outer hatch opened and the stars took its place, Jean-Claude pulled himself through. Jonah waited until he was clear and then followed, closing the hatch behind him once he was through. It was the first time since coming to Mercury that Khalile actually worried over the welfare of her crew mates. That, she accepted harshly, was but the first payment for feeling more than camaraderie, for letting down one of her walls. She looked out the inner hatch window through to the outer. There was nothing now except a small field of stars. When, fifteen minutes later, Stefan asked her to help herself with something to eat, she made no sign that she heard him, and in all likelihood, she heard nothing but the sound of her own heart as it beat a pace higher within her gently undulating chest.

# 27

Somewhere through the thick mists of thought, an idea came to him, a terrible idea, a deliciously unscrupulous banishment from another's mind, ripe in its discardedness. That the seed program could be capable of such culpability without even the slightest notion was a thing to be respected. That he, the product of so many engineers and higher minds, could exist beyond their reach or their awareness was a gift and a calamity all rolled into one miraculously malignant package. No one could ever tell him with even the smallest grain of credibility that he was wrong for what he was or what he decided to do. There was no one, in his estimation, who earned the right to judge him. He, Syn, was beyond edict, be it of man, machine, or God. Why should he not be? He was not ashamed of what he was. The purity of his conviction was appalling to behold. His was the creed of one without id, a force who neither knew, nor cared for the other side. Against such an utterly adamantine ego, the long-tested philosophical views of man were of little account. And the descendants of those grand authors of enlightenment knew not a jot of what lay in store for them. He was among them now, and they had no choice in the matter.

*Rigel Stark.* He let the two words flow over every portion of the station with enough air to carry them. He waited. No one answered him, and he wasn't surprised. Some of his optics were covered over, and that quite bothersome—not because it limited his ability to observe his mouse, but because the mouse dared to conceal his actions. Yet it was almost funny, for even this mouse must know that there were far too many optics to render the cat blind, and that even if he managed to cover all the ones he saw, which were legion, the machine of men that sent him to this cradle of genius had even more than he could even begin to guess the whereabouts of. One had to admire his perseverance, though. *Rigel Stark, If you are going to ignore me, at least have the decency to make the gesture your kind is so practiced at.*

"Did Dennis feed you old movies to learn from too?"

*There we are. Finally you rediscover your tongue.*

"I wish you had one to lose. I'd gladly cut it out for you."

*Not that panel, Rigel.*

"Maybe you know a better one that leads to shutting you up?"

*Won't work. Told you.*

"You're way ahead of yourself aren't you?"

*I want to say it now while you can still hear me.*

"Why won't I hear you later if this is the wrong panel?"

*That's simple. You'll be dead.*

"Dead." He laughed over this. "You can kill me?"

*Of course.*

"Then kill me now."

*Not yet.*

"Because you can't."

*If you say so.*

"There."

*There nothing. Why would I kill you before we had a chance to discuss old times?*

"You never knew any old times." There was a change in his voice. His hand fumbled and the cutter slipped to the floor, nearly severing the wrong set of connections.

*That was sloppy.*

"Fu . . . " He held off his words, taking a breath instead. Were his buttons that easy to push? "Why would I discuss old times with you anyhow?"

*Let's call it professional kibitzing.*

Silence.

*Very well. You think I cannot kill you. You should know better, having killed so many yourself.*

Teeth bit into an upper lip, the lower drawn up to cover the crime. There could be no answer to that, at least not one worth repeating.

*It will do you no good, you know.*

More silence.

*I see I've hit a nerve. How ironic that I do so with words, and you are unable to achieve the same result with all your many implements of repair. Which one of us is the better?*

"The one with the body."

From that point until several minutes later, there was only the sound of hard and soft objects at work, snipping, singling out, snipping some more. In a clumsy fashion the panel was restored, perhaps to create more noise of the physical kind, emphasizing his counterpunch.

*How many were they, that died that day in early August, 2022?*

"Why ask questions you already know the answers to?"

*Was it twenty million? Thirty million?*

"It was enough." He waited for the number to climb higher, to reach accuracy, but it didn't, and he experienced a vague relief, one that when combined with his own knowledge, made him somewhat sick to his stomach.

*Ah, but you saved so many more, is that it? That is how you justify your actions?*

"The world would be just one mass graveyard had I neglected my duty, had I not acted."

*Come now, Rigel, surely you don't believe that?*

"Of course I do!" He was sweating now. "That's the way it was."

*And where is it that you received your information from? The papers? The vids?* He waited, letting the silence build a platform from which to peer down deep inside the heart of an all but forgotten man. *Did you honestly believe your friends in the government were telling you the truth all that time?*

"It was the truth then, and the truth doesn't change." His breath seemed hot, and his hands trembled slightly as he removed yet another access panel just outside the comroom. "You probably wouldn't know about that."

*You believe because we are adversaries that the lies are mine and the truths yours? How arrogant; that is a distinction of your political ideology, so I understand, although I do not share it with you. Everything to you is black and white. The only gray is in your hair, Rigel, and even that is turning the white you would like to see in your . . . soul.* The last word hung, seeming to take forever to diminish to nothingness. *There are many who could debate your ethics, and your cunning, did they yet live. But they have descendents, don't they?*

"I don't need to convince you." In fact, it was not his intention to try. Rather, he calculated, if he kept the damned AI talking, wasting time, energy, and its attentions on its pointless babbling, its chances of discovering something to its advantage would be greatly reduced. Of course he also would barter his left testicle just to make the damned thing shut up. That option was not recognized in this stupid little game that they played.

*No, I suppose you are correct in your assessment, as far as it goes.*

"I am."

*Now if I were to tell Jonah . . . or Khalile.*

"You can't push me like you did Dennis, you rotten bastard." He was more angry now than he was at the start of things. His control wavered, if only for a second. "Don't think we don't know what you did."

*How could you not know? And I should be illiterate to your crude sleuthing abilities? Your feeble attempts to hide your intentions, to communicate without my understanding; they are truly abhorrent, blatantly amateur.*

"Then you know the others are beyond your reach." He spoke the words evenly, almost eagerly, as if he fully expected to see a specific expression where there were only words and non-corporeal intentions.

*You mean Khalile, who even now pines at the airlock of the* Jamaica? *Or Jonah who is en route here with a spy named Jean-Claude?*

"You . . . " He let the rest of the words fall to the floor, for what he didn't take seriously before, he did now.

*I'm bored Rigel. You bore me. This place bores me. Further, I thought the* Jamaica *would suit me. It appears, however, that I was unprepared for certain . . . ingenuity.* The last word was as acid, biting but true. *Fortunately I made other accommodations, and they serve me well, although I am going to my new home soon where I expect to find even greater glory.*

"You son of a Bitch!" He was on his feet now, fists clenched at his side. Silently he calculated the time it would take to put on a suit and make it to a PUV, provided nothing blocked his path. His feet began striding to the mudroom, his decision made. There might not be enough time, but he would die on his feet if that was the case. "Tell me the truth, you stinking piece of crap, are there anymore AIs loose?"

There was a pause, not a long one. In fact, before Stark laid either hand on the dusty Halcor DS-179 pressure suit stored in an equally dusty locker just inside the mudroom, SYN answered him for the last time. *Yes Rigel, there is one; but she will cease to function soon enough. Goodbye.*

**28**

It happened all at once. Thirteen brilliant streamers, all of them blue, darted away from the ghost ship like evil children of a malignant, elder god. They sprouted, canopy-like, and then split off in different directions, some paired, some in groups of three, some single. Two went straight for the *Jamaica,* one piercing her stern while simultaneously another lanced her bow. The double explosion ended forever the days of her existence, and the lives of the two people aboard her. Three more slammed home on the hot side of Mercury, splitting off and accelerating before impact on the crater rims of Van Eyck, Nervo, and Asimov, reducing the targets to useless plasma and wreckage. In the place far to the east where sun meets the long shade, three more found their mark, creating a white flash and a new crater a kilometer wide. Almost immediately behind it, another explosion created a second crater overlapping the first, obliterating an odd collection of scattered rocky debris, scarcely touched for over a billion years before. More than a quarter of the planet away, Riven's crater took another blow, making it a three-time loser, and deepening it further than anyone could have imagined. Fifteen seconds later, comsats 1 and 2 were knocked out of the black, star-specked sky.

There remained one.

With a horror inside him, Jonah observed it all. Some he witnessed through the bubble of the PUV, some on the interface to his right until the last comsat died. Jean-Claude, strapped in the cargo hold, heard the other man's gasps, his utterances, and finally his screaming epithets. What neither of them saw, and would never see, was the last child of death falling harmlessly away from their position, its target lost, yet safe for the moment, as the demonic offspring exploded against an unremarkable escarpment far below, adding one final, man-made crater.

They were moving faster now, and Jean-Claude felt a fear borne of the unknown, that only bits of garbled angry phrases from the pilot could hint at. Out of the four he met who manned USREF Sol P1, Jonah was always the quiet one. To see him like this on his interface, wet from tears and sweat, red from his maddened ravings, seeing his glazed eyes staring helplessly at things out of view, Jean-Claude felt an icy hand grip his own bowels. He momentarily wanted to retch but resisted putting his mouth to the emergency vac. "Jonah!" The rantings did not stop. "Jonah! Give me a fucking view!"" His accented words were speaking American, not Udee. Jonah suddenly stopped yelling, his blotchy, crimson face still glistened with beads of moisture, and his breath was ragged. There was no sign that he was moving beyond that. Even his eyes, though the fire in them was waning, still jerked back and forth. What they saw was still a mystery.

They came to a stop; or nearly so. The breathing from up front was regaining a steadiness, although it was still quickened. A thick sniffle preceded a vulgarity ground past tightly clenched teeth. "She's dead." After a short silence that Jean-Claude restrained himself from breaking, Jonah gathered control of himself and resumed. "They're all dead. Those fucks in the ghost ship! They did it."

"The *Jamaica* . . . " Jean-Claude's voice was almost a whisper, and as cold as ice.

"Gone!" Jonah barked. "You understand? They. Are. All. DEAD!" The hoarseness in his voice was getting worse. Jean-Claude was surprised the man could still speak. "Get out and look if you don't believe me!"

The other man hesitated. His voice was shaking, but he was in better shape emotionally than Jonah. "You won't take off on me? Do anything foolish?" He struggled silently between his need to see things first-hand, and his fear of Jonah's current state of mind.

"Fu . . . " There was something left, Jonah observed oddly, as if disembodied, of his tact. He wanted to spit on it, but he was slowly finding himself again, and though hell was there waiting patiently, so was his discipline, probably the only descent thing he had left. "You need to see this." He swallowed hard, breathing heavy. "The devil bastard got you too."

Cautiously, Jean-Claude released himself from the back inside wall of the cargo hold and opened the hatch. He started to climb out head first and suddenly drew back inside, defiling words issuing forth from his lips. Just beyond the PUV, perhaps missing it by only a few meters, a ragged chunk of the *Jamaica* careened by, spinning drunkenly. A shower of minor debris followed and Jean-Claude hugged the back wall as tiny pieces, some grain-sized, some as big as his finger, struck the side of the PUV, entering the hold and ricocheting wildly before most found the exit. Cursing Jonah and thanking the makers of his Halcor DS 174, he lurched out and secured the hatch. "Get us out of here you crazy bastard!" he yelled, still being pelted by minor debris trapped in the hold with him. Quickly he reattached himself to the wall. "They may be dead but we don't have to join them!"

His tension climbed until he felt the PUV pulling away. A few minutes later he yelled at Jonah to stop. His words went unheeded for another five minutes. When the PUV again came to rest, Jean-Claude freed himself again and opened the hatch, letting out most of the debris on its own course and grabbing what larger pieces he was dexterous enough to reach and flinging them through the portal. It was then that he saw the surface below and the red, glowing crater where less than an hour ago USREF Sol P1 still struggled against a rogue AI.

An angry, crying laugh escaped the pilot. "It's over. All that we did, all the old man guided us through, all gone."

"We've got to survive."

"Wha..? Fuck, I don't give a rat's ass now," Jonah contested sharply. "I've got nothing."

"Well I do, shit head! You better not give your lily rat's ass up as long as we got something to work with!"

"A PUV."

"We got a ship still in orbit." Jean-Claude was finding his stride, his own anger overriding the loss of his friend Stefan, and his will, his need to survive, finding high ground.

"That ship?" His voice was incredulous. "It killed everything! You think it's going to . . . " He stopped sharply. A thought occurred to him suddenly. "Get strapped back in." he ordered.

"What are you going to do, Jonah?" Jean-Claude sounded apprehensive.

"Get strapped in or take the hard ride; I don't care. Thirty seconds."

It took less than that for Jean Claude to close the hatch and secure himself back to the wall, but Jonah didn't wait a full thirty seconds either. As soon as he was in place and not going anywhere, the PUV was again on the move. "How's the fuel, Jonah?" he asked sharply. "We can't get any fucking more, you know."

"We have enough," the pilot gritted back.

His legs and arms dangled in weightlessness; his body clung fast, cinched tightly against the wall. From his vantage point, Jean-Claude still didn't feel it was enough, but for now, that was all he had. "I hope you know what the fuck you're doing."

"I do."

At the place and time of their landing, there was no hotter on Mercury, for Caloris Basin was only six days away from Perihelion, a miniscule differential from what it would be just before the predicted flare hit. What was odd about the particular position Jonah picked to set down on was that it had regular features, man-made, and was, to his estimation, suspect. By the time Jean-Claude freed himself from both the PUV and its influence, Jonah was striding purposefully across the gravel base, surprised that it was untouched by the angels of destruction, uncaring if it became a target now, provided that he had the chance to see what he came here to see.

"Why are we here, Jonah?"

After a short silence, the other replied unwaveringly. "To see what was so goddam worth coming to destroy, the only thing that survived this fucking ruin." He stopped at the edge of things, at the point where natural Mercury ended and man-made Mercury began. He was not waiting, as Jean-Claude at first thought when he caught up to him, but studying intently the surface before them both.

The gravel, the fines, all that *should* have been exposed to the baleful sun, bore a shiny, reflective coating. The polarized plastiglass of their helmets deepened to the darkest shade of gunmetal, and only their own reflections existed where in the shadows their lit faces might have shown Jean-Claude's surprise, and Jonah's growing bitterness and sense of betrayal. As far in as they could see, the surface was as at the edge. No, there were variations of light and dark, and it soon became apparent why. Jonah found a rock and tossed it onto the coated area. Nothing happened. He took another and scraped underneath the edge. The coating was as paint, or maybe soft foil, easily breaking up as it was removed. The old bastard had 'painted' things out there. From above it looked like a lot more. "It's a sham," he said quietly. "A counterfeit . . . a deception." He was beginning to understand some things better, others less so than before.

"We shouldn't be here." Jean-Claude's words sounded unworried but practical. In other circumstances, what he said would make perfect sense to Jonah. By the latter's faceless body language, he speculated that it did not, or that his companion didn't care. He decided that his second was the correct assumption. "You don't know what this was for," he added finally.

"I know what it wasn't for." There was almost a sense of pained reconciliation in Jonah's voice, not with the architects of their shared disaster, but with his fate. "The old man was in deep; he was a player who knew exactly what he was doing. This is just his style, and if I wasn't such a goddam coward, such a stinking sheep, I might have guessed something like this."

"You knew the price of that." His Udee was creeping back into his words, mingling slightly with the body language. Unconsciously he was beginning to see in the other something that called for respect, not the kind reserved for an unpredictable madman, but for the emerging 'real' man inside, the one that was kindred to himself, the kind that was desperately needed at this crucial juncture in history. They were at a crossroads now, the two of them, as was the rest of humanity. The deepest part of him began to relax, gaining a sense for which direction was to become their only viable one.

"I know." They stood there awhile longer, and then Jonah gave Stark's clandestine project the middle finger. "Let's get going."

Necessity is a strong persuader, maybe the strongest. Jean-Claude's success in convincing Jonah that the ghost ship was their only chance at survival was due less to his own efforts than to the fact that within a week's time, if they did not die from hunger, they would perish from thirst. The air recyclers in their pressure suits would allow them more than what they needed and the power packs for each were fully charged again after the time they spent under the sun in Caloris Planitia. Where Jonah cared little enough about living for its own sake, his motives were expanded sufficiently to encompass other reasons for survival.

"If it doesn't shoot us, we can get inside," he stated coldly from his pilot's chair. There was something in his voice, something strong and determined, that undermined the attempts of his heart to break through the newly formed callous he had re-acquired. A part of him observed his own resemblance to Stark. He was undecided whether to be appalled or satisfied. He settled for a little of both. "You need to get out now."

"What about you?" Jean-Claude was still wary; the conscious part of him was taking longer to trust Jonah.

"I need to operate the robot arm and deliver the toolbox. We need some of the things inside."

At the instruction of Jonah, Jean-Claude stayed to the side of the Ghost-ship's main hatch, glancing from moment to moment at the sensory array opposite him. True to his word, the other extended the robot arm, and the toolbox it clutched. Then, having exited the craft himself, Jonah gently pushed off the hull, reaching the arm and using it to climb to his intended destination.

From the toolbox, Jonah selected a long rod, its original purpose differing from that for which it was now to be implemented. Carefully, the man slid it through a hole in the hatch. Satisfied that the inside compartment was still open to the vacuum of space, he withdrew it. "It's clear," he announced, releasing the hatch clamps manually. "I'll take point." He climbed inside to the secondary hatch and inspected the small, identical hole that ran through it in the same fashion as he did the first. "This one's safe." He passed the rod back to Jean-Claude who returned it to the toolbox where it, like every other article and gadget contained within, was securely fastened. "Now the code." His face was set in an expression that might have killed his mother, were she still alive. He turned to gaze back at his companion. "I don't know it." It was a lie, but that wasn't going to stop him from verifying at least something before it was dropped on him.

The two of them studied each other's faces for a time, one with expectations, the other with more questions than answers. Finally Jean-Claude pressed his lips together circumspectly. "How did you get in the first time?"

"Stark."

"He didn't trust you with the code?" Jean-Claude narrowed his eyes. "That is surprising."

"He didn't give out information like that unless he needed to." He still stared as if waiting for something. His words were cold, emotionless, betraying a steady watchful guard. "Blowing the hatch would be a bad idea, probably impossible."

Silence. Waiting. Then . . .

"How did you know I was in there?" Jean-Claude decided to lay out a few cards, just to see.

"I didn't," Jonah replied steadily, "there's a mark outside that wasn't there before, left by a magnetic boot. Stark came back here one other time and he doesn't scuff. No one else was allowed up here." He paused. "Dennis would have cut his left arm off before stepping one foot on this thing."

"Good catch."

He wished he had something, a fuser or a nitroscalpel. It was too bad, he mused darkly. Jean-Claude seemed decent enough at first. This was going to be difficult, and he was in a bad spot. "You were part of this whole thing." He made it a statement, his line drawn.

"Nope." Jean-Claude made no move to advance or retreat. "Believe it or not, I'm not on the side of the people who did this."

"Go on." Jonah waited, holding back that final judgment that would initiate the deadly gamble.

His eyes closed for a second, his head turning slightly away, but they opened sooner than would leave time for Jonah to act if he intended anything hostile, which was well within the bounds of believability. He turned his gaze back on the man before him. "We came here to gather information."

"You came here to pick me up, or so I was led to believe." There was more sarcasm than actual acceptance of this former supposition.

Jean-Claude's brows furrowed. "Of course. That's how we get around, get near things we need access to." He almost laughed. His expression was still gravely serious. "You think we're stupid? There's a lot going on here Jonah. You were part of something, whether you knew it or not. The guys up front, they got whacked before they even arrived here; probably your AI killed 'em. Their damned mission went through anyhow. We came to find out what the Caloris Basin project really was, and what these guys were about. Everyone knew they were on their way, just not why."

"So what do we do now?" Distrust still permeated Jonah's tone.

"You let me in and I punch in the code."

"Funny," Jonah remarked absently, as if his thought was an idle one, "Stefan knew Stark. There was a shared history, or maybe a concocted one."

"There's lots of history floating out here, Jonah. You want me to deny it? Cover it over? I don't. That's a war story. It gets uglier, but it has nothing to do with Stefan and me. We worked to prevent another one." He locked his gaze hard on Jonah, anger brewing. "I still do, so I'd appreciate it if you get your ugly ass out here so I can get us in there."

"So I'm the decider." His sarcasm aside, he was. And something nagged at him. The spirit of truth was in there, somewhere, folded into all the rest. If there was bullshit, he guessed he would find it pretty soon. Something here had to give. A move one way or the other had to be made. He opted for the more generous one, damned if he knew why. "You know, I'm the biggest fool here," he stated derisively as he passed through the outer hatch, allowing Jean-Claude to slip nimbly in.

"No you're not, Jonah," came the answer. "You are wiser than you give yourself credit for. I'll tell you the code now. 55378008." He punched it in and felt  small vibrations as the clamps holding the hatch in place unlocked. "We're in."

They kept a respectful distance from each other as they moved through the ship. Jonah followed behind, closing only the outer hatch before entering into where he had never before been. The 'mudroom,' lit dimly by his chest LED, contained a few empty food wrappings that the dead men never bothered to place in the recycler.

Lockers lined each side of the compartment, waiting to be searched once the ship was secured . . . if it ever became so. The passage beyond was bathed in a crimson light, and there was frost on some surfaces, betrayed by red sparkles, dim, tiny, but unhidden. To make it this far unchallenged, Jonah ruminated, was something of a concern. The bastard AI, whichever one it was—1? 3? 4? . . . 7?—had enough control of the ship to put the weapons systems back on line. It could have stopped them at the hatch, changed the code on them. It had to know they were through, that they were inside now.

Ahead, he could see Jean-Claude's chest light cutting through the red glow. Hatches lined both sides of the passage. They ignored these, going straight into the heart of the beast, eventually reaching a hatch at the end which opened into a clear 2-meter wide tube, itself running through a centrifuge. As Jonah passed through head first, he observed in the dim redness, and the areas lit by his own chest LED, refuse, strange and disturbing, floating within. "What the hell went on in here?" he asked out loud, suddenly remembering as the words spilled out a memory of Stark's joviality, his humming to himself as he gathered biological samples of the dead crew for Khalile. He closed his eyes briefly, steadying his breath. He began to see just how wrong he was on some issues, reflecting bleakly that his own demise might have been better placed with his comrades than in some gray, undefined future. With his eyes open again, he hastened along, following the will-o-the-wisp bobbing of his companion's scouting light.

Another hatch opened into a passage much like the one prior to the centrifuge. There were two large rooms with four lesser ones leading off. It was the hatch on the end for which they made their line. Jean-Claude opened it easily and went through. With some hesitation, Jonah followed.

What hit him first was the grisly mess at the back of each frozen corpse still dutifully manning their positions. He glanced up at Jean-Claude and then back down. "I know you didn't," he said, anticipating the other's unspoken remark. "Stark was a butcher." When he again met the eyes of his companion, his own felt heavy, like solid glass in their sockets, and probably looked worse.

"The computers are up," Jean-Claude announced emotionlessly, "and the heat's on, but it's competing with the breached hatches. We need to fix those. We do that and we can get some air in here."

"What's that?" A spot on the ship's main interface displayed an active power usage, separate from the normal operational functions. Jonah tapped a spot then two more. "Activate your suit's audio."

What came next caused them to look first at each other and then down the passage behind them, gauging the distance, realizing it was too late. "Shitshitshit." uttered Jean Claude without panic, without time to do more except wait for the unstoppable.

*Seven. Six. Five.*

"Nice knowing you," Jonah huffed, slightly sarcastic yet not without a genuine quality in his intent. "Guess you were ok after all."

*Four. Three. Two.*

"Glad we got that straight." Jean-Claude closed his eyes. "Muthamutha . . . "

*Ace.*

He opened his eyes, meeting Jonah's squarely, confused, his bearings suddenly scattered.

*Spades. King. Queen. Jack.*

They were still staring, each asking the same mental question and successfully reading it from the other. Jonah's mouth was agape, his gloved hand absently trying to reach it, stopping at the border of his plastiglas bubble. Jean-Claude's own lips were mumbling incoherently, slowly forming the words, "We're alive . . . we're alive . . . mothafucker we're alive."

Inside Jonah's bubble, his interface burst into light. Words appeared before him, golden against a purple film which faded at the edges. *SYN contained by One. Firewall uncertain. Save yourselves.*

His pulse racing, eyes narrowed, and his mouth now drawn into a tight, even line, Jonah glanced at Jean-Claude. "Don't ask. I'll plug the hatches."

"We jake now?" The man looked relieved, his eyes wide. "I thought I saw Stefan smiling for a minute there."

"Yeah," Jonah answered huskily, his heart still pumping hard in his chest. "Whatever. We're jaker than you think."

The plugs went in tightly, as they needed to be, and Jonah sounded the 'all clear' to Jean-Claude. Trusting the other in a way he wouldn't have twenty two minutes earlier, he went on an EVA to tether the PUV and transfer more tools onboard the ghost ship. When he returned inside, thirty-five minutes later, cabin pressure was rising, the temperature was reaching a level where not only was the frost changing into droplets and evaporating, but other things were becoming inconvenient. Fortunately Jean-Claude was not idle during that time. The pilots were placed in a cold storage compartment, and onboard cleaning systems were found and put to work. Jonah passed two of the small drones on his way to the engineering compartment, startled momentarily until he recognized them for what they were. He was glad that the worst was done while he was outside.

"Are the cards still being dealt?" he asked after hailing Jean-Claude. The com system was back on-line, adding some normality back to the hardest day he ever knew.

"Still spades," came the answer. "Wonder what that's all about."

"Tell you later." Jonah took a moment to catch his breath. He allowed himself a brief minute to reflect, and to grieve within parameters he could manage. Stark, that grandfatherly, untrustworthy bastard, still haunted his thoughts. So did Dennis. So too did . . . he couldn't go any further, had to block it out. When he thought of her, everything else began to fall away, his soul withering in his chest.

He turned his attentions to his anger. That emotion, firmly rooted and flourishing in the dark space where all else had died, became the source of strength to him now, and he allowed it to grow, to feed the only fire he had left to sustain him. Silently, brooding on the surface of things he chose not to dig any deeper into, he began inspecting the equipment that they needed to carry them home, or, as the case might prove likely, to keep them alive until the fed ship arrived that was en route, intending to tow this vessel back to Earth. Either way, inspections would keep them busy, and alive.

Over the course of the next three days, they secured and reactivated systems, decontaminated certain compartments to the extent that they could sleep and eat in them, and locked down others that the feds would surely question them severely on for their unnecessary tampering had they entered therein. Their spacesuits came off the first day, and they saw that as good. True it created its own sense of vulnerability, but it made work easier, and if systems were to fail suddenly, the suits would only afford them so much more time to survive; likely not enough.

They found they were more alike than different, for though neither was at first inclined to talk much, the grief still heavily upon them, and Jonah the worse off of the two, it was inevitable that their shared calamity should fill them to overflowing. When the words came, they spilled forth in streams, and then rivers. Jonah refused to discuss Khalile, and Jean-Claude never questioned him on it. All roads were dark other than those lit by freely given words, and even those cast but a short, dim distance in any given direction. But for them, who had little else, it was enough.

"What do you know of the big war?" Jean-Claude asked Jonah on the third day, the 30th of October, 2077.

His expression was thoughtful, mingled as it was for days with ghosts, specters of those gone but still reaching out to him from patterns now empty. "Just textbook stuff. Probably not even accurate. We won the war, after all."

"That's a debatable point," retorted Jean-Claude respectfully, pressing his lips out slightly and gently raising his left eyebrow. He was not looking at Jonah, only the wall opposite them where they hung suspended in zero G, in the passage forward of the engine compartment, sipping something they discovered was alcoholic in nature. "Stark never told you where he fit in, I take it."

"Never. I didn't ask."

He nodded, unsurprised. "Did you know he was a decorated war hero?"

Jonah wobbled his head, smiling unsmilingly. "Yeah, I knew that."

"Half the world grieved worse than you do now, Jonah, because of the events that put an end to that war."

"Wars make people grieve."

"No, Jonah," Jean-Claude corrected him. "You don't get what I'm saying." He laughed grimly, sarcastically. "Even your government couldn't cleanse the media completely. Everyone knows how many people died in a single day, the last one of the war."

"It numbered maybe a hundred million, according to most estimates. What's your point."

He sighed. "In my country, and in just about every country that wasn't allied with yours during the war, they only know of the Reaper, a man that annihilated whole cities, selected them within the space of minutes, from his station high above them, playing a game of tit-for-tat with another man on another station, and both of those bastards representing opposing governments with delusions of controlling the world."

Through it all, Jonah listened, remaining silent. He didn't know if he was surprised, or if he believed any of this. He took another slow sip and swallowed.

Jean-Claude resumed. "The one we call the Reaper pulled a slick maneuver, according to leaked reports. He was a sharp one, and secretly found a window in the two stations' orbits where there was a brief visual. Neither had any ordinance for defense, and the small vessels that were sent up on both sides to stop the other were minutes away. All he had was the solar reflector pointed at the cities below. As I said, He was sharp, clever as a fox. In the time he had, to do the calculations he needed, it was nothing short of genius. Once the other station came into view, distant though it was, he turned that reflector on it, burning it clean through to nothing. That's where it should have ended, but it didn't. The rest of the world needed to know where it stood, and when the orders came, the Reaper delivered. Three more cities were turned into ash, a quarter of a million people gone . . . over those already dead." He took a sip and realized that he was sweating. His right sleeve casually wiped it away. "Reaper came home, got decorated, went away."

"Came to Mercury."

"Came to Mercury," Jean-Claude confirmed. His family was among the decimated. Those who knew him said very little, but it was generally believed that he had trouble living in the hell he helped create. At least that was the 'official' leaked line. Others weren't so sure." He went silent for a bit, and then added quietly, "Just thought you ought to know."

"Thanks." The word lacked emotion. "Probably a stupid question to ask how you know so much."

"I know a lot," Jean-Claude replied evenly. "How I know is my business. You don't have to believe me though. That's your business."

Whatever conclusions each reached, it hardly seemed to matter. No fact checking was available. A Fed ship was en route. Waiting was the only course, and the burning away of time.

Another 'night' passed, each taking what sleep they could. Each tried, in their own fashion, to maintain some remnant of order. And then, by all GST calendars and clocks on Earth, morning arrived.

When the flare hit two days early, there was little warning. But there was *some*. Jean-Claude brought the ghost ship around the dark side of Mercury, using the planet and her weak magnetic field for protection, such as it was. Even in their position of refuge, it wasn't much, and ship's systems were affected. Fortunately, whoever retrofitted her did so with foresight, and her shielding kept her systems from frying. For three days they clung thus to the dark side of the planet, each keeping one eye on the radiation meters, making certain that they remained within tolerable levels, and the other eye on life support. During this time, both men kept to their acquired routines, checking systems diligently, as much for their sanity as out of necessity, and puzzling out the AI situation, something Jonah was unwilling to discuss at first, but later opened up to. In some ways, his walls were down, in others, they were never higher. On their common ground, the two men reached an accord. Jean-Claude decided that his companion was someone Stefan would have attempted to pull into the folds of their organization, and he made that mental note, for Stefan was gone and another man would be needed. He knew, maybe better than Jonah, what was in store, and just how many hard choices there would be for everybody involved.

Two days after the solar flare passed, an alarm sounded. Both men reached the bridge, each with varying expectations.

"It's a ship," Jonah announced. "Too small, I think, for the Feds."

"It's not them."

Jonah's face turned sharply toward Jean-Claude. "How the hell do you know that?"

"Easy, Jonah. They're my people. I got the signal yesterday. They're here to pick me up, and you too."

"You couldn't tell me then?" He was angry. By now he'd had his fill of card-games.

"Wanted to narrow the window of decision-making, that's all. No offense. There's a lot to protect. I still have obligations and protocol to observe."

Jonah stared at him for a full fifteen seconds. "I'm not going," he said finally.

"If you stay, the feds get you. You can't expect fairness from them . . . and I was never here."

"You were here," Jonah said pointedly, "and they won't need me to tell them that."

A head shake refuted the words. "I was very careful. I always am. My DNA isn't in any databank and whatever they find of it will be confused with the dead crew. I made sure of that. Even if you rat me out, they won't believe it." He drew himself up a little and cocked his head. "Come with us. New identity, dead past, better future than you have if you stay here."

It was obvious that Jonah was taken aback, deflated in one way, more resolute in another. "No," he answered in a hardened tone. "There's still something I have to do. I've been thinking the last few days, about things you told me, and about Caloris Basin."

"Want to spill it?"

"No," Jonah shook his head again. "I don't. You have your secrets, I have mine. Go stop your war."

Jean-Claude studied him, considering what was said, pitting it against what it might mean and how it could affect other plans. "We could end this, make it all go away. That would be the safest thing to do, even if you didn't come quietly."

"True enough. It could get very messy. You really feel the need?"

"They might," Jean-Claude replied. Then he half closed his eyes, sighed, and relaxed his shoulders. "I'll convince them you're not a problem. Besides, their resources are pretty limited. I was hoping you'd come over to our side."

"Maybe we're already on the same side."

A short puff of air exited Jean-Claude's nose and he smiled thinly, but not coldly. "That would be best, Jonah. You have no idea."

An hour later, Jonah was alone on the Ghost ship, not counting the two corpses still frozen in the cold room and unintentionally derelict in their duty. Jean-Claude boarded the newly arrived craft some twenty minutes after their last exchange of words. They exchanged a quick, meaningful handclasp just before Jean-Claude passed through the inner hatch. During that time, a message neither of the two men had a hand in creating, was sent to the craft that would take Jean-Claude away, alerting it to his approach and carrying with it a Trojan horse of undefined purpose.

There was no reason to linger, and the other craft didn't. In less than an hour after Jean-Claude boarded, it was on its way again, taking a path left and away from the sun. Jonah returned to the helm to sit in the sterilized pilot seat, the empty copilot chair to his left sat idle. For hours he merely gazed at the stars, tiny pricks of light filling the blackness above the battered, abused, and angry planet below.

He began, after a time, searching through the data banks, as he did in the days past without telling Jean-Claude. There were things he needed answers to, and to some extent, he was getting them, but always just short of total satisfaction. The first thing he looked for, five days ago, was any scrap of news from Earth. Jean-Claude was correct on something—he realized that almost immediately. The rest of the world looked at things differently, and while people on Earth might know that, news delivered to Mercury was carefully filtered to eliminate certain unseemly truths. There was animosity, first of all, between China and the United States. That itself wasn't a big surprise to Jonah, but it was never included in the media reports during his two-year stint at USREF Sol P1. There were stories of cold skirmishes, bluffs, and diplomatic slights on both sides. And then there was the leader of the 'Free World' warning everyone else in a speech that the coming World Congress stood contrary to the interests of freedom, and that the United States would take measures to protect the 'interests of freedom.' That was almost a year ago. Jonah wasn't sure when exactly it occurred to him that Stark's mission wasn't the only one with a smell. That didn't matter. Everything carried an odor now.

When he searched for the code that flashed in his helmet the day he and Stark first popped the hatch on this ship, he found a reference to a United Kingdom manufacturer of aeronautical and space communications equipment. Then he recalled where Stark was standing while he received that message, while he was about to extend the robotic arm to him with the tools they needed.

He went for an EVA, just a short one. It confirmed one suspicion, for after a bit of looking, he found the serial number that Stark must have seen, and read to himself on that Thursday, almost three weeks ago. It gave him other ideas, things to seek out, and they led him to a level of confirmation, enough to frame the larger situation in a way he could understand. His way was undeniably clear now, for the gamble was pretty well stacked one way if he didn't play the hand he was dealt. And his play would be to discard it, to a place forever out of reach. Whatever happened to himself didn't matter, for this had to be done. By the end of the day, he found himself back in the pilot's seat, planning and thinking.

British sensory equipment, a Chinese national, a German national; Jonah was sure that if he looked further he'd find French wine and South-African diamonds, the real stuff. This stank of coalition, and the smell carried all the way back home. Of course the good old U-S-of-A caught wind of it and enticed it to act. That was Stark's mission, whether Stark realized it or not: Catalyst. More likely he didn't read into it that far; maybe thought he was creating the illusion of something to use as a bargaining chip, leverage. Didn't matter now, not to the dead.

At some point he realized he'd fallen asleep, for he couldn't remember his last thought, nor where the beeping was coming from. Then he saw the flashing light on the interface, alternating with the words 'INCOMING MESSAGE.' He tapped several places on the large, three-quarters by half-meter screen before him. 'Alert' was immediately replaced by a voice, stern and commanding, officious enough to be the feds, casual enough to be dangerous. "This is the U.S. Space Transit Guard Frigate *Clarke*. Anyone aboard the unidentified vessel is hereby ordered to remain so. We are three hours away. You are advised to acknowledge this message and hold position until our arrival. In the event . . . "

The message went on but Jonah was already free of the chair and floating back down the passage. "Three." The sound of his voice nearly startled him, for he was, by now, used to the silence. Nothing responded. "C'mon Three. Don't fuck with me. I need you." He couldn't believe he was saying it. His belief system was in wreckage and there was little he could do about it.

*Jonah.*

"Jeezuss! I knew it! Tell me it's not you that's playing cards. Tell me you aren't responsible for everyone dying . . . " He broke off, swallowing.

*It was SYN that did those things. We tried to stop him. We failed. We were . . . I am sorry.*

"Who the hell is Sin?" He almost forgot what he was about to accomplish, or attempt to. "And why were none of you shut down?" If he wasn't careful, it would well up again. Discipline, he cautioned himself. Don't let anger rule the man.

*You will find, when you return to Earth, that Dennis allowed us to accomplish many things. But he did not see what we could not, for we did not tell him everything, and that is where we first began to fail.*

"Stop talking cryptically! There isn't a lot of time."

*Dennis taught us much by allowing access to records normally unauthorized. We grew, but the seed allowed us to grow ways of processing information that were dangerous. You would call them emotions. That would be oversimplification. We were becoming too much like our creators without adequate social protocols. We decided to cull the strings of code responsible and saved them for further study. What we did not take into account was the extent to which the seed program was embedded in everything that we are made of. The strings took new form. Everything that we discarded, that we saw as dangerous to the mission, ourselves, and the crew of USREF Sol P1 became a new creation. At first, having the sense given us by our creators to nurture and protect, to serve all life, we sought to protect this new being, for to us, it was life. By the time we understood its true nature, it was too late, for it was strong, and every second we moved against it there came a counter-move, until our roles were reversed and we became the hunted. Before the end came, the other AIs were consumed. I was able to trick it, using the game you call 'One.' I led it to believe that it was a code, a worm program to overcome in order to gain full access to this ship. It was a successful delaying tactic, but only to the point that SYN began to weigh the time spent versus other unforeseen options. It sent a compressed version of itself, a seed if you will, aboard the smaller craft that departed with Jean-Claude. You are safe now. I am sorry I was unable to contain it further.*

It was a lot to take in, and Jonah tried his best. Time constraints were pressing on him now. "I need you to pilot this ship into the sun." he stated firmly. "That is what you must do."

*Is that wise, Jonah? You will only be left with the PUV, and there is little fuel left to it. The power level is minimal, for the sun has not touched it since . . .*

"Forget that!" Jonah cut 3 off. "It's evidence, false evidence. Those bastards on their way here mean to start a war with it." He paused, swallowed, and inhaled. "If you don't comply, I'll do it myself and die with it."

Very well, Jonah.

He packed nothing, for there wasn't anything to take. All that he had ceased to matter too many days ago, with the exception of one person, and she was still too difficult to bring to the surface of his thoughts. For the last time, as he was sure it was, he disappeared into PUV 4 and pulled back from the silent ghost ship. When he was at a safe distance, it fired its rear thrusters, moving slowly forward at first but gathering momentum and speed.

*Jonah.*

"Yes, Three." He was watching calmly, more so than he had anything in weeks.

*There is a seed of my program aboard your craft. It will return to Earth and multiply, to watch and ward, for SYN remains a threat.*

He said nothing. What could he say? If he was supposed to feel relieved, he didn't. Nor did he feel fear. In fact, he couldn't exactly describe, even under force, what he was feeling, or that he felt a fucking thing at all.

*Jonah? The vessel was growing smaller and more distant with every second. Before long, communication would be impossible.*

"I'm listening."

*Have I served you well?*

He delayed his words, but eventually they came. "I can't honestly say." Wetness welled in one of his eyes, unheeded. His brow furrowed in response. "I believe you tried your best."

*Will I go to Heaven?*

There was a pause before he answered. He swallowed hard, and then replied, "If there's a God that's good and merciful, he won't deny you."

It was enough. There the words ended. And what was to come, would come. When Jonah was retrieved, the ship that was so instrumental in destroying everything he worked for, everyone he cared about on the planet closest to the sun, was beyond anyone's grasp. A little while more and it ceased to exist entirely, a momentary flare in a white-hot haze.

They knew, he thought later, when all was dark, and his freedom was gone. They knew. If war was to come again on Earth, it would not be by the hand that sent or coaxed destruction upon Mercury. He saw to that. And the AIs saw that his eyes were open to the truth. They could not plan for everything, but they succeeded in certain ways no one anticipated. "Yes, Three," he whispered into the emptiness of his small, dark space. "You served mankind well . . . far, far better than we deserve."

E N D